King of the Moon

A Mike Forde mission

VW Selburn

SGP

GOLD STONE PUBLISHING

Published by Gold Stone Publishing

PO Box 6415 Leighton Buzzard, LU7 6EL, United Kingdom

First published in the United Kingdom in 2013

ISBN (Paperback) 978-0-9927668-0-1

ISBN (Ebook) 978-0-9927668-1-8

Printed and bound in the United Kingdom by

Charlesworth Press, Wakefield.

www.vwselburn.com

For my Parents

Grateful thanks

Producing a book is not a singular experience. I am grateful for the assistance, guidance and encouragement I have received from the many colleagues and friends who have been so generous with their time in reading or sharing their experience and skills with me. I am especially grateful to Penny, who edited the early chapters, and to Gillian, Philippa, Sarah, David, Glen and Neil, for their help with editorial, design and print issues. Special thanks also to Lorraine, and to Sean and Luke, whose faces are thinly disguised on the cover.

To you who are reading this novel, I hope you enjoy the story as much as I enjoyed writing it.

V W Selburn

One man's great idea is another
man's secret weapon.

PROLOGUE

Somewhere over the Indian Ocean

Carrying twenty-five passengers and crew, the aircraft flew high in the bright blue sky, heading away from Diego Garcia, a tiny dot of an island in the vast expanse of the Indian Ocean. The men and women aboard the metal bird were at last going home, talking, drinking and singing with happy relief after their six-month long tour of duty on the military base.

'Hey, Schumacher, pass over a beer!' Stevie Brent shouted from two seats in front of the aforementioned man. 'I'm drying out down here!'

The 30 year-old owner of the loud voice was in fact a good mate of Schumacher, who was a tall and athletic, fair haired German. The two men had worked and played together ever since they joined the services seven years earlier and then were posted together to Fort Pierce. Verbal sparring was par for the course.

'Come and get it yourself!' Schumacher replied, laughing. He stretched over to the box of beer cans disguised as a package of gifts under his seat, picked one up and threw it at Stevie, who bent over sharply to his left and just managed to catch it with his right hand in mid flight.

'Thanks!' Stevie retorted drunkenly, pulling the ring off the lid of the can to open it then he threw the metallic debris back to where his friend sat. 'Next time throw the bloody thing straight!'

Laughing, Gerd Schumacher dodged sideways, hearing the ping as the metal ring bounced on his can and fell to the floor of the aircraft. He waved his arm at his friend. 'Next time, get your own, Stevie!'

He was trying to get a date with Lana Guilders, a soldier from Oklahoma in her late twenties who was sitting on his left by the window. He thanked his lucky stars that the Americans had leased the remote small island from the British, to be used as a military base, and that he had the good fortune to be posted there or he would never have met her. He was even more thankful that his commanding officer was not on board or the journey might not have been as much fun.

Lana was not particularly beautiful but she had quite a character, which Gerd had fallen in love with. He was desperate; he adored the woman and had been trying for a date with her ever since they met on his late night watch when they first arrived and still he had not succeeded. Once they landed she would be gone forever. Her service ended when her tour was over, a matter of hours away.

Schumacher picked up and returned the metal ring in Stevie's direction with a quick flick of his thumb and index finger and turned his attentions back to Lana.

The main topic of conversation between the departing soldiers was what they would do when they reached their home base. Some had planned holidays with their families and others were taking a well-earned rest before returning to civilian life. Those who had drunk enough alcohol lay down however comfortably they could and slept it off.

Below them the Indian Ocean sparkled in the bright afternoon sun and barely visible white crests fluttered like birds on the top of the tiny waves. They flew on, heading north-west toward the Arabian Peninsula.

Within two hours of leaving Diego Garcia the soldiers who had drunk their fill of alcohol before and after leaving the base were lulled into a deep sleep by the monotonous purring of the aircraft engines

Diego Garcia, Chagos Archipelago in the Indian Ocean

Sam Willis sat at his desk staring at his flight monitoring screen in the air traffic control office facing the landing strip on Diego Garcia. Several aircraft call signs blinked their bright orange glow on the screen in front of him. Some aircraft were leaving and some were landing minutes apart, all in an orderly queue. There were quiet times of course but there were sometimes hours of activity, particularly with military exercises. It was not an unusual day.

Nothing extraordinary ever happened to Sam. He was not a pilot. He would never fit into the cockpit anyway so he did not have the excitement in his day that some of his friends did who at least had the time and opportunity for flying. He used to fly many years ago when he was younger and thinner but his eyesight was no longer good enough. Every day was the same. He was bored out of his brain and looking forward to dinner.

Food was on Sam's mind most of the time. Food was his passion. He loved to buy it, cook it, and eat it, and this was clearly evident in his very large girth and rolling waddle as he walked around the base. He had tried to diet but nothing

3

worked so he had given up trying.

Looking up for the fiftieth time at the clock he could see it was time to go out for a coffee, thank goodness. He had a hangover the size of the Enterprise after the drinking session in the mess last night... and he was hungry.

As his gaze moved away from the clock face and returned to the monitor his eyes widened in shocked disbelief as one of the three-digit, flashing flight icons disappeared in front of his eyes. In a panic, Sam shouted to his shift manager, Tes Burnside.

'Tes… get over here quick! We've just lost Flight 198!'

In that historic moment he forgot about the coffee and food as his insides contracted violently in alarm.

CHAPTER ONE

Washington DC

Jumping on the man from behind, Mike grabbed the intruder around the neck with his left arm. The man was thick set and strong and fought back, fiercely biting Mike's right arm and trying to stretch his upper body away from his captor in his effort to escape, but Mike held him fast in his grip. His strength was more than a match for the man. With great effort he stretched his right hand forward to reach the man's right wrist to try to wrest the gun from his hand.

Just to the left of the two men locked in their fight, Lisa, dressed in her night dress and robe, pressed her back hard to the front of the kitchen cupboard door in her effort to pass in front of the two struggling men. She still held the knife in her hand with which she had tried to fight off the man she had found in her darkened kitchen after leaving her bedroom to investigate a noise. The knife had lain where Lisa had left it earlier and she had instinctively picked it up as soon as she felt the stranger grab her arm. Mike had returned home from his meeting in Washington a little earlier than expected. He saw the intruder holding on to Lisa as soon as he opened the door and switched on the light. Distracted by the light, the man had let her go.

Determined to stop Lisa's escape the intruder kicked out with his left foot and the frightened woman tripped over it falling face down onto the floor. Again Mike tried to reach the gun but he was not quick enough to grasp it as the man stumbled off balance with the effort of his kick and he fell heavily forward over Lisa. Suddenly a shot thudded into Mike's ears just as he in turn fell over the body of the man. Immediately afterwards he heard the crack as the intruder's head hit the hard tiled floor. The noise of the shot echoed like a cannon in the quiet of the night and the gun slid forward as the man dropped it when he was knocked out by the blow to his head.

Mike pulled the unconscious man off Lisa's strangely still form. He saw and felt the warm, wet life seep uncontrollably from a deep exit wound in his woman's neck as he picked her up in his arms and cradled her to him. Her eyes were open and lifelessly staring at him. He gasped, horrified as he realised that she would never answer him as he called her name over and over again.

'Lisa... Lisa...Lisa...!'

He felt himself being shaken and heard a voice calling his name. 'Mike! Mike! Wake up! Mike!'

Mike groaned. 'Damn it!' It was December 11th, Lisa's birthday and he was having the same nightmare which he had endured each year since her death. He was relieved as it ended and he opened his eyes to return to the familiarity of his friends' bedroom in which he was a guest, as he often was. The alarm clock blinked five forty-eight in the morning. Lisa had died around the same time five years earlier.

Craig was concerned and Maddy, his wife walked into the room with a glass of water. Mike sipped it gratefully saying,

'Sorry. This happens every year. I'm sorry to wake you both. I'll be fine now.'

'It was a bad time Mike, and I'm sorry to see that you're still suffering like this. Try to sleep a little more. We'll see you at breakfast.' Craig said sympathetically. He and Maddy returned to their bedroom. They knew that Mike would never talk about that night. He was all talked out. It was a painful memory and one he wanted to put behind him.

Mike was English by birth. He was a tall, physically fit and athletic man. For over two years he had worked as a senior agent on secondment to the American Special Intelligence Unit, referred to in-house and by the limited number of people who knew of the department as ASIU, and he had no plans to leave. The unit fulfilled an important role in the country's security but was not as well known as the CIA and the FBI.

Craig, who was almost sixty-five, had been Mike's boss for almost ten years and a friend even longer. He had retired early at 60. Maddy, younger than her husband, was one of the kindest, sweetest women Mike had ever met. The older couple lived in an exclusive suburb of Washington.

Mike's mother was English and his father an American air force officer who had been on a posting to Biggleswade when he had met and fallen in love with her. They had died in a tragic motoring accident in thick fog on the M25 when Mike was two years old. Fortunately Mike was not in the car with them on that particular journey to join friends for dinner. After the funeral he had gone to live with his Uncle John, his father's younger brother and Aunt Caroline who lived in Alton, Hampshire in England at the time. His childhood was happy and his teenage years were spent in Alton and Oxford where he had gained his various degrees in mathematics, languages and management. He followed his father's profession, but into the English air force.

At thirty two years of age after a busy and distinguished career with the Royal Air Force, his last posting at RAF Odiham, Mike transferred to an American air force base in Florida to participate in the first of many special missions. Two years later he joined the Washington office of ASIU.

John and Caroline eventually left England to be near him and with Mike's help they became the proud owners of an art gallery specialising in English art in Laguna Beach, where Mike had a private residence. The gallery was a gift from Mike to demonstrate his love and appreciation for all his aunt and uncle had done to make his childhood a happy one.

In pride of place on the wall near the counter in the gallery hung a beautiful, large painting of Mike's parents, which John had painted at the time, depicting his mother holding him as a baby. Mike had no memory of his parents except through the photographs of them in the family album which was now in his home near John and Caroline's. His disposition, despite the loss of his partner Lisa, was optimistic.

CHAPTER TWO

Laguna Beach, California

Mike returned to Laguna Beach the following day. It was his habit to take a week away from his work in Washington on the anniversary of Lisa's death and he usually spent that week with Craig and Maddy, who considered him part of their family.

He picked up the newspaper from the tiled floor of his light and airy porch and threw it habitually on the sofa on his way upstairs to take a shower. He was hot and sweating from the usual morning jog that followed a five-mile circuit.

After his shower, Mike poured himself a cup of coffee and sat down, turning his attention to the newspaper. His eyes widened in disbelief. The headline shouted the disappearance of the aircraft from Diego Garcia. Mike's heart sank as he read the article. Twenty-five soldiers and three of the crew were missing, feared dead. He looked at the list of names; a lot of the men were from his old unit and there were other men he did not know. He was horrified.

The article described how the aircraft disappeared from the air-traffic control screens between the Indian Ocean and the Arabian Peninsula the previous day, and how rescue aircraft had been despatched from bases all over Europe and Southern Asia to search for wreckage or survivors. At the time of going to print, the newspaper said, not a trace had been found. All that was known was that the pilot had not communicated with British or American military personnel since leaving the base on Diego Garcia and Sub Commander Elroy Green was heading for the island to direct the search teams. There were a few photographs showing relatives anxiously waiting for news in the public relations area on the base in Fort Pierce, Florida and others from English military bases. A telephone number and website address was given for relatives to make enquiries.

Mike knew that the new, specially designed aircraft, on its second long haul outing, was invisible to conventional radar and that the tracking mechanism depended upon a specially coded digital signal being bounced between the air traffic control centre and the aircraft antennae via satellite. A telephone conversation with Chief Special Intelligence Officer, Jackson P Johnston, more commonly referred to by all at ASIU as JP, confirmed the status quo. There had been no indication that the equipment was defective on the aircraft during service in Diego Garcia or at any time since it had been installed.

To find out how the search was progressing, Mike rang the island base to speak with Elroy whom he knew. His hands flew over the telephone buttons as fast as he could make them.

'Yes... camp communications!' The response was almost instantaneous.

'Commander Mike Forde, ASIU here. I'd like to speak with Elroy Green.'

Immediately a voice responded. 'Hello, camp security, this is senior security officer John Matthaus speaking.' Mike could hear faint voices talking in the background.

'Hi John. Mike Forde ASIU here...' He was seriously concerned, but it was not reflected in his voice, which was calm and steady.

'Hello sir. Sub commander Green is speaking with your boss at the moment. I will put you through as soon as his line is free.'

Momentarily, the line went dead as he was diverted then a minute later breathed into life again as Elroy Green responded.

'Mike. Thanks for contacting me. I take it you have seen the newspapers? I'm sorry no-one has informed you yet. JP has just given me the go ahead and I expect he'll be contacting you soon; obviously he knows you were one of us before you joined his team. I've been directing rescue teams between here, the Arabian Gulf, and the north-east African coastline throughout the day. We just don't know what to think.' He tried unsuccessfully to stifle a yawn. 'The pilots were experienced guys; they've flown that route hundreds of times without any previous problems. It's a hell of a mystery, so you can appreciate we're pretty busy at the moment.'

Elroy sounded harassed and tired. Mike knew the effort the officer would already have expended to try to locate the missing aircraft. The man liked to look after his 'boys' as he would call the troops affectionately, though not to their faces. Like most of the older generation of officers, he was everybody's father, confessor and confidante.

Mike's head drooped slightly as he rubbed his brows with his fingers, feeling devastated. He had visited Diego Garcia shortly after joining ASIU on an official visit with JP.

'Haven't they found any sign of them, anything at all, any clues?' he asked with despair in his heart.

Elroy paused before he answered. He just did not want to

say it. 'No.'

'What about communications. Exactly where did they last signal from?'

'The last call was just five minutes after they left the island. Nothing has been received since then and the tracer has shut off completely. We'd be lucky not to expect at least one defective tracer from time to time but this is the first time I've encountered it.' Elroy sighed. 'We just don't know what to make of it,' he said, 'Communications teams are running checks every five minutes but no luck so far.'

CHAPTER THREE

Camford University, England, United Kingdom

Abstractedly, his mind agog with a sense of achievement, biochemical engineer Dr Bill Willington turned off the burner on the bench in his lab and picked up his notepad. Composing his thoughts in his mind, he scratched his ear with his pen through his rapidly whitening hair then started the first paragraph of his report. He stopped. He would do it tomorrow when he was less tired.

The English doctor had worked in San Diego with an American, Dr Marsha Kepler for four years on a joint classified project funded by the British and American governments. Dr Kepler was an eminent neurobiologist who specialised in researching the effects of various chemicals on the functions and biology of the brain as well as being a well-respected haematologist at a San Diego hospital.

Bill had returned to England to continue his work for the project in the Camford University lab. An extension to the project due to an unforeseen development had meant that for the last six months Bill had been experimenting with a new chemical compound, which he had called Tintomin. It was the most important component in an antidote to Riofactol, the drug used in the treatment of genbriotic hypnotherapy.

Genbriotic hypnotherapy was the very latest treatment which utilised the drug Riofactol. It had been tested some months earlier in San Quentin prison in an effort to find humane ways in which to rehabilitate criminal and violently inclined prisoners. Some of the inmates volunteered to participate in the research experiment in the hope of an early release. Not all volunteers were accepted into the project.

After an injection of Riofactol, which promoted a deep psychological withdrawal from consciousness and subjugated subconscious aggression, it became possible to chemically induce a deep trance-like state. Using auto-suggestive therapy, the patients could be influenced to irrevocably forget their criminal past. Only volunteers who had no known relatives were accepted at first, because along with forgetting their past life, their only remaining memories would be those they made in the future after completion of the treatment. This meant that they also forgot the people with whom they had associated in their past misdeeds. There was more work to be done on memory retention for those prisoners who had relatives but that was to be the next step in the treatment.

Before the use of Riofactol some criminals had returned to their old ways despite themselves following the more conventional type of hypnotherapy, but after a period of observation and tests, criminals who were treated successfully with Riofactol were eventually released into society to lead normal lives. None had so far regressed.

Success had not been achieved without failure. During the experimental period some volunteers had suffered serious allergic responses to the drug and because it was an event which could occur without warning, it was difficult to avoid.

After the tenth case of an allergic response in which the unfortunate volunteers sank into a catatonic state, human rights activists had somehow found out about the treatment and through unwelcome demonstrations and other public and political activities, had succeeded in forcing the government to end the project. The team members were asked to review the use of genbriotic hypnotherapy as a treatment for criminals but, more importantly and if possible, to find a cure for the affected prisoners who remained in the prison hospital being cared for by specialist medical staff, an unwelcome expense.

The doctor had committed himself wholeheartedly to achieving a cure for the comatose patients. Now, at long last he knew he had a viable antidote to Riofactol, which satisfied the medical, legal and ethical requirements dictated by the two governments and that it was a solution that would enable the treatment program to re-commence. It was vital to continue the project. Prisons were overcrowded and prisoners' criminal tendencies only increased each time they served a sentence. The system had to be changed.

Bill opened a chat window on his computer to Glen, his overworked research assistant, asking him to pack up for the day. Glen responded moments later.

'Hi Bill, are you ready to go now?' wrote Glen. He hoped so as he was ready to crawl into bed himself. Like his boss, he had worked a long night and an even longer day.

'Yes, can you call Leo and have him meet me outside in twenty-five minutes. Thanks. See you tomorrow.'

Leo was Bill's usual driver from a local transportation company. It was a private arrangement. Bill looked at his watch; it was four fifty-five. 'Ask him to pick me up outside the hall as usual. He needed to see Larry before he left. Larry was his friend and Bill habitually popped into his office to see him before he left the campus.

'OK.' The chat window disappeared.

The tired doctor put away his papers, locked up the lab and once outside the building, walked through the wild gardens of the university. The wild garden was never mown so teamed with wildlife. Bill always found it a relaxing place to enjoy his lunch when he could force himself to stop working.

Across his path ran two grey squirrels playing chase around the trunk of one of the dozen or so oak trees in the open area between the buildings. Some of the trees had grown higher than the three storey buildings next to them. Bill's gaze followed the lively creatures as they effortlessly clawed their way higher up the trunk and onto one of the wider branches.

A group of university staff members on their way to the campus shop passed Bill, smiling acknowledgement as he headed through the doors toward Larry's office in the white building, which was all that remained of the grand old Hall. Apart from the large rooms which had been turned into offices and a very grand staircase, the building was no longer as imposing as it once was in its heyday as an opulent home for rich landowners.

Larry, busy typing on his computer keyboard, took off his working spectacles, looking closely at Bill as he walked into his office and stood behind his desk. He could definitely detect a spark of euphoria in the doctor's tired eyes but he never asked any questions. If Bill wanted to tell him what he was doing, he would do so in his own good time.

'How are you, Bill?' he asked.

An exhausted Bill sat down on the chair opposite his friend. He was so tired he could hardly keep his eyes open.

'Hi Larry... I'm in dire need of a good night's sleep, but otherwise I'm fine, thanks!' he put his hands on the side of his head and briskly rubbed his face, willing himself to stay awake.

They talked briefly about the coming weekend. Larry and his wife Joan were due for dinner at Bill's home on Saturday evening. At dinner the previous week Joan had discreetly begged Bill to remind Larry about her birthday. Her husband was terribly absentminded about birthdays. Bill lived alone so he had no birthdays to remember except for his friends'.

Smiling, Bill looked at Larry. 'You've got the card then?'

'Yes. I got it this morning. Thanks for reminding me. Larry waved the card so that his friend could see it. 'I won't get away with forgetting it two years in a row!'

'No you won't. Now I'm off home to have a good night's sleep. I've been in the lab since eight-o clock yesterday morning and I'm exhausted.'

'Ok Bill. Sleep well. You'll be in tomorrow as usual?'

'Yes, as usual.' Bill laughed wearily, shaking his head to resist the heavy weights that were trying to pull his eyelids down and his eyeballs upwards into sleep as he walked out of the door. 'See you tomorrow!'

In front of the old Hall was a parking area. Bill could see his driver Leo, he was leaning casually against the passenger door waiting for him.

Bill disliked driving. The truth of the matter was that often he was too tired to drive because he worked such odd and long hours. Driving home late one night three years earlier, after

17

working for two long days and nights in the lab, he had almost killed himself when he had fallen asleep at the wheel of his car.

The car was written off and Bill ended up in a sorry state in the local hospital with several badly broken bones and complications for three months. He realised after he returned to work six months later that it was much wiser and safer for him to use the services of a driver after working either late at night or early in the morning, if he had to work that way at all. Doing the easy thing like cutting down on his hours was not going to happen.

Bill looked upwards; the sun was starting to hide itself behind a large cloud. He walked towards the car feeling exhausted but despite his tiredness, mentally elated. It was all he could do to keep his eyes open. He intended to sleep first and then update his colleagues in San Diego personally by telephone with the news of his achievement when he knew they would be in their office, and he was not too tired to think.

Leo Forrest smiled at the man whom he had come to know well as he drew near, noting the sparkle behind the weariness in his passenger's eyes as he opened the rear door.

'Hello Dr Willington.' he greeted him pleasantly. 'Had a good day?'

'Hello Leo.' Bill replied. 'Yes thanks, you can take me home now. I am well on my way to an overdue sleep.'

Gratefully the exhausted man sank into the back seat of the car and after clipping on his safety belt, closed his eyes. Leo shut the passenger door then walked around to the driver's side, climbed in and started up the engine. The car moved smoothly, purring silently forward then slowed near the junction with the main through road as a car completed a right turn. He headed for the south exit.

Just as he moved off, Leo saw a large metallic grey car pull up sharply from his right, in front of the car, forcing him to brake hard to stop. The car had black windows and he could not see the driver. The passenger doors nearest to him burst open and to his horror he saw that the two men who jumped out were dressed completely in black and wearing ski masks. They were also carrying automatic weapons, which they pointed directly at him.

Remembering his anti-terrorist training from years back as a private chauffeur, Leo switched into reverse gear and backed away from the junction at high speed back up to the parking area in front of the old hall. The wheels screamed and smoke poured from the burning tyres as he rapidly reversed the car to keep as much distance as possible between his vehicle and the weapons. Leo saw the men return to their car and drive up the road toward him at great speed. He veered left running over the damp, grassy lawn, churning up the flower beds in the process, which had been planted up each side of the road. The grey car turned back and passed him on the grass on his left, forcing him back to the road. Leo continued to drive ahead

In the back seat, Bill opened his eyes in alarm, looking about him and outside the car windows in tired confusion.

'Get down, Doctor!' Leo shouted to him over his shoulder. The glass dividing panel between himself and his passenger was down and he quickly pressed the button to raise it. It wasn't bullet proof but it was reinforced and might absorb at least some of the impact of a bullet should one be fired into the car.

'What's going on?' Bill shouted back.

'There's a bunch of crazies with guns outside!' Leo shouted loudly, 'Keep down!'

Bill unfastened his safety belt, grabbed the end of a seat belt fastener, and sank down to the floor of the car as much as he could comfortably manage with the high-speed manoeuvres Leo was making. He felt helpless. Bullets ricocheted off the body of the car.

Just as he neared the entrance to the west car park, Leo was dismayed to see a huge lorry ahead of him was making a u-turn into the junction of the road with the H9, completely blocking it. His only alternative was to drive into the west car park and try to dodge his pursuers.

The men in the car had the same idea and by the time Leo had driven around the rows of cars and returned to the entrance there were two men standing by the gate, weapons pointing in his direction, waiting for him. The grey car was very close behind him and he could see that he had no chance of escape. Trapped, he placed his hand on the gear stick and his right foot just above the accelerator, watching the gunmen in fearful trepidation but poised for any chance to escape.

Bill sat up on the seat again, hardly able to believe the scene before him.

Another two men dressed alike, with their faces covered with the same black ski masks, emerged from the grey car and walked towards him. One of them opened Leo's door.

'Out! Now!' the man snarled, taking hold of the shoulder of Leo's jacket and dragging him from his seat. With great strength the man hurled the driver to the ground.

Leo landed on his left side coming to rest on his left elbow. He was shocked by the brutality of his aggressor and wondered what would happen next.

Immediately Leo landed on the ground the gunman raised his weapon and shot him twice in the chest. The impact caused Leo to fall back and he watched in terror as he saw the man was aiming for the third time directly at his head. He heard the crack as the bullet ejected from the chamber and hit home, and with a cry of pain he twisted on his side again.

He had made an effort to turn away as the bullet hit his head but he was unable to support himself as he took the force of the blow and fell onto his stomach. Now he lay facing to the right, his eyes staring straight ahead. Blood was seeping onto the ground from a gaping head wound on the left side of his head. The gunman started to walk towards Leo with the gun pointed menacingly at his head, intending a final blow.

'Leave him Decker, he's dead already,' a second man confirmed, looking down at Leo and pushing him over with his foot. Leo flopped over onto his back like a rag doll, staring dead eyed at the gunman. 'Come on, Neko is expecting us back by Sunday. Let's go, we're later than we planned. They won't wait.'

The other man turned back to the car.

The gunman replaced his gun in his leather shoulder holster, looked back briefly at Leo then walked back to the car. One man opened the rear passenger door of Leo's car and the other dragged Bill out, who had watched the horrific scene in helpless terror and could see Leo lying quite still on the

21

ground.

Pushing the reluctant passenger who was shaking with fear, toward the grey car, the gunman ordered, 'Get in Willington. Get in the car!'

When the rear passenger door was opened the man pushed Bill unceremoniously onto the back seat, jumped in beside him and shouted to the driver. 'Go....! Go!' The other three men were already in the car. They drove off at great speed heading for the east gate and the M1.

In rapidly increasing pain and with superhuman effort Leo raised his head, trying to take note of the registration of the car just before it sped off. He failed.

'I'm not dead yet, you bastards!' he mouthed slowly and with great difficulty.

It was hard to get the words out and he could hardly breathe. Almost immediately he collapsed again, his head pounding. He felt as if he was constantly fainting. He could feel a warm wetness spreading all over his cold chest and became alarmed. His ear felt warm and the same feeling of wetness was spreading down his neck. How long before he bled to death?

In between bouts of dark unconsciousness Leo vaguely heard the noise of people around him but was unable to respond to their faraway cries.

'The ambulance is on its way. Hold on! Hold on!'

Something was pressing on his chest and he could feel his head bursting with pain as if it was being squeezed in a vice, then the sky turned black and the driver fell into the mercy of providence and a speeding ambulance.

CHAPTER FOUR

Location unknown

Bill was terrified. He had been blindfolded, gagged with tape and forcibly held down in the grey car. Shaking with fear, he thought, was Leo really dead? He hadn't moved after he was shot. There was nothing he could do; the men had left him as he lay bleeding on the ground.

There had been three single shots as well as the rapid fire of an automatic weapon, Bill was reasonably sure of that, and it was more than enough to kill a man. Surely someone on the campus would have heard the gunfire? It had all happened so quickly and although it was late afternoon, quite a lot of people had been walking around the grounds. The car park was full. He knew staff would be walking to their cars to go home. Somebody must have seen something, he thought desperately.

The men had kidnapped him in broad daylight on the university campus and in full view of the security cameras in the car park. It can't have gone unnoticed. With deep sadness he hoped that by some miracle the gunman had been wrong when he said Leo was dead. Visions of the driver haunted him and dark, sad thoughts flew around his brain one after the other.

Eventually the car stopped and Bill was pulled from the car and accompanied by someone as they walked over some ground and up a metal ramp. He was then pushed roughly down until he was sitting on a rigid metal surface. Immediately afterwards he was lifted quickly by two people and tied into a seat. He felt ropes bite into his neck, arms and ankles. A safety belt was clipped shut around his waist.

They obviously weren't going to kill him yet! He could hear people moving about and an odour that smelled like the strong musty smell of old, dry wood permeated the air. There were loud bumping noises in the background as if a piece of furniture was being moved around. Louder than anything he recognised the sound of an aircraft engine. Was he at an airport? What was going on?

'Is that the lot?' a man's voice asked of someone else.

'Yes. You know what to do.' another man's voice replied. 'Have a good trip my friend.' the man addressing the voice moved closer to Bill.

'Make sure he survives the journey,' another foreign sounding voice said to someone else. 'He is an important man!'

Bill heard them all laughing sarcastically as departing footsteps made loud, flat, slapping sounds on the metal floor.

Someone else was standing near him. Bill felt his jacket being cut in a line up the left sleeve and the point of a sharp instrument was stuck into his upper arm. He winced at the pain of the roughly administered hypodermic. Now what?

'That should knock him out for a few hours.' he heard a voice say.

Moments later a creeping cold feeling moved up the nape of his neck. His throat dried up, a strange smell and taste seemed to seep up his nose and down the back of his throat as he lapsed into blissful unconsciousness.

After what seemed a short time afterwards, Bill awoke with a pounding headache and feeling nauseous. He did not remember the journey and had no idea where he was. The blindfold and gag had been removed but it was very dark and he could just about make out the shape of a room. Something sharp was sticking into his head. He put his hand up and brushed it away. It felt like straw. Good lord, he thought, now where am I? At least he was free to move around.

He had no jacket on, only his shirt with its torn left sleeve, and his trousers. His feet were cold and he realised that he had socks but no shoes on. His eyes gradually got used to the darkness but he could see only vague shapes. Standing up, he walked tentatively straight ahead, swaying unsteadily, hands outstretched. He stopped as he felt a cold stone wall. Crossing one hand in front of the other on the wall, he turned right, moving slowly and placing each hand in front of the other.

The room was quite small, only about two and a half metres square as far as he could estimate. By the time he reached the point at which he had started it became clear that the only means of rest in the room was a stone block, the bed he had been lying on, which was covered in straw. There were no blankets.

Bill eventually concluded that he was in a stone cell that had no windows but had a wooden door, which he found to be locked and the bottom edge of which was raised about twenty-five centimetres from the ground. In the dark he had felt around the edges of the door when he came upon it.

Sitting down on the bed he tried to work out what was happening to him. It was clear that he had been kidnapped. Why? For the Riofactol? It did not make sense. The drug had proved to be risky, flawed even, so why would anyone want to use it? However, that appeared to be the only sane reason for his kidnap. No one yet knew about the antidote, he had only just developed the compound for the pills, so whoever had kidnapped him must want the liquid Riofactol. The antidote to the Riofactol was still his secret.

Bill's research was a subject known only to a small circle of professionals, and on campus he kept the exact details strictly to himself because of the sensitive nature of the research. Some articles about the project naming Riofactol had been leaked and published in the newspapers, so that drug was already known about but no-one except he and Professor Marsha Kepler knew about the antidote. The project was his highest priority.

Eventually Bill gave up thinking and lay on the bed hoping it would not be too long before he would find out what would happen to him. Sometime later he heard the faint sound of shouting followed by cries of pain in the distance. He could not make out what was being said but it alarmed him. Was someone being tortured?

Would they torture him, he wondered, growing cold with fear? He had a low pain threshold, which had made itself known to him at the time of his last car accident. The pain of his broken bones had been excruciating and he dreaded the thought of having to go through such an experience again. The memory of the sight of his broken bones sticking out of his leg and arms made him almost faint at the thought.

The seriousness of his predicament sank home as he realised that he would be unable to cope with being tortured, he just wasn't that brave. Despair and exhaustion combined with fear kept him awake as he leant against the prison wall but sleep, as it always does to a tired man, eventually overcame him.

Bill slept erratically and each time he woke up there was no way of telling how long he had slept. His watch had been removed, presumably when he was drugged. It was a good watch, a gift from the Faculty Dean last Christmas and he doubted he would ever see it again.

Gradually, he became aware that a light was approaching his cell through the grille in the door. He heard footsteps outside and the squeaking of the bolts being drawn back. The door creaked as it opened and a man in uniform walked in. Two other men stood outside in the corridor, armed with automatic weapons similar to those that had been used in his kidnap. Bill stood up defensively. One of the soldiers stepped inside and placed a lamp on the floor.

'Dr Willington. So kind of you to join us here!' the man said pleasantly. 'I have been looking forward to meeting you.'

'You seem to know who I am. Who are you?' Bill asked coldly.

'I am General Paulo Bhoti. This is my military base and you are my prisoner. You cannot escape so I suggest you do not even try. There are guards at every exit even supposing you could leave this cell, which you certainly cannot without my orders.' Arrogance poured out of every word.

'Where am I?'

'You may find out in due course.' Paulo said imperiously, 'but for the moment, that is not important.'

'Why have you brought me here?' Bill demanded 'Are you

going to kill me?'

'Oh no, doctor. If I had wanted you dead you would be dead by now. No. I have something I want you to do for me.'

'Whatever it is you cannot make me do it.' Bill replied, somewhat afraid. He wasn't too sure about that brave statement. He had not forgotten the cries of pain he had heard.

'Oh, but I can, doctor. You yourself have made it possible for me to do so. I am aware of your genbriotic hypnosis. I have a friend who is very interested in it and is studying it at this very moment. He is learning fast!'

'I don't believe you. You are lying!' Bill retorted. 'There are only three other people who are involved in the treatment. They would never help you!'

'I agree, two of them would not, but the third would!' he laughed. 'You underestimate us, Doctor. We have been following your work with interest for years. We knew about your first discovery and the subsequent updates that led to your work in San Quentin prison. There is nothing we don't know about genbriotic hypnotherapy now thanks to you and Professor Kepler, but especially to Dr Symonds!'

'I don't believe Dr Symonds would help you!' Bill spat the words out.

'No. I agree but he is teaching all he knows to my friend, Elio. He is an excellent teacher!' The man laughed in his face.

Elio? Dr Elio Garcia? The doctor realised he meant Dr Symond's assistant. 'He is working for you?' he asked in astonishment.

'But of course, doctor. You would never have known, I know. However, he will be with us soon!'

The arrogance of the man made Bill want to strike him if he could find the guts, and the strength. He was a scientist, not a soldier and he was woefully unfit.

You don't know everything, he thought.

The General continued, unimpressed by the doctor's presence of mind.

'The fact of the matter is, either you help me or I will kill you. If you will not cooperate, your death will not matter to me but I am sure you don't want to die yet. What do you say? Help me and you can leave this cell for more comfortable surroundings. Refuse and you will be left to die. I will give you time to think about it. In the meantime, my men will bring you some food and drink. You must not lose your strength, doctor. We need you in good health. It would be a shame if you were to fall ill!'

A soldier picked up the lamp as Paulo walked towards the door. The General turned around to face Bill.

'By the way Doctor, it gets very cold in these cells at night. Would you like some blankets? I will ask my men to bring some for you. Sleep well.'

The door slammed shut, the bolts squeaked home and Bill was left alone. The light was switched off in the corridor and darkness once more descended. He lay on the bed thinking about his predicament. What Paulo had said was true enough. With the aid of genbriotic hypnosis he could make him work for him.

If Garcia did come to wherever this place was, Bill could indeed become a victim of his own treatment. The man had studied with his colleague, Doctor Symonds, for nearly two years and knew quite a lot about the project. If he didn't help the man he would either be left to die, or be drugged with his own chemical. Perhaps it was better to work for Paulo apparently willingly and find an opportunity to escape if one should present itself. If he were unwilling and Paulo used his own chemicals against him there was no telling what he might be made to do whilst under Garcia's control, especially as he had no access to his antidote.

Bill curled up to try to keep warm and closed his eyes. His captor was a sadist when he asked if he wanted blankets. He must have known that the cell was cold, very cold and it was difficult to stay warm. However, he was still sleepy and soon dozed off, only to be woken up again sometime later with the smell of food greeting his welcoming nostrils. One of the soldiers brought a tray into the room whilst the other stood guard at the door, pointing his weapon at him.

They also brought with them two thick, warm blankets and a lantern which they placed on the floor by the end of the bed before they left, locking the door behind them. It lit up the cell with white light, exposing how grey and dirty it was. The floor seemed alive with crawling insects coming and going from the holes around the junction of the walls and floor. The thought of them creeping all over his body in the night made him shiver even more than the cold. He hated insects, always had. The man knew how to make him feel afraid!

Bill was pleasantly surprised when he lifted the cover from the plate. The delicious smell was coming from a hot succulent roasted half of poultry of some sort... it looked like chicken, accompanied by unknown greens and what turned out to be a type of potato. He ate them gladly as he had been so wrapped up in his predicament he had not realised how incredibly hungry he was.

Included on the tray was a can of lager, an orange and a mango. The lager was not very cold but it was welcome all the same. The mango was soft sweet and very ripe, so very messy to eat. Bill sucked at its flat, slippery seed to get the last drop of juice until it slipped through his fingers to the floor. The seed lay there for only a second or so before the hungry insects found it. The sight of them crawling all over it bred the seed of nightmares into his mind.

He slipped the orange into his trouser pocket for later, in case it was a while before he was given anything else to eat. It didn't matter where the food had come from, only that he was hungry and he had to eat and drink to keep his strength up. There was no point in starving himself out of misguided martyrdom, he thought.

The soldiers returned some time later to remove the tray, leaving the door open as they left the cell. Bill waited for them to lock the door and walk away but they did neither. Moments later he heard the sound of boots crunching their way to his door. The General walked into the cell and stood three feet away from him.

'Well, Doctor Have you given my request any thought?'

'Yes.' Bill locked away from his captor's eyes. He knew what he had to do. He had to survive.

'What have you decided?' he asked, as if Willington had any choice in the matter.

'I will help you. I don't want to, but I do not want to die

31

either. You have left me with no other choice!' he snapped angrily. Bill knew he would try to escape if he could.

'That is a good decision, doctor!' Paulo smiled with satisfaction, ignoring his captive's bitterness.

'Come. Let us get out of here.' He placed his hand on Bill's shoulder as he guided him through the open door then looked around with disdain as they left the dirty, insect ridden room. 'These cells depress me!' he said, haughtily.

CHAPTER FIVE

San Diego, California

The men stopped the truck on a quiet road outside the city of San Diego. Decker lay motionless on the ground in the middle of the road at the beginning of a long bend; an upturned motorcycle was four metres away opposite him. It lay on its side burning brightly on the unlit road and visible to traffic only as it turned into the left curve of an 'S' bend on the main road entering and leaving the south of the city.

No one else could be seen. To anyone driving into the scene it would seem to be yet another speed induced accident in which some damn fool speeding motorcyclist had misjudged the bend going too fast, had taken a tumble and the fuel had spilled out during the fall, to be ignited by a spark as the metal ground its way across the rough surface of the road. It happened every day... somewhere on the network of roads.

Nat Anderson, lulled by the soft music he was so fond of, saw the accident just in time. He pumped the brake lever hard, hearing the excruciating pain of the brakes of his eighteen-ton truck as they screeched and strained to stop the wheels.

'Jesus, Holy Christ!' he shouted aloud. Adrenaline surged through his body as his heart pumped furiously in cold fear. He pushed and pumped the brakes even harder, just managing to stop the truck somewhat askew, five feet in front of the figure lying, apparently dead on the opposite side of the road.

After switching off the engine he jumped lithely out of the

vehicle and dashed over to the body. He thought he saw a foot twitch. Was it still alive?

Bending on one knee over the still figure he tentatively touched the leather jacketed shoulder.

Concerned, he called, 'Hey... hey mate, are you okay? Are you ...'

Nat fell back as the inert corpse came to life and the gun in its hand shot him once through the middle of his forehead. He died instantly, shock registered in his eyes, his mouth slightly open with the next unspoken word.

Neko and four other men stepped out from behind the shrubs at one side of the road. They had been watching, well hidden by the dark and the foliage and had seen the truck heading towards Decker.

They all admired the courage of their comrade as Decker had set the cycle alight then lay down on the ground nearby with his gun hidden underneath him. He had passed the truck five minutes earlier on the way to his murderous rendezvous. His timing was perfect.

Neko had ordered him to hijack a truck to transport the guns they intended to steal, to the warehouse. The unfortunate driver of his target was simply in the wrong place at the wrong time. Any large truck would have done. It was the first they had come across and it was to be used only once then abandoned. That way there was less risk of being caught.

His accomplices appeared out of the shadows. Their leader, Neko, took off his balaclava and rubbed his hand roughly through his very short hair. His head itched after wearing the balaclava and it had become unbearable. Six foot two, of wiry build and thin faced, his eyes would be considered sensual and exciting with their dark, long lashes in the right circumstances, but they were cold and piercing to his men, of which he demanded absolute obedience.

Even though he was thirty-five years old, when Neko smiled he looked like a mischievous boy. He was a cold-blooded killer and among his friends his skill with a knife was known and feared. He had no family except for Paulo, his brother, whose life had followed the same murderous path. He was a fanatic, dedicated to punishing the British, the Americans and any and all other countries who dared to interfere in the running of the Yemen, his beloved country, but his main aim was to fatten his bank balance by dealing in weapons, drugs, and the business of managing a band of mercenaries. He hated westerners but he wanted the luxury of a western lifestyle. Making money was an obsession and there were no boundaries to how he made it. He would do anything.

'Well done,' Neko laughed admiringly, his dark brown eyes full of praise as he greeted Decker. He was well aware of the great risk his friend had taken but it was the only way to get a truck driver to stop. Drivers never picked up hitchhikers or stopped for accidents unless they were obstructed by or involved in them. Taking the risk of forcing a truck driver to stop by driving alongside could cause an accident. A damaged truck would attract unwanted attention and stick in the memory of anyone who saw it. They had not wanted to risk the cameras at the truck stops. Decker's idea was definitely the best, although the most dangerous way to do it on that stretch of road.

35

Decker did not reply. Neko Bhoti was his boss and he was too busy recovering his composure. His heart had gone cold as he saw the truck approach at high speed! If it had skidded over to his side of the road he would have been killed.

Not a man easily impressed, Neko had a healthy respect for Decker. They had not fought each other only because they were both unsure who would emerge triumphant at the end of it. It was as well to stay friends and as long as Neko paid well Decker would go the distance with him. He only took the risks to show his boss he had the nerve when it counted. He wondered when he would see Neko display the same level of bravery.

Neko didn't need to. He had more sense while there were men like Decker working for him. Decker liked killing, money, and women, though not necessarily in that order.

When buying the bike, Decker had appeared to the dealer to be yet another bike bozo, admittedly a little old for the scene, looking for fun at the weekends on a cheap and cheerful 'set of wheels'. Not that unusual; there were always some tearaways who never grew up. Suits during the week; bikers at weekends. He had seen them all. Decker had paid cash and that was all that mattered. If the cops managed to trace the source of the motorcycle, which he had not registered, Decker and his friends would be out of the country long before they could ever trace its last owner.

Clean shaven and clothed in a suit and tie, with his long, white blonde hair neatly tied back, it was unlikely anyone would have recognised Decker for what he really was, a merciless killer. That was partly why Neko employed him.

Knowing how sadistic he was had really impressed the brothers. Kadella, another member of Neko's gang, had arranged to meet Decker after hearing about him through a former inmate with whom he had shared a cell in San Quentin many years ago.

'He had me worried for a while. He was a good driver, was he not, my friend, yeah?' Grinning, Neko indicated the short distance between where the truck stood and the spot where his friend had lain.

Decker was still shaking. 'Yeah! Bloody fantastic!' he retorted sarcastically. He removed his helmet. 'I hope your brother appreciates the risks we take to deliver his weapons!'

He watched Neko's back as the man headed for the front of the truck. Decker was still sweating; he had lain on the ground thinking it would never stop; it had been too bloody close for comfort

Benny and Kaddella, also working for Neko, stood beside the truck. They had silently picked up the dead driver, opened the metal door at the back, hauled the body inside, laying him face up on the floor and then climbed in beside him. Three other men who had kept a respectful distance during Neko and Decker's conversation, joined them, leaving the door open for Decker.

Neko sat patiently in the front passenger seat as always. He watched as Decker cleaned up. He wanted no evidence left on the road. Most of the burnt fuel traces would be washed away by the next heavy rainfall and the pounding of traffic in the rush hours during the week.

Decker pulled on his thick leather gloves and walked to

the burning motorcycle. After dousing the flames with an extinguisher he pushed it into the deep but narrow shrub covered incline on the inside of the bend. He waited until the crashing sound died away, assuming it had probably hit the bottom and was now well hidden in the overgrown mass of weeds, trees and shrubs, then he climbed into the back of the truck. It would be weeks or months before anyone found the bike, if they ever did.

Neko was a demanding boss but he made sure there was always a plentiful supply of young, sexy women once the job was done. Decker had his favourite of course.

Sheree was a very attractive woman whom he had met in a bar five years ago when he was in San Diego on one of his missions for Neko. After several weeks when he had visited her almost every day, he became so used to her company that he preferred to stay with her when he was in the city. He was not that keen to waste time with Neko and the boys in their hideout. The woman had endeared herself to him because she had made him laugh. Sometimes he needed to laugh, and what a woman! He would be seeing her soon enough.

Dalton, who was to drive the hijacked truck to the coach maker's garage, stood watching Decker and saw him jump into the back of the truck. Walking slowly to the driver's cabin, he climbed into the seat, closed the door behind him and with black leather gloved hands pressed the starter button.

They drove back through the city, most of the way in silence. Neko only spoke to Dalton to give him directions. Dalton was a new man and Neko watched him closely. It would be a while before he would feel that he could trust him as he trusted Decker or any of the men he had known for years. It took time. That was normal.

Their job was to transfer the stolen weapons and explosives from their hideout, a coach makers' garage owned by Kaddella's brother, using the truck they had stolen, to an old, disused warehouse. There they would leave the truck and its dead driver.

Four smaller vans, also recently stolen, were waiting at the warehouse. The weapons would be transferred to the smaller vans and driven one at a time at suitable intervals, to the terminal of the air freight company owned by Neko's brother in law, Bart Nixon.

From there they would be flown to a private airfield owned by a terrorist cohort of Paulo's in Sana'a in Yemen, then shipped to Rakhyut in Oman, where Paulo's men would pick them up and transport them by truck or helicopter to his base.

Paulo had built up an impressive network of contacts which enabled the trading route between Sana'a and Oman to operate through bribery, corruption and terror.

Using the small, anonymous white vans was less conspicuous. It was quite common for small vans to be seen around the hangars. Suppliers used them to transport spare parts and tools to the maintenance crews. The boxes holding the weapons resembled the boxes housing the spare aircraft parts.

There were also several other boxes of detonators and explosives waiting to be taken to the plane. It would take quite a long time to load the goods on the aircraft using the vans, but the risk of discovery was a lot less than bringing a cumbersome stolen truck to the airport. Security was tight and they had already taken enough risks.

CHAPTER SIX

Paulo's desert hideout

Bill followed the arrogant general, glad to be leaving the dark, cold cell. One of the soldiers walked immediately behind him pointing his weapon at his back, the other brought up the rear with the tray. They climbed up a long, narrow stairway which appeared to have been hewn out of the sandstone rock. The stairs were just wide enough for two people to stand side by side. Then they walked along an upward sloping sandstone passage until Bill found himself standing at the back of a crescent shaped cave approximately one hundred yards wide. The ceiling rose up to ten metres high at its highest point and curved down at the back until it reached the bed of sand and rock upon which the occupants stood. Four heavily armed soldiers guarded the parts of the entrance that opened up to the sunlight of the outside world.

Paulo signalled to Bill to remain where he was as he walked over to two of the men and stood talking to them for a few minutes in a low voice. From time to time he indicated with his thumb toward his captive. The soldiers looked at Bill and nodded their understanding of Paulo's instructions.

'Come.' Paulo called to Bill once more.

Bill walked toward Paulo who stood at the mouth of the cave. Outside of the exit was a wall of sand, the top bank of which rose some metres above his eye level but beyond that the surrounding area seemed to be completely devoid of any other sign of life, natural or otherwise. Dismayed, Bill found that the entrance to the cave was in a deep well of sand dunes. The unaccustomed scorching bright sunlight burned his eyes.

'You see Bill,' Paulo said as he turned to him, smiling the deceptively pleasant smile that his cold eyes belied, 'You cannot escape, my men have orders to shoot you if you try. You would die before you got very far even if you could get away... from dehydration! There are no oases for many miles. You could not walk that far either at night or during the day, so I suggest you remember that.'

Paulo led him toward the back of the cave and pushed Bill in front of him as they took one of several stairways to a lower level, eventually stopping at the end of a poorly lit, winding corridor. Turning to a wooden door to the right, Paulo took a key from his pocket and unlocked it. The door opened inwards.

'These are your quarters,' he said then walked to the opposite wall through an archway covered by a crude curtain made of coarse woven fabric.

Bill followed him through the curtained doorway into a low, narrow tunnel about two metres long and less than two metres wide, which led into another larger room. It had been set up as a laboratory with a huge bench in the centre of the room. Light shone down from fluorescent tubes suspended from a large metal frame fixed to a very high, uneven stone ceiling. The muted sound of a generator hung in the air. It would never fall silent.

Paulo sat on one of the metal-framed stools by the bench, indicating that the doctor should sit on the one next to him.

'Now to business, Doctor.' he said. 'I am sure you know what I want from you?'

'No.'

'Come, do not underestimate me. I have already told you I know about the Riofactol. I need you to manufacture some for me. I have urgent use for it.'

'What urgent use?' A sense of cold foreboding crept into Bill's heart.

'That is none of your business!' the other man snapped, his pleasant demeanour vanishing. 'All you need to know is that I need it. You have said you will help me. Are you now saying you won't?' His evil eyes glinted impatiently. 'Are you so eager to die?'

Paulo sprang to his feet, gun in hand, kicking over the metal seat in his anger. It bounced noisily away from them.

'No, no, I w...will h...help you.' Bill stammered, shocked at the intensity of anger in Paulo's voice. He realised that it would not take much provocation for Paulo to kill him. The man is crazy, he thought.

Paulo relaxed slightly. 'That is better. I will arrange to buy all the chemicals and equipment you need. Anything else you want will be brought to you. Just ask. In the meantime you will be locked in your quarters and will not be allowed out until I have what I want and you demonstrate to me that it works perfectly. Do not try to trick me,' he warned. 'If you do, you will die and we will have the inconvenience of bringing one of your other colleagues here. Whatever happens, I will get what I want. Do not doubt that!'

Bill did not doubt it. His captor left, locking the door

behind him. He sat in a chair with his head in his hands, wondering how he would ever get out of the mess he was in. There was no choice. He had to make the chemicals. People working for Paulo could not be fooled because they would be loyal to him. He had to do it.

CHAPTER SEVEN

A warehouse in San Diego, California

The two boys ran into the old warehouse. They had found a way into the compound through a missing fence panel. Their parents had warned them to stay away from it but that only made it a more exciting place to go. Cautiously they crept around the wall and into the open doorway.

Twelve year-old Gary, the elder of the two boys, spotted the truck first and ran toward it. The front of the cab faced the door as if it had been backed into the warehouse.

'Hey, Jimmy, come on over here; there's a big truck in here and the driver's door is open!' he cried gleefully. He had always wanted to drive a truck.

Ten year-old Jimmy ran to join his brother and one after the other, they clambered into the cab. There were no keys but Gary had fun turning the steering wheel, finding that he could turn it quite easily.

After five minutes of watching Gary, Jimmy became bored. 'Come on, it's my turn. You've had long enough. Let me do it now!' he moaned. 'Come on, come on, it's my turn. You've had yours '

After another two minutes of Jimmy's moaning, Gary got out of the cab and Jimmy took his place at the steering wheel. Standing below the cab the elder boy watched as the tyres strained, although they didn't actually move very far as Jimmy pulled and pushed the steering wheel around.

He wondered why the truck was in the warehouse and decided to take a look around. It was a large warehouse but it was definitely in need of some repair. The roof was intact and the skylights were dirty and impossible to see through. Many of the side windows were broken and there were no doors to bar entry at the huge front entrance. For some reason they were lying flat and looking a little battered, on the floor of the warehouse.

Maybe someone crashed into them, thought Gary, as he walked to the back of the truck. He looked up at the vehicle's huge rear doors. They were not quite closed. Curiosity got the better of him and, using both hands to grip the corner of the right hand side door, he pulled hard at it until he could feel it move slightly. There was a peculiar smell of something unfamiliar but it was not too strong. Keeping the momentum going, he pulled it backwards until the door opened suddenly causing him to trip backwards and he fell into a sitting position on the ground. The door just missed the top of his head as he fell as, with an almighty crash it swivelled all the way around until it hit the side of the truck and bounced back slightly before again settling against the side. The boy was shocked by his sudden meeting with the ground and was dusting himself off as Jimmy ran to him.

'Wow! What did you do that for? I nearly fell off the seat!' he cried.

'Well, I got it open anyhow.' his brother retorted. 'Come on, let's see if there's anything inside.'

The boys walked to the back of the truck and gasped as the stench of decaying flesh met their nostrils. Just inside the door was a mass of clothing that was only just discernible as the clothing on a body. Maggots were crawling all over its mouth, inside the nostrils and eye sockets.

In shock, the two boys stood transfixed for a moment and then Jimmy let out a long, high-pitched scream as Gary, realising the meaning of the sight in front of them, grabbed his hand and dragged him away and they both ran home in fear, as if the devil himself were chasing them.

CHAPTER EIGHT

DI Kassar

Detective Inspector Alfredo Kassar sank into the rich brown leather seat, the only emblem of rank and luxury in his office. The chair was there by chance, not from choice. He had inherited it from the previous incumbent, Tobias Abraham Singer who had retired seven years ago.

Singer had been Station Superintendent before his retirement after forty years service. He lived most of each day in the office on the ground floor even though he could have had a bigger room upstairs among the elite. His ample frame made him hate climbing stairs. He used to be fit and strong but age had taken its toll. On his last day, all of the officers were surprised to learn Singer actually did have a home to retire to! It had been his habit over many years to keep a sleeping bag in his cupboard and he was often to be found sleeping the night away in one of the empty cells. The men would joke about not filling the last cell in case Singer needed it. Many a woefully deserving case was ousted from one of the dry cells into the wet streets to make way for a tired captain when they were filled to overflowing on busy nights.

It had taken the officers of forty-seven precinct a long time to get used to someone like Detective Inspector Alfredo Kassar. Like Singer, Kassar was dedicated but unlike him, not married to the force. He had a family, although his colleagues knew that his wife had died. After Kassar was promoted to

Detective Inspector he was allocated Singer's office because no one else wanted it. Kassar did, he liked the homely feel of it. It was small, overcrowded with old furniture and housed an equally old computer terminal, which did the job for Singer but not much else. Singer hated computers. The first thing Kassar had done after he moved into the office was to replace the old computer terminal with the latest laptop and other technological marvels as time went by. He had an iphone, which he used to keep in touch with his daughter, and he knew about facebook but had no interest in it only because he had no reason to have an account. He liked a peaceful life and just wanted the end of each day to arrive, uninterrupted by villains.

It was two thirty in the morning and a mug of hot coffee, which was a perfect fit for a faded ring mark embedded in the worn red leather inlay, was steaming on top of his desk. He pulled out the ginger crunch cookies he stored in a plastic box in the bottom desk drawer, picked one out and dipped it into his coffee. Eating dunked biscuits was an art and despite dunking biscuits every day, he had never mastered it.

'Damn!' he said in frustration, as the soggy mess dropped onto his papers. He scraped off the mess directly into the waste bin with his desk key fob, which he wiped clean with his handkerchief.

For half an hour he sat deep in thought, head down, elbows resting on the arms of his seat. His hands were clasped together and his two index fingers were pressed against his lips. It was clear to anyone looking at him that he was oblivious to the world around him.

Which low-life bastards were operating in his territory?

50

The mess the bomb had made would take months to clear up. He had seen the injured and the dead and he felt like throwing up. His stomach retched with the memory. As if that wasn't enough, he now had a dead body which some kids had found in the back of a truck that was parked in an empty warehouse.

Kassar's dusty grey hair was straggled about his ears and stuck upwards on the top of his head. Looking tidy was the last thing on his mind as he 'pff - pff'd' absentmindedly through his fingers.

Vickers, one of his team, knocked on the glass window and walked straight into his office.

Kassar looked up startled by the intrusion.

'Sorry Al. I didn't mean to disturb you. Here's the coroner's report on some of the victims.'

Tad Vickers laid a red card file in front of him. The dead bodies always got red files. His men were out notifying the relatives of the injured victims and those among the dead who had been identifiable.

'Thanks. Barbara spoke to Mrs Delgardo just an hour ago.'

Barbara was another member of his team. Delgardo was the only police officer to die in the bombing. Kassar felt sorry for Mrs Delgardo, she had given birth to their second child only three months earlier.

'I haven't managed to contact Mrs Franklin, Doctor Franklin's wife yet, but I'll keep trying.' Tad said. The state of his stomach matched Kassar's.

Dr Franklin had also died. He had been driving a block away when the roar of the explosion forced him to jam on his brakes and get out of his car. Seeing the smoke billowing along the street, he ran to the scene, leaving his car parked by the kerbside. As he tended to the injuries of a child inside the building, some masonry had collapsed, killing them both. If they had both lived, he would have been a hero. Now he was dead. What use is being a hero if you're dead? Kassar groaned inwardly at the cruelty of it all as he looked at the news article recounting the growing list of dead appearing on the webpage on the screen of his computer.

'Have you got anything on the driver in the back of the truck yet?' he asked Tad.

'I'm working on it, sir. The forensic team has almost finished and the coroner is standing by to take the body to the morgue. I've contacted the company who owned the truck and left a message with the secretary asking the manager to phone me back when he gets back into the office. The secretary is a temp so doesn't know if there's a driver missing. She just started work today and all the regular drivers are on the road.' Tad just wanted to finish his shift and go home. He hoped he wouldn't throw up until he was out of his boss's office.

Although Kassar was sad about those who had been killed in the bombing, he was relieved about one thing. Thankfully, his daughter Maria was not among them. He had sent a text to her immediately he had heard about the bomb. If Maria had not taken the day off to visit her husband's folks, she could have been one of the dead as she worked right next door to the carnage. He decided to go home. Maria was expecting him for dinner and the investigation could wait. Surely nothing else could happen today?

CHAPTER NINE
San Diego to Milton Keynes

Mike Forde was also in San Diego when the bombing occurred. After Bill Willington was kidnapped he had been recalled to ASIU headquarters in Washington.

JP met him at the airport. As ever he was friendly but absorbed with the business of the day.

'Relax! Let's have a drink before lunch.' JP offered. He could see tension evident in his agent's demeanour. He was a perceptive man. 'Is there something on your mind?'

Mike shook his head as he hoisted his luggage into the back of the vehicle. 'Yes . the missing planes; the loss of my friends.'

'Anything else?' JP was not convinced. He could sense there was something more.

Mike was thinking about Lisa but he knew it would not have been a good idea to mention it. 'No... nothing else, thanks,' he replied. He could not get her out of his mind completely. Work would help. It always did.

It was a short ride from the airport to the offices of ASIU, and once they were safely within the compound it took only minutes for the two men to get to a secure conference room near the entrance to the building.

Mike looked back expectantly at him. 'Are you going to tell me what this is all about? Why I'm here?' He had been given twelve hours notice of his recall to headquarters.

'Let's drink first; there'll be plenty of time later.'

They talked about the recent terrorist bombings in Dallas, Texas. Four oil wells had been destroyed, the fumes polluting much of the surrounding area as much as the smoke following the explosions. It had taken almost three weeks to put the fires out. Those responsible had not yet been caught. The figures on the surveillance camera tape were dark human shapes moving in the night, with no distinguishable identity.

No-one had yet claimed responsibility and FBI and NSU operatives were frustrated with lack of progress in their investigations. In recent weeks bombs had also gone off within days of each other in Salt Lake City, Chicago, Philadelphia and Washington. San Diego centre was also bombed, causing billions of dollars of damage to the local economy. Nothing so devastating had been seen since the terrorist events of 9/11 in New York.

Mike and JP were only interrupted once when his assistant brought in a tray of sandwiches. JP poured another drink for Mike who lifted his glass in salute.

'Your good health.' he took a sip of the ice cool malt, 'Now, are you going to tell me what this is all about?' he asked for the second time that day.

JP returned to his seat. 'For obvious reasons, this is classified but I don't doubt for one minute that you will find the job interesting.'

'I don't doubt it; you don't get me here for dull projects. Tell me more,' he said as he faced the man attentively.

Mike's boss spoke quietly, 'Last month, a Dr William Willington was kidnapped from Camford University in

Buckinghamshire, England. His driver, a guy named Leo Forrest was shot and very badly wounded. Luckily for him, he survived but it was touch and go for a while.'

Mike whistled softly, he knew only too well about the devastation a bullet could wield and he had not forgotten the pain of injuries he had sustained in the past.

'Forrest was unable to talk or move for some time and has only just recovered the use of his voice. He still uses a wheelchair to get about but the doctors are hopeful that he will be able to walk again sometime. One of the bullets went clean through his chest and chipped a couple of his vertebrae. Luckily, it missed his spinal cord. He owes his life to a couple of medical students who happened to be on campus visiting friends. They saw what happened and took care of him after Dr Willington was driven away. He didn't get the license plate of the vehicle and neither did the students unfortunately, but with his injuries he was lucky to be alive.'

Silently, he passed five photographs of Leo's injuries which had been taken at the hospital.

Passing them back to JP, Mike whistled softly, 'He was very lucky! So where are we with the kidnapping? I take it you want me to find him.'

'Yes, that's right. We do. There has been no ransom note.' JP went on, 'In fact, there have been no notes or telephone calls. Absolutely nothing has been heard from anywhere regarding the man. He has just disappeared, vanished completely without a trace. We just can't understand it. Kidnappers would normally have been in contact by now. We have heard nothing and as yet no body has been found, though as I'm sure you know, that in itself is no guarantee that the doctor is still alive. However, for anyone to go to the trouble to kidnap him it does not sound as if death is the intention.'

JP drank from his glass, then continued, 'For reasons that you will come to understand, knowledge of the doctor's disappearance has been kept between as few people as is absolutely necessary. We can't be absolutely sure that someone in England isn't responsible for his disappearance so we are taking no chances. After the story broke the British government allowed no further publicity. Owing to the nature of his last work for ASIU we don't want too much information released about his disappearance. Dr Willington is a very important man these days. He was working on a classified project at the time of his disappearance.'

'Do you think someone on his staff could be responsible for his disappearance?' Mike asked.

'I don't know. No-one knows. Two hand-picked special intelligence agents have gone through his papers at the university.' JP answered. 'We took them out of his office on Friday. They found nothing of significance.

Mike took another drink. 'Nothing at all?' he asked.

'Absolute zero!' echoed JP, returning his glass to the table.

'So who do you think might be responsible for the Doctor's disappearance?'

'We don't know,' admitted JP, 'Janet Kepler, Professor Kepler, his counterpart over here, is as baffled as we are. She was concerned because the doctor had not made his weekly report and we had to let her know about the kidnap because of his involvement with her over the genbriotic hypnotherapy trials at San Quentin prison over a year ago. On top of all that there are the bombings. We just don't know who may have planted them. What little intelligence we have managed to pick up so far indicates that it wasn't any of the usual suspects here at home.'

'Have they picked anything up in the war zones?' Mike enquired.

JP frowned, 'Not a lot I'm afraid. That's the problem, they can't find anything definite to go on. We are drawing blanks from all quarters.'

'I'm wondering how you think I am likely to succeed when you and all your resources have failed to find anything.' Mike was perplexed, 'Isn't there anything you can give me to go on?'

'Well, I have to admit we really have nothing conclusive to go on.' JP said. 'We have hit the proverbial brick wall, to coin an old saying. The best we can hope for is that you might find something we have missed if you go over the kidnap situation in detail. Fresh eyes sometimes see more. The British police and our men spoke to everyone who came in contact with him that day but they found nothing.'

'Maybe they didn't ask the right questions.' murmured Mike thoughtfully.

'Maybe not but you can try. Len Bowater's men could have missed something or there may be something in the information which they do have that they aren't aware of.' JP said. 'Len couldn't guarantee a good job because he wasn't there.'

Len Bowater was one of the senior investigators and the only agent who worked permanently on site. He had lost the use of his legs after being shot in the lower spine so could only get about in a wheelchair, which meant that his field days were over. It had happened during a shoot-out at an attempted hijack at Los Angeles airport some years earlier. The plane never left the ground and the hijackers were all killed, except one, who was eventually captured and imprisoned in San Quentin. Now Len was the brains behind the desk at ASIU, the 'godfather' of the field agents, the man who trained 'Intelligence' to be intelligent.

'When do you want me to start?' asked Mike, knowing the answer before he had finished the question.

'I was hoping you can start today?' JP raised his eyebrows hopefully.

'I thought you might,' he replied.

'We will find an opportunity for you, Mike, to meet with Professor Kepler. She knows the doctor well and may be able to give you some useful information about his lifestyle and work habits. She has also met all his friends, either socially or at meetings. She can tell you who to contact for information about him when he was away from the prison during the trials. You will also need to meet his driver.'

In the middle of the afternoon Craig called in to see JP. Mike stayed on and after JP left them they spent the rest of the afternoon drinking and reminiscing about the good old days when Mike and Craig were out in the wilds of the Iraqi desert, and about the latest news of enemy disasters from the war zones. By six o-clock both men were rather inebriated but hid it well as they left the building. Craig's driver drove them to his home for dinner. As he always did, he had arranged that Mike would stay the night. Maddy was delighted to see Mike again, even though her sharp eyes noticed the signs that the two men had drunk too much. She scolded Craig for not bringing him home earlier.

Mike flew to San Diego the following day. One of the companies that supplied some of the chemicals required to make the Riofactol drug was located just outside of the city centre. Mike spoke with Karen Clarke, the account manager through whom Bill would have ordered the chemicals, but she could offer no helpful information. The doctor was a client and they met only occasionally when he was in San Diego. 'A nice man!' she enthused.

Mike worked hard, earnestly following up every line of enquiry but he found no further clues to Dr Willington's disappearance. The head of home affairs from the British Intelligence Service, MI5, had sent him a full but uninformative report to him about the disappearance of Dr Willington. There was nothing in it that he did not already know from his briefing at ASIU headquarters. The mystery surrounding the disappearance of the man grew as large as Mike's determination to solve it.

In frustration, he decided to take a break and called to see Ben Harrington, an old friend from his military service days, who was a pathologist working at the coroner's office. Mike needed a drink and Ben's office was nearby. Ben was an old ex-soldier who also knew Craig and had retired early from the SAS due to a back injury. He had married an American woman from San Diego whom he met during his years of service and chosen to remain in the city after his wife died.

One of the assistants in the main office directed the visitor to Ben, who was drinking coffee in the pathology lab next to the mortuary.

'Hi, Ben... is any of that coffee going spare?' Mike smiled as he greeted the slim, bespectacled man sitting at the desk munching on a cinnamon doughnut in one hand and holding his mug of coffee in another. The combination of formaldehyde and mild smell of rotten eggs in the air did nothing to diminish the man's appetite, it seemed.

Ben looked up at the invader to his space, 'Oh, hi Mike, where did you spring from? Long time, no see! Coffee? Help yourself. There are some mugs on the bottom shelf of the cupboard above the coffee machine.'

Mike picked a mug from the shelf. 'I was in the area so I thought I'd pop in to see you. How are you?'

'Well. Quite well lad. What are you doing in San Diego?' The man was surprised to see his old colleague.

'I'm investigating a case at the moment and not making much headway. I'm afraid I can't say much more than that at the moment."

Ben looked down at his papers and gestured with his thumb at the window behind him then said, 'I understand. I'm sorry to hear you're stuck. I'm a bit busy myself, actually. I've got a John Doe on the table. He got shot, presumably after his truck was hijacked. Nobody has missed him for some time because it seems that no-one has reported him missing. Maybe he was always away from home somewhere. One shot to the head. Whsssht! Dead as a doornail! I'm just about done. All I need now is a name then we can inform the relatives if there are any. One of the local cops is going to get back to me later today or first thing tomorrow, hopefully with a name. It makes life a lot simpler when we can put a name to a corpse, otherwise we have to hang on to them for ages and we just don't have the capacity.'

Mike held back the nausea as he looked at the badly decomposed body through the viewing window. He had seen dead bodies before but not so badly decomposed. Wars were a quick business these days, with the type of smart technology used. The dead were usually gathered up from the battlefield, and if they were lucky, in a fairly recognisable state, and then wrapped for shipment home.

Except for really exceptional circumstances, there was no time for advanced decomposition to occur. With his back to the window to shut out the sight, Mike poured coffee into the mug and sat on the chair opposite his friend.

'I don't envy you working in this field. I don't know how you do it,' he said humourlessly, indicating the corpse. His stomach just would not settle.

'As a matter of fact, I used to hate the smell but you get used to it.' Ben said with a wry grin, 'I was just talking about this particular case earlier, to a colleague in Scotland Yard, England. We were discussing the bullet found in the driver's head. My assistant put the details on the International Weapons Activity Database just two days ago. I had a call from the police in Buckinghamshire late this morning. Apparently it matched bullets taken from the body of a driver who was shot three times... in broad daylight too!'

Mike looked up in amazement. Something sounded

unbelievably familiar. 'What was the driver's name?' He was almost certain that he knew what Ben was about to say.

Ben shuffled through some sheets of paper in a file, looking for the details he had scrawled hastily during the call.

'What was his name?' he muttered to himself. 'Ah, yes. Older black fellah called Forrest.'

'Forrest? Would that be Leo Forrest?' Mike repeated incredulously.

Ben nodded in agreement. 'D'you know about that?'

'As it happens, yes I do. What an amazing coincidence! Let me have the details. I wish I had known about this sooner!'

Briskly, Ben walked over to the filing cabinet. 'You couldn't have had it any sooner. The tie up on the IWAD didn't occur until this morning. John Doe's body was only found a few days ago. Pretty bad shape it was in, too. He had been dead for some time. Some kids found him in the back of his truck in a disused warehouse. It must have given them quite a shock. Somebody had driven the truck through the doors and left it and him, to rot. Out in the open air the body decays quicker, you know. That was no way to hide a body at all. It is quite a mystery. The police are still working on it. Speak with a chap by the name of Detective Inspector Kassar; he's in charge over at the local precinct.'

'I can't say why, but I need as much information about Forrest as I can get. Can I copy some of the information you have received from the police?' Mike's interest in his assignment had gained a new momentum by this mind-blowing stroke of luck.

Ben handed him the file he had extracted. 'There isn't

much, but copy what you want, the machine's down the hall next to the water dispenser.'

'Thanks, I'll do that.' Mike walked toward the photocopier.

After Mike returned to Washington, a printout from an emailed photo of the dead driver and his truck was linked by a length of green tape, to a photo of Leo Forrest, on Mike's case board in his office at ASIU. The driver had been identified from the company that owned the truck but his relatives had not yet been traced. Apart from an old group photograph of the man and his colleagues celebrating Christmas, no recent image of the man was available. Mike was not sure where the lorry fitted into the diagram but he was determined to find out! By the end of the day he had spoken to detectives in Milton Keynes who were involved in the initial investigation into the kidnap and shooting.

Very early the following day, Mike returned to Laguna Beach, threw a few clothes in a bag and drove to the airport to take the next flight to London. The journey was a long one, but he needed the time to think. He couldn't even imagine a link between a truck driver and a biologist. He could have spoken to the driver, Leo Forrest on his mobile but Mike thought the situation demanded personal contact.

Promptly at seven thirty that evening, British time, the plane landed and Mike picked up a hired car. Within thirty minutes of arrival, he was driving north around the M25 and up the M1 towards Milton Keynes, turning off at junction 13, the Camford exit. The traffic was not too bad and once off the motorway he reached his destination in minutes. The Camford Hilton was a large modern hotel in its own grounds of about three acres. His room, with en-suite was on the first floor. It was also conveniently close to the university.

CHAPTER TEN

Milton Keynes, England, UK

It was a fine day. At nine thirty next morning, Mike drove the short distance from the hotel to the security centre at Camford University. The Head of Security, Maurice Edmunds walked with him to the site of the kidnap then took him to the Research Centre to talk to Larry Oxton, who had been the last member of staff to speak with Dr Willington.

Larry related how the Doctor had called in to remind him of his wife's birthday. He suggested that the doctor's assistant would be the right person to ask about Bill. Unfortunately, Glen was unable to help because his car had been parked in the east car park and the men had not left the lab together. He saw nothing of the kidnap but he did hear the gunfire.

'Who on earth could have missed it?' he said incredulously. 'I can't believe it happened here; this place is so boring, nothing ever happens except the occasional arrival of a member of royalty or a politician, by helicopter. That's the noisiest it gets except when that bloody awful grass-cutting machine is doing the rounds!' He hated the infernal thing because he couldn't think for the noise when it was outside his window. Worse still, he had to shut the windows, especially during a high pollen count because it affected his hay fever.

After making sure he had all the information he needed, Mike left and with the help of the satnav in the car, he managed to find his way to the central police headquarters in Milton Keynes.

He spent an hour talking to Chief Superintendent Potts who arranged for one of the officers to go with Mike to Leo Forrest's home fourteen miles away in Leighton Buzzard. It was a pleasant drive up and down the rolling country roads and he nearly missed the left turning for Linslade off the bypass.

He continued driving up and down a couple of inclines, and took the first turning on the right as Chief Superintendent Potts had advised in his instructions, into a well established housing estate.

After a couple of irritating wrong turns and at the fifth attempt, Mike managed to find the Forrest's bungalow. He parked the car on the road and walked up the long, block-paved driveway.

He rang the doorbell and a woman opened the door. She was a short lady of mature years, probably of Caribbean descent from her bone structure, he thought. Her eyes were brown and her short, dark, neatly styled gray hair was streaked discreetly with some unruly silver and white strands.

Showing his identity card, he smiled. 'Good day, Ma'am. I'm Mike Forde and I have an appointment to meet Mr Leo Forrest.'

The woman carefully scrutinised his face after looking at the photograph. 'Hello. Come in, Mr Forde. We were expecting you.' she offered her hand and Mike shook it briefly. 'Chief Superintendent Potts contacted me to say you were on your way. Leo is in the conservatory, please come this way.'

'Thank you, Mrs Forrest.' Mike returned his identity card to his wallet and stepped onto the doormat. He rubbed the soles of his shoes, hoping they would not leave damp patches on the shiny wooden floor and then closed the UPVC door behind him.

'Call me Anne. Mrs Forrest is so formal. We don't stand on ceremony here.' She smiled.

Anne led the visitor to the back of the house, going first through a tastefully furnished and immaculate living room.

Leo sat in a wheelchair, reading a book. If he were on his feet his height would have almost matched his own, Mike observed. The driver was dark skinned, with an athletic physique and looked the sixty-four years the incident notes showed as his age. He removed his spectacles as he looked up at the approaching party. His Trinidadian descent was obvious but well controlled as he spoke.

'Hi!' he said, putting the paperback on the table next to him. 'Sorry I can't get up, take a seat.' he indicated the four cane chairs in the spacious glazed room.

Anne left for the kitchen, having ascertained that the two men would welcome coffee.

'I see you are recovering well. You must have suffered some with being shot.' Mike spoke empathetically, borne of painful experience. 'Three times, wasn't it?'

'Yes, it was and yes, it was hellish painful, but it's funny how soon you forget it. I'm quite well now and the doctors tell me I will be able to walk again so I'm not so badly off.' Leo replied. 'I go for physiotherapy twice a week. I have to practise with those.'

Leo inclined his head to his left, indicating the crutches leaning against the corner of the conservatory. Mike followed the man's disinterested gaze; he wasn't fond of crutches, that much was obvious.

'I gather you still remember what happened. Would you mind going over it once again for my benefit?' Mike asked.

Leo grimaced, 'I haven't forgotten any of it, except being saved from bleeding to death by three very brave students. They were lucky the kidnappers didn't shoot them too. They were so sure I was a goner! They got to me just after the car sped away and it was thanks to their efforts I was in hospital inside fifteen minutes. It isn't far away you know. Just five minutes up the road from the university.'

Mike listened as Leo related the event. He was amazed that Leo had survived at all and very lucky that the bullet shot at his head had not killed him. The wound looked so bad the doctors had told him afterwards that the kidnappers would have thought the bullet had penetrated his head deeper than it actually had. A lot of flesh had been torn away but the bone had only been grazed, fortunately for him, not deep enough to break his skull and damage his brain.

Remembering his own agony when he had been shot four times, Mike felt a tremendous admiration for the way in which the man sitting in the wheelchair opposite him had let the kidnappers think he was dead when he must have been suffering indescribable agony and fear.

'Do you remember any names being mentioned?' he asked eventually, taking a bite of the cake Anne had offered with the coffee she placed in front of him.

'Only the one... after I was shot somebody said "Leave him Decker, he's had it." I remember that particularly because I thought to myself after he said it, oh, no he hasn't, and hoped they would hurry up and drive off because I didn't know how much longer I could hold my breath. When that bastard kicked me over, I nearly choked.' Leo's face reflected his anger as he was reminded of the pain, then he remembered he had company. He looked at Mike and shook his head with a shudder as if to block it out.

Mike raised his eyebrows in surprise.

'Decker? That name hasn't come up before!' he said to Leo, 'That's useful, thanks. I can be reached through Chief Superintendent Potts at the Milton Keynes Police HQ. He can contact me at home and at work if you remember anything else after I'm gone. In the meantime, thanks for your help. It can't have been easy for you to go through it again.'

Leo smiled grimly. 'I was lucky. My concern now is for the doctor.'

Mike understood. 'Yes, I will do all I can to find him. However, you must know you couldn't have prevented the kidnap, Leo. You were shot, and even if you had not been, you could not have changed anything. Nobody can possibly place any blame on you for not stopping it, so don't even think it.' he said firmly but kindly. 'We don't know where the doctor is or if he's still alive, but if he isn't alive it isn't due to anything you could or couldn't have done. If he is alive, we'll find him and bring him back home. You can count on it.'

'Thanks.' Leo said, 'I'm sure you will.' though he was not. Why had he stopped at the gate? Why hadn't he just run the

69

bastards down? Maybe the truck would have gone by the time he got down to the bottom of the drive again. Maybe he could have got to them before they could have shot him through the windscreen. Why hadn't he tried?

Mike saw the anguish in the man's eyes as he finished his coffee and stood up. There was nothing of comfort that he could say to him. They shook hands and he left. Within a day he was back in San Diego.

CHAPTER ELEVEN

Tracing Decker

Mike was satisfied that he had accumulated all the information he could about Dr Willington's kidnap from Leo. If only he could find out who Decker was and how the bullets in both the kidnap of the doctor and the death of the truck driver came to be fired from the same weapon. It was an amazing coincidence that he happened to be in Ben's office when the information was made available via the IWAD! Perhaps the International Criminal Intelligence Database would also provide a clue. ICID was a new database that held every piece of intelligence on criminals and criminal activity across American, Europe and Australia. Not all countries had signed up to it, but it was an invaluable source of information for any law enforcement office with a link to it. No matter how small, whether the data came first or second hand, a record was created and the information shared with any of the agencies signed up to it. Sometimes it was even more efficient than the police files. New information was added every minute of every day. It recorded known associates, partners in crime, type of crime, prison records and any information which could be found to be of use, now or in the future, about criminals and crimes.

From Mike's perspective, this seemed an appropriate time to enlist the help of the local police, perhaps they had moved forward on the truck driver murder case whilst he was in

England.

That afternoon Mike visited the local police precinct in San Diego. He was introduced to Detective Inspector Kassar and he took an immediate liking to him. There was something about the man that exuded trust and confidence, which was probably why he was in the role. They discussed the hijack of the truck, which had taken place in his territory and without revealing too much about his own assignment, Mike informed him about the link between the bullets shot at Leo Forrest and the dead truck driver.

Together they scanned ICID, looking for Decker. There was an entry against his name showing that someone by the name of Decker had been mentioned before in connection with a crime, but there was no forename, address or prison record. The two men spent an hour scanning the database, and cross referencing the crimes the names were linked to in the 'Known Associates' table, which eventually brought up the name 'Hibbot', who had a small apartment in a large block of apartments not too far away from the central shopping centre in San Diego.

Kassar ran a check on Hibbot's personal details. Two minutes later he said, 'Here's an address for Hibbot. I could put a couple of men to keep an eye on his place for a few days, to make sure he still lives there unless you prefer to enlist the help of ASIU personnel?'

'I'll arrange for some ASIU personnel to place a surveillance team in the area. Your men have enough to do coping with the bombings.' Mike confirmed. 'Leave it with me.' He left Kassar and took a taxi to the airport.

CHAPTER TWELVE

The Inquiry

In Washington, Mike brought Craig up to-date with the information he had learned during his trip to England. He also mentioned the link to the killing of the truck driver, who had now been formally identified by his clothing and dental records as Nat Andersen by his boss at the company for which he worked. It had been established that the man had no living relatives. Craig was quite surprised to learn about the hijack, and even more amazed by the link between the bullets fired at Leo Forrest and Nat Andersen and their discussion ended when they realised that the threads of the investigation were not yet ready to make sense. Mike was about to leave when Maddy arrived home and insisted he stayed for dinner.

'I haven't had much of a chance to see you since you arrived. We've both been so busy.' she said. 'You must stay for dinner!'

So Mike stayed. He sent an email to Grigor Irons at ASIU, asking him to arrange a surveillance team to watch Hibbot's home, with sound and recording equipment.

'Don't involve anyone else from any other agency. They can get a bit heavy in a situation like this. We need to be discreet to maintain control of this stakeout. Use only ASIU agents and keep the local police out of it. Pick the best of those available and keep a light touch. If this all goes wrong you will be held personally responsible. We need Hibbot alive.'

Two days prior to JP's meeting in Washington that day, the results of the Diego Garcia inquiry into the missing aircraft had been made known to the US president, Grant Carlton. JP's last task was to take care of the legalities regarding the missing men. Many of the relatives were demanding either a formal declaration of death in active service, or a continuation of the search, which had all but ceased for their loved ones. Added to their grief was the loss of earnings of those spouses and parents who had been unable to return to work because of their need to cope with the grief and fears of their children or siblings. Incredibly hard though it was to bear, all the affected relatives needed closure and future security.

In sombre mood at quarter past four, Mike and JP who was clothed in his military uniform, walked in silence in a steady, evenly matched stride to the conference room in which the meeting was being held. With their heads held high, they looked every inch the respected and professional men that they were.

The last few months had seen sweeping searches of the Indian Ocean and intelligence gathering from the area of the search, with no tangible results. To date, the troops and crew were unofficially listed as MIA. With no trace of wreckage or bodies, the only conclusion that could reasonably be drawn at the inquiry two days earlier, was that the aircraft had gone down somewhere, probably at sea and sunk to the bottom of the ocean. A new, technologically advanced aircraft had been lost and the whole business was a devastating mystery.

Two armed soldiers stood outside the large double doors which were closed. They recognised the two men and saluted in unison. The soldier on the left opened a door and the men entered the large, sunlit room. There were six men and four women seated at the polished maple, twelve-seat table. The outside wall of the room was mostly made of glass, except for a ten inch metal plate at the top and bottom of each pane. The panelled and soundproofed inner walls kept the room private.

All of the other people present were in military uniform except for the communications assistant, who was a woman probably in her early thirties, Mike would have guessed. She was dressed in a grey suit and white blouse. Her face was expressionless but her eyes were sharply attentive. She held a pen in her right hand which was poised above a writing pad on the table on which, he had noticed moments earlier, she had made several notes during the discussions that were taking place as he and JP arrived.

The room fell silent.

JP took his seat and Mike sat next to him looking straight ahead. He could not stop thinking about the men, women and crew who were probably lying dead on the bottom of the ocean. His thoughts were also with the missing doctor. He bowed his head, knowing what JP was about to say.

The faces around the table turned to JP, who looked around the room; the seriousness of what he was about to say was reflected in his heart but his face and manner reflected official representation. Addressing the listeners around the table in a formal voice, he began the summing up of his discussion with the President following their teleconference that morning.

'Following our meeting earlier today, Commander Forde and I have formally informed the President of the findings of the earlier inquiry that took place two days ago in Diego Garcia into the disappearance of the soldiers on the military aircraft, flight 198.'

'It is with great sadness that the President has agreed with the findings of the inquiry that in the interests, and for the welfare of the relatives concerned, those twenty-five men and women soldiers and the three crew members be officially declared as deceased, killed in action.'

Several listeners bowed their heads respectfully.

'He has asked that it be formally placed on record that he has acknowledged that all that could have been done, has been done to trace and recover the aircraft, its passengers and crew. He is in agreement with our conclusion that we must regretfully close this case as unsolved on the basis that some new information may come to light at sometime in the future.'

There was a murmur of voices and sad faces turned sideways, looking at their neighbours.

JP paused and the room again fell silent. 'It only remains, ladies and gentlemen, to thank you for your participation today. This meeting is now formally closed. For those of you whose duty it is to inform the relatives of this decision, the President sends his thanks to you for taking on this sad task. It will not be an easy one.' He paused, then sat down and pulled his papers together to put them away in his document case.

To Mike he said quietly, 'That's it. It's over for now. Perhaps one day we may find out what happened.'

'Maybe,' said Mike. Even though it was months later, he still felt the loss of his friends just as if it had happened yesterday. Tragedies like the one they had just closed would take a lot of forgetting.

The other representatives filed past them, saying their

goodbyes and shaking hands, until only JP and Mike remained in the room.

Mike looked down the empty table, a deep sadness in his eyes.

'I just can't believe it, even now. Twenty-eight people have just been written off forever.'

'Come on Mike, you know we've done all that we could,' JP said, putting his hand briefly on Mike's shoulder.

He knew how Mike felt. He was feeling it too, but it served no purpose, they were both professionals and had to cope with such things. Mike would too in time; he was much younger than his boss and had many new experiences to come that would help to put all this in perspective.

'Time to go,' he said quietly.

They left together, each deep in private thought.

CHAPTER THIRTEEN

Surveillance

It was twelve thirty and a news flash appeared in the middle of the film Kassar was watching. The newscaster stared out of the screen as he announced with concerned intensity that a bomb had just gone off outside the Capitol Building in Washington. Two people were killed instantly, another twelve were injured and several windows were blown out. There was footage of shocked pedestrians and taped off areas covered with debris.

The voiceover declared, 'Following the pattern set by the earlier bombings in San Diego and Washington, no-one has claimed responsibility and it is not known when the bomb was planted. Police are currently studying security tapes. Further details will follow as soon as they come in.'

Kassar switched off the screen, too tired to pay much attention.

Let the military handle it today, he thought, and closed his eyes. He prayed the bombers would stay out of San Diego today, or at least until he could get a good night's sleep.

Just as Kassar turned off his television, Mike arrived at his hotel in San Diego. He ate his dinner in the hotel restaurant and spent the evening in his room looking over Kassar's notes on the death of the truck driver. He had a map pinned to the wall and was marking it up with the location of the bombings and the warehouse when the telephone rang.

Peter Grainger, an ASIU agent assigned to the stakeout near the home of Decker's associate in crime, informed him that Hibbot was still living in his apartment. The agents who were tracking him twenty-four hours a day wanted to know if Mike wanted the man picked up.

Mike asked Grainger just to let him know when Hibbot was back in the flat. He wanted to see the man himself.

At four o-clock the next day, Mike received a text message from Grainger, telling him that Hibbot was home. Arriving discreetly, Mike parked his car around the corner from the unmarked van from which the surveillance team was operating. He knocked and jumped quickly inside the side door of the vehicle. The two men turned as Mike climbed in.

'Hi, I'm Peter Grainger, I'm new to ASIU.' one said as he shook Mike's hand. 'You must be Mike Forde?'

Peter had recognised him instantly from footage and pictures taken of him and JP at the meeting in Washington, which was announced on the television the same day. The decision had as expected, been the subject of newspaper articles every day since the beginning of the inquiry in Diego Garcia.

'Yes. Glad to know you.' Mike greeted him and turned to the other man whom he knew, 'Hi Piers.'

The tall, blonde man shook his hand heartily. 'Hi Mike, I was sorry to read about your men. It's a terrible business.' He showed Mike a map of Hibbot's home. 'We've placed fibre optic videocams in all of the rooms and the phone line is tapped. When do you want to go in?' he asked as if they were simply walking into a hotel lobby.

'I want to listen to him for a while. See if he makes any calls. Let's monitor him tonight and maybe tomorrow I'll pay him a visit. I don't want to scare him off.'

Surveillance could sometimes be a boring job but it was a necessary one in this case so Mike was happy to hang around. Throughout the evening no one visited or left Hibbot's apartment. At two twenty early the following morning, Mike saw the light blink on the monitoring equipment indicating a call being received by Hibbot. The phone rang for some time before Hibbot eventually got himself out of bed to answer it. Mike and Piers quickly picked up their headphones and listened in.

'Hibbot?' a voice asked.

'Who's asking?'

'Swanson. You know who is pulling another job. Are you interested?'

'What job?' Hibbot asked.

'A heist. Weapons. Partridge's warehouse on East Street.'

'What's in it for me?'

'Two thousand.' the voice replied.

'I want four.'

'Three. No more.' He'd been given permission to go up to five but three was enough, he would keep the rest for himself. Hibbot would never know

'Okay. Three thousand. I want two up front or I'm not interested.'

'Okay. Two before, one after.' the voice sounded impatient.

'When is it and where are we meeting?'

'Tomorrow night and we're meeting in the alleyway behind the warehouse. Call me tomorrow afternoon for the time. We'll be waiting for your call. You had better not let us down!'

The connection went dead.

Mike whistled. 'Wow, some call! We'd better tell Kassar. He ought to know about this. In fact, we could let him pick the other guys up and we can take Hibbot.'

'Yeah, it would save us picking him up beforehand and possibly having nothing to pin on him to keep him in custody.' Piers said.

Mike left and drove to the precinct.

Kassar was on the premises and available to talk to him so he walked straight to his office, knocking briefly on the window before opening the door.

'Hi!' Mike greeted Kassar.

Kassar sat down and Mike took a seat opposite him. 'How can I help you this time, Commander?'

'As a matter of interest, I have something for you!' Mike said, smiling, 'There is going to be a robbery tomorrow night at Partridge's on East Street. I want one of the men involved. Your guys can stake it out and when you have rounded them up, I want the man called Hibbot.'

'How do you know all this?' Kassar asked.

'The usual way; will you do it?'

Kassar dunked his ginger crunch cookie into his coffee. It melted quickly and he only just managed to get it to his mouth before it fell apart.

Mike looked at him in earnest. 'I need this man urgently

82

but I want you to have something that you can hold on to him for when I am finished with him. I don't want him to spill his guts out to his friends because I want to get one of them in particular. If he goes free they'll all fly and I'll never catch up with them!'

'Tell me more.' Kassar picked up his pen and started to write on his notepad.

Still monitoring Hibbot's movements, the ASIU agents were unable to hear the conversation that took place between Hibbot and the other man the following day, because Hibbot used a mobile in the middle of a crowded and noisy area so it was impossible to listen in. They had no alternative but to ask Kassar to get his men in place early in the evening.

CHAPTER FOURTEEN

The Heist

Later that night, eighteen police officers and six dogs waited on the perimeter of East Street, out of sight of either end of the alleyway. Another ten undercover officers were entrenched in hiding places inside the warehouse as they waited for the robbery to begin. A member of Kassar's team had warned the owner of the warehouse to stay away after closing up for the night. He was easily persuaded to do that.

At three forty five in the morning a large car with black tinted windows parked in a small loading bay halfway up the alleyway behind the building. Four men alighted from the vehicle and walked towards the back doors of the building.

Kassar waited until they had broken into the premises and ordered his men to close in, ready to light up the area. He watched as the shadowy figures disappeared into the blackness. When he was sure that all of the exits were covered he shouted, 'Now!' and his men ran silently into the building.

'Police officers... freeze or we shoot!' one of the officers yelled loudly.

The lights were immediately switched on and the four men tried to hide behind the stacks of wooden boxes. The officers were ready for them.

'Drop it!' one officer yelled at one of the armed men who had not seen him emerge from his hiding place immediately behind him.

The man dropped his gun and put his hands behind his head. The officer expertly grabbed his wrists, deftly twisting them behind the man's back to handcuff him. There was no resistance. Seconds later, two other officers escorted him unceremoniously outside to the security van which had screeched to a halt at the rear exit door as soon as the lights went on in the warehouse.

Another of the four men was seen hiding behind a stairwell and began shooting at anyone who approached. Carlson, another police officer, belly-crawled out of sight behind the nearby racking and approached the offender from his left. The man was distracted by officers Davies and Smith as they fired convincingly accurate shots at nearby targets.

'Freeze you scumbag!' Carlson yelled loudly, now almost touching the panicking villain.

The man turned suddenly and fired at him, falling backwards as he did so. The bullet missed Carlson and hit a light above him. Carlson twisted to one side and returned his fire immediately, jumping with great agility to his feet. The gun fell from the man's hand as he cried out in pain. The officer jumped forward and kicked the fallen gun away from the man, pointing his gun directly in the terrified man's face.

'Get up scumbag and walk straight ahead to the officer over by the door!' he ordered, holding out his arms with his finger poised a hairsbreadth above the trigger.

The man walked toward the door grimacing with the biting pain and clasping his bloody hand to his chest as he attempted to stop it from bleeding.

Kassar had a grip on a third man and was holding his left

arm high up his back. The man was yelling at him.

'You're breaking my arm you bastard. Let go of my arm!' and he tried to kick back at Kassar who kicked his legs from under him so fast he was on the ground before he had finished his sentence. Two officers held him down as they cuffed his hands behind his back then dragged him to his feet and led him out to the van.

The fourth man was exchanging fire with two of the officers at the front of the store. In a desperate attempt to escape, he shot out the window of the glass front door and as he made a dash for it, one of the officers shot him in the leg. With a cry of pain, he crashed through the broken glass. As he fell forward through the door he landed on a large sliver of glass, which stabbed him in the chest. He slumped forward, dead within seconds as a piece of glass still fixed in the door frame pierced the main artery to his heart. Kassar contacted the coroner's office as he made his way back to his car. 'That's one less villain' he said, with an air of relief in his voice to Carlson who had watched, wide-eyed with horror, as it happened. Seconds later, Carlson dashed outside and threw up the Big Mac and chocolate bar he had consumed only two hours earlier. He hated the sight of blood!

Back at the police station Kassar put each of the men into separate interview rooms.

'Hibbot is in room six. He's all yours!' he told Mike as he walked into his office. 'Let me know when you're finished with him.'

Mike entered interview room six. Hibbot was sitting at a table with his back to the wall, his hands cuffed behind him.

Mike sat opposite him, rocking on the back legs of the chair, with his feet crossed on top of the table. For a full five minutes he said nothing, just looked at Hibbot who became visibly agitated as each minute passed. He didn't know what to expect from the man sitting there, just staring at him. Mike's gaze never wandered.

Hibbot, a coward at heart, grew even more nervous. 'What is this? What're you doing here? Who are you?' he looked at the door, 'Guard! Guard! Get me out of here!' he yelled, panic rising in his throat. No one came to his rescue.

Mike continued to look at him. He knew what he was doing; he had done his homework on the man. Hibbot had been in prison twice before. He would become paranoid when he was stared at by people in a stronger position than he was. Hibbot probably thought he was in for a beating. Mike wanted him to think that.

After twenty minutes, Hibbot was constantly shifting about in his seat. He didn't dare move out of it. Mike's gun was sitting in his shoulder holster, very visible. The strap was loosened and Mike could take out the gun anytime he wanted to.

'What do you want, you've already caught me. I want to see my lawyer!' Hibbot shouted, looking decidedly scared.

CHAPTER FIFTEEN

Paulo's desert hideout

Paulo had supplied all of the items on Bill's list, after some fabrication by him as to their use in some cases. It had taken weeks after his kidnapping before they were delivered. Part of his deception had been to let his captor think it would take another month to produce the amount of Riofactol in the primitive conditions in which he was working, especially to produce large quantities, which is what Paulo wanted. Bill was relieved that for most of the time Paulo left him to it, and pleased because he knew that his stalling tactics had worked.

It seemed to Bill that the man was either not in a hurry for the drug or that he was involved in some other business at the same time. He cared little as long as he was left alone. As a precautionary measure he had, unknown to Paulo, included on the list the chemicals and substances he needed to produce a quantity of his antidote in case he needed it. It was unlikely that his captor would know the difference.

Bill was afraid but cautious by nature. He thought that once he had successfully demonstrated the quantities and routine application of injections, Paulo would have no further use for him. He feared that the insane madman might decide to use the Riofactol on him. He had decided to produce the antidote because it was his only protection against that possibility.

The days came and went monotonously and he very rarely

left his lab except to sleep in his bed at night. There were a few occasions when Paulo was drunk and he had sought him out, then the doctor had been allowed to walk about in the mouth of the cave. It was a relief to breathe the cool night air of the desert.

One evening, Paulo again called him from his cell. He was even more drunk than usual and had an almost empty bottle of spirits in his hand. 'See how kind I am. Come... let us go up into the outside air for a walk.' An armed guard followed them both as they made their way up to the cave entrance.

Bill followed the man up the stone staircase. He did not particularly want Paulo's company but the fresh night air was always welcomed. The lab was stuffy and his room stank of unwashed clothes. If only he had more clothes to wear.

'How are you... um... liking your... work, Doc...tor Willington.' Paulo's accent was stronger and his speech was hesitant and slurred.

'I would like it more if I knew what you were going to do with it.' Bill replied.

'Ah... my dear... doctor. I have a great... plan…' Paulo stumbled on the last stair as they walked up towards the mouth of the cave, '…in mind!'

'And how can my work help you with that?'

They had reached the top and Paulo walked unsteadily into the moonlight. The sky was clear and the stars were bright. Bill wished he knew more about astronomy, maybe if he did he would be able to get a clearer idea about where he was. This desert could be any desert!

Turning suddenly, Paulo, sweating and almost falling

down, put his hand on Bill's shoulder to steady himself as he took a slug from the bottle. Then he whispered in a low voice, 'I am going to become the richest man in the world, my friend, and your genbrictic hypnosis and your drug are going to help me!' His vile breath disgusted his prisoner as much as his words. The four guards stood attentively at the mouth of the cave to ensure they did not attract Paulo's attention.

At first Bill thought he was just trying to scare him but something in the man's demeanour eventually made him realise that the evil bastard was serious. Paulo said no more, and sat on one of the hewn sandstone seats watching him as he finished off the golden solace.

The guards watched them both and as on many occasions, without reacting when Paulo drew out his gun and shot wildly into the outside sky. They knew it would be madness to move away from their posts or to approach Paulo when he was so drunk.

Thoughts of escape did not enter Bill's head; he knew it would be foolish to attempt it. He had seen no sign of transport at any time, although he did once or twice hear a noise that sounded like a helicopter landing. He had often wondered how people arrived and left the camp; perhaps there was a helicopter somewhere? But there would be no comfort in knowing that. Even if it were true and if he did manage to escape, he couldn't fly a kite much less a helicopter.

Within three weeks of receiving the contents of the list he had given to Paulo, the doctor had produced enough of the drug to be prepared for a demonstration. He had stalled for as long as he dared. Paulo's patience visibly wore out on his last visit to the lab and his rage was so great that Bill was too afraid of his captor to attempt another delay.

Some weeks later, at eight o-clock in the evening Paulo arrived in his lab, very much the worse for alcohol and looking decidedly enraged. 'I want to see what you have done. You have had enough time!' he snarled drunkenly. 'Show me! Where is my drug?'

Bill walked over to a small glass flask supported on a metal stand and full of clear yellow liquid, marked with the letter 'R' for Riofactol. 'Here it is,' he said.

'What! You have spent so many weeks working on that? Why is there so small an amount?' he stormed.

'This is a test batch and it is necessary to refine it otherwise it is dangerous. The drug must be as pure as possible, if not, you will kill the subjects. The refinement is a long process. It cannot be rushed. Even such a small amount takes a long time. Larger amounts would take even longer. Remember that this is not my lab, the equipment is not the best available and you did not let me select anything myself. I have had to make do with what your men chose for me!' Bill was desperate to fool the man into believing him.

Paulo looked at him suspiciously. Abruptly he said, 'You will demonstrate the process to me tomorrow!' and staggered out of the room, touching the wall in an effort to prevent himself from falling over.

Relieved but shaken, Bill knew it was going to be a very long and sleepless night. He was thankful that he had managed to fool Paulo for so long. Most of his time had really been taken up with secretly making the antidote. As far as any of

Paulo's soldiers were concerned when they walked into the lab, he was grinding refining powder. They were none the wiser. So far he had managed to tuck away almost two hundred antidote pills in a sterilised, sealed container hidden inside the underlining of the sofa in his room because he had no idea how long he would be kept a prisoner. As a precaution he took two pills each day.

Also hidden away at the back of the lab, Bill had secreted enough pill mass for another sixty-four pills. It had taken him a long time to make them because he did not have a proper machine. With some effort he had managed to make a very rough and basic pill-making frame from two blocks of soft wood, which he found at the back of the lab. They were probably off-cuts from when the benches were built. The frame had taken some time to make because he could only work on it when he knew Paulo was asleep and there was little risk of discovery.

The wooden frame, which was thirty centimetres long and about fifteen centimetres wide, was quite smooth. He had carefully cut eight v-shaped grooves, each about one centimetre deep and ten centimetres long, side by side, across the narrow top part of it. The only means of sterilising the frame without risking discovery was to pour boiling water over it.

Bill made the pills by mixing up a smooth pill mass with the new form of Tintomin, combined with syrup, which he made from sugar, to which he added a proportion of calcium and eighty five percent dried root powder. After he had rolled the paste-like mixture over the grooves in the wood, by

93

pushing it hard over them with another piece of wood, he was left with eight ten centimetre triangular strips of pill mass. It took a lot of time and patience to cut each strip, using a fine wooden scalpel, into halves, quarters and then eighths, repeating this until the pills were the correct size. Bill was proud of the wooden scalpel, which he kept hidden in the hem of his jacket. He had made it himself from another small piece of waste wood from that which he had used to make the pill-making frame. He knew nothing about carpentry and had relied on his instincts to make the scalpel. It was short and very thin, and not strong enough to strike a deadly blow but it served his purpose well enough.

Paulo did not allow him to have any metal items that could be turned against himself or his men. The knife he used to create the pill-making frame was an accidental discovery under one of the benches in the darkest corner of his room. The blade was broken but it was sharp enough to cut the soft wood. It was too short to be used as a weapon. In any case there was nowhere to go so it was easier not to risk death by trying to escape, or angering his captors.

When the pills were cut he rolled each one individually in his palm until it was round, then he pressed it flat. He left them all covered over and hidden at the back of the cave with the others to dry out. With the right equipment he could have made thousands in the time it took him to make sixty-four. He thanked his lucky stars that he had studied the history of medicine at college, which was how he had learned the primitive method for making up his pills. His carpentry skills were not great but the frame was as good as he could make it.

At about nine thirty the next morning Paulo sent one of his soldiers to carry Bill's equipment and chemicals to a small room. A table and four chairs stood in the centre of the room. Bill placed his equipment in a particular order on the table and sat down on one of the chairs. One of Paulo's soldiers stood guard at the door, which remained open.

Shortly afterwards Paulo and another man arrived with a white-faced soldier walking in front of him. The accompanying guard had his gun pointed at the handcuffed soldier's back. Fear showed in the man's eyes as the guard ordered him to sit on a chair.

Bill was shocked but not surprised to see Dr Elio Garcia walking beside Paulo. His captor had boasted once before of the traitor's loyalty to him. All hope of a miracle rescue seemed to fade. He wondered if anyone else from the project team might be working with the madman. Marsha Kepler would never turn traitor, he was certain about that, but there were a few other, less influential individuals working with her.

Garcia would not meet his eyes and behaved as if Bill did not exist.

Paulo surveyed the hypodermic syringes on the table and gestured with his thumb at the soldier. 'Inject him!' He commanded, looking at Bill.

Bill hesitated, seeing the fear still in the soldier's wide eyes as he approached him.

'Inject him! Now!' ordered Paulo, pointing his gun at Bill's chest.

It was clear that to Bill that he would be shot if he didn't do as he was ordered. Pushing the needle of the syringe into the small jar holding the liquid, Bill drew out a measured amount of Riofactol. Squirting a small amount of the liquid out of the syringe, he carefully injected the young man who, not knowing what was going to happen to him, gasped as the needle went into his arm.

The three men watched for five minutes until the soldier relaxed, his eyes glazed over and he stared unfocussed, straight ahead. Garcia ordered the man to follow him, and took him out of the room. Ten minutes later the two men returned and Garcia ordered the soldier to sit. The soldier sat next to Paulo.

'Now what?' Paulo asked Garcia. 'What do you do now?'

'Ask him questions. Tell him to do something, anything. He will do it.' Garcia replied arrogantly.

'Are you saying that I can ask him to do anything?' Paulo asked, astonished.

'That is correct.' Garcia was smug.

'Will he remember doing it?'

'No. Not unless you ask him to remember what he has done.' Garcia confirmed.

'This is wonderful!' Paulo cried, excitedly. 'Just think what we can do with this!' Then he turned to Bill. 'Do you see now why I brought you here? I can achieve anything now!'

Bill looked at him in disgust. 'No. I don't. What proud deeds can you achieve with that!' he pointed to the soldier, who did not move or speak.

The expression on Paulo's face changed. 'I would be very careful if I were you!' his features hardened. 'You may have done too good of a job!' He walked over to the soldier who had supervised Bill's activity. 'Take him back to his lab.'

The guard grasped Bill's arm roughly and pushed him out of the room then followed, closing the door behind him.

Paulo walked in front of the chair where the soldier sat. He looked at his face and saw compliance in his eyes. He was like a child with a new toy.

'What is your name, soldier?'

Looking straight ahead at nothing in particular, the soldier replied evenly, 'Gerd Schumacher.'

'Where are you from, Gerd?'

'Orlando.' he said without expression, his eyes continued to stare straight ahead as if he was focusing out of an invisible window.

Paulo stopped walking around the chair. 'Have you killed anyone, Gerd?'

'Yes.'

'Who did you kill?'

'Terrorists.' The man frowned slightly, as if he was trying to remember something.

'Can you make bombs?'

'Yes sir.'

Paulo sat on one of the chairs, smiled his evil smile at Garcia and leaned excitedly towards Gerd. 'How very interesting!' he said. He turned to Garcia, 'We have another messenger. Get in touch with our friend. Tell him I am sending him another package.'

Bill sat in his room, gutted to his very core. The poor soldier; Garcia knew that a lot of psychological counselling went into the treatment and he should never apply the drug without it. Without rehabilitation the man would behave almost like a zombie. It was cruelty to an extreme. He wished he had never invented the damned drug.

What would his captors do with him now? Paulo had what he wanted. Would he shoot him or use him as an experiment? In a panic, he checked that the guard had locked his door and took out the box from the back of the sofa. Picking up a handful of Tintomin pills, he put all but one into a small plastic bag. Using his scalpel, he hacked out two inches of stitches on the inside hem of his lab coat. Afraid of being caught, he worked quickly to ease the bag into the inside of the hem and then secured it again with a few knotted threads. He swallowed the remaining pill with a glass of water, reminding himself again that he ought to take one every morning and at night before he went to sleep.

On their own the pills were harmless enough. If Paulo had him injected with Riofactol, the chemical already in his body would counteract the effect. At least he hoped it would, he had only tried it on his lab volunteer as an antidote after the injection, not before, and taken a series of blood samples to monitor the circulation of the drug in his system. The volunteer was under the impression that he was contributing to research about a sleeping pill. It had been vital to keep the research a secret at the university. The volunteer had come to no harm. The results looked promising but the doctor had no catatonic patients to experiment on. Was he to be the first?

CHAPTER SIXTEEN

Interrogation

Mike was determined to find out from Hibbot where Decker was hiding. When he was sure that the man was sufficiently scared of him, he stood up and walked slowly behind the man's chair. Hibbot looked over his shoulder nervously, his face pale, palms sweating from fear. He could sense the strength of the man behind him and had seen the determination in the set of his strong jaw. There was something resembling violence in the demeanour of the man and he feared the cold, steely eyes which his had met briefly when he plucked up the courage to look into them. He gripped his handcuffs to stop his hands from shaking.

'Decker. I want Decker.' Mike finally said, his mouth almost touching Hibbot's left ear. 'Where is he?'

'Wh...who's Decker?' the man stalled, his face turning even paler than before. He was relieved when Mike stepped away from him.

'Don't take a chance on fooling with me, Hibbot!' Mike replied coldly, his voice deathly calm. 'Where is he?'

He returned to his seat in front of the man and with unblinking eyes, continued to look directly at the scared face. He took out his gun without removing his gaze and slipped the safety catch off then casually extracted a silencer from his pocket and screwed it onto the nuzzle, hoping his bluff would work. He had no intention of shooting the man but Hibbot did not know that.

Hibbot watched him, his mouth open and eyes wide with fright.

'I want Decker. Where is he?' Mike repeated.

'Hey, man. I don't know anyone called Decker!' The balding scalp damply reflected the light from the ceiling. Hibbot wanted to wipe the sweat off his face but he could not because of his cuffed hands. The sweat rolled from his forehead into his thin eyebrows, and then down his face.

'You do.' Mike said simply, looking directly into the frightened eyes and pointing his gun directly at Hibbot. He got out of his chair and again walked slowly behind Hibbot and stood menacingly close behind him.

'Haven't you wondered why it is there's just the two of us in this room? Do you think someone is going to run in here? They won't hear the shot!' Mike laughed. 'Nobody here cares about you, Hibbot. To the men in this building you are just another loser! Scum! There's no one here to see or hear me shoot you. I'll dump your body in the sewers and the coroner will conclude you were killed by your mates.'

Mike waited to see the impact of his words.

Hibbot's body tensed up and he looked at the door, wishing he were fast enough to get through it and away from the maniac behind him.

'If you don't tell me, someone else will!' Mike said carelessly. He pushed the silencer into the nape of Hibbot's neck so that the man could feel the cold steel next to his skin.

Hibbot swallowed, almost choking in terror. 'You can't do this! I should be protected here! You can't shoot me!' he moved forward in his chair. 'I have rights!'

Mike laughed wickedly. 'Can't I? Do you think any cop in this precinct is going to protect someone who is prepared to shoot at their friends? We both know what happened back there. You threw away your rights when you attacked police officers.' The gun was pushed harder into the sweaty, hot neck. 'I'm going to count to three. When I get to three, I shoot!'

'One ...!'

The man shook constantly with fear as he continued to squirm stiffly and uncomfortably in his seat.

'He'll kill me! He'll kill me. I can't tell you... I daren't tell you!' he cried.

'Two ...!' Mike leaned over his head, threateningly and whispered harshly in the man's ear, 'What difference does it make. Either he kills you or I do! Or you tell me and live. You'll get a fair trial.'

The man struggled to reason within himself, realising he was trapped, either way.

'Three ..!' Mike knew the chamber was empty of bullets but Hibbot did not. His finger pressed lightly on the trigger knowing his victim could feel the vibration as the gun moved slightly under the pressure.

'Okay! Okay! I'll tell you! D...d...don't shoot! For God's sake don't shoot!' He cried pitifully, his voice rising two octaves. He tried to curl into a ball on the chair away from the gun, drawing up his knees as if to protect himself. He was afraid he was too late and waited for the impact of the bullet.

Mike returned slowly to his seat, making a show of pressing the safety catch back on, removing the silencer and returning his gun to its holster.

'That's better!' he said, returning to his seat. 'Tell me!'

Hibbot relaxed cautiously, his white knuckles kneading together. He was ready to sing. Decker wasn't worth dying for.

'He has a girlfriend. She lives in an apartment in Harbour Drive. Her name is Sheree and she works in a bar at the Pasadena Village Hotel. He goes to visit her there sometimes. I don't think he lives there all the time.'

'What does he look like?'

'Tall... above six foot... athletic build, about forty-six. Long, white hair, blue eyes, you can't miss him! He wears a tan leather jacket sometimes; he stole it from someone he killed.' Hibbot was thoroughly miserable. 'You'll protect me from him won't you?' he begged, anxiously. 'He'll kill me if he gets to know I told you all of this!'

'He won't kill you, don't worry. When was the last time you saw him?' Mike replied.

'Four days ago. He was with someone; they were planting a bomb in the city. He never said anything to me about it. I just overheard him when he was telling his boss he had done it. As far as I know the bomb hasn't gone off yet. That's all I know. Honest!'

Shaking with relief but still frightened, Hibbot's voice trembled uncontrollably as he spoke.

Mike asked, 'You don't know his friend's name?'

'No. I never saw him before the day they planted the bomb in the city centre. The other guy acted kinda funny, like he didn't know where he was half the time. He was a white man and he did what Decker told him to. Everything. I never saw anything like it!'

'What do you mean?' Mike asked. The man's words seemed to make no sense. Only people who knew what they were doing would get involved in planting bombs in the middle of cities.

'I don't know. He never spoke, even when Decker spoke to him.' Hibbot stared momentarily unseeing, at the table, a picture of the weird man appeared in his mind. 'A kid! He was like a thirty-year-old kid' he looked up. 'I never saw anything like it before. It sure as hell spooked me!'

Mike pressed a button on the communication console. A guard walked into the room.

'Look after him for a while.' Mike ordered.

The guard stepped inside, drew his weapon and locked the door.

Mike made for Kassar's office. The inspector sat writing at his desk. He looked up as Mike walked in. 'Well, did you get what you wanted?'

'I got enough for the moment. Apparently Decker was involved in planting a bomb somewhere in the city centre four days ago. As it obviously hasn't gone off yet you'd better get a search set up.'

'What do you want me to do with him?'

'Keep him for the moment. You have enough evidence to hold on to him. Thanks for your cooperation in catching him.' Mike yawned. 'I think I'll go home and catch up on some sleep now. Goodnight inspector.'

'Goodnight. Thanks for the information!' Kassar picked up his mobile and dialled the number for the bomb squad. He sighed heavily; it was going to be yet another long night and

103

tomorrow promised to be an even longer day!

An hour earlier on the East Coast, another bomb went off outside the rear of the Capitol building in Washington. It had been hidden out of sight at the side of the steps leading up to the main entrance to the building. No-one saw anything, it was a foggy, rainy day, but the security tape showed two men who had emerged from a car at the rear entrance.

The tapes from the internal security cameras showed the two men going through the various rooms but at some point they both just simply vanished.

The body of the guard who would normally be standing outside the door lay on the floor beside it. The camera lens on the wall nearby had been sprayed with a silicon polish from the stairs behind it, rendering the tape useless from that point onwards. The only clue to the identity of the perpetrator was the hand that sprayed the polish, which wore a black leather glove, but it could have been anyone's.

Worse still, the guard's body had been booby-trapped. Bomb-defusing experts evacuated the building and after ensuring that it was kept well guarded on the outside, defused the booby trap in little under an hour. At least the guard would get a decent burial.

Kassar sighed when he heard the news. The exhausted detective inspector already knew there were not enough officers available to search for bombs over such a wide area. Just after eight thirty the next morning a huge explosion rocked one of the shopping Plazas in the heart of the city. Half an hour later and the numbers would have more than trebled.

CHAPTER SEVENTEEN

Deception

After each batch of Riofactol was made Bill would pass what seemed like weeks in absolute boredom. There was no night and day in his existence. He had read all the books in his lab from cover to cover and often either sat for hours with nothing to do, or slept fitfully, often reliving the kidnap and he would awake feeling the same terror.

The supply of chemicals and raw substances was exhausted, which meant that Bill was unable to make more Tintomin. He had three hundred pills left but as he didn't know how long he would be held prisoner he decided to worry about the consequences only if the well hidden supply ran out. He had taken every opportunity to increase his stock of the precious antidote, and there was nothing more he could do to protect himself. Staying alive was all that mattered. He had no way of telling how long he had been a prisoner but it seemed like an eternity. He had also stopped counting the number of times he was given a meal because there was, with only few exceptions, nothing in the food to indicate whether it was a breakfast or a dinner.

Eventually, after another very long and boring day, Bill heard the door being unlocked and Paulo walked into his room. 'I must congratulate you, Doctor Willington. Your genbriotic hypnotherapy really does work!' Paulo handed him the Washington Post, which was dated ten days earlier.

Bill read the headlines as Paulo tapped arrogantly with his finger at the newspaper.

"More bomb blasts in the cities! Shocked pedestrians and security guards ran for their lives as a bomb exploded at the Capitol building yesterday..." Paulo grinned wickedly and passed the newspaper to his horrified prisoner.

Bill read on, shocked to think that his teams' development of genbriotic hypnotherapy was responsible.

"The force of the blast blew out several windows and was felt over three hundred yards away. San Diego is also in mourning for the thirty eight people who died and over one hundred members of the public who were injured.

No-one has claimed responsibility but Police are studying security tapes from both areas in the hope of finding clues to the identity of the bombers…"

The article went into more graphic detail and Bill couldn't read any further. He was sick with shock and horror as he realised what Paulo was congratulating him for.

Throwing the newspaper to the ground he shouted, 'You bastard! I never intended it to be used for that!'

Paulo just laughed. 'Maybe you didn't doctor, but I did! Do you know how much money I can make setting bombs for my friends, thanks to you of course? There is a certain justice in this!' he said harshly, 'They are killing themselves anyway with all their pollution and fast food. I am helping them to do it better!' He walked out of the door, locking it afterwards and left Bill shaking with rage and despair.

Half an hour later Paulo returned with Garcia who was dressed in a white coat, and carried a small tray.

106

Bill couldn't help shaking as he saw the hypodermic syringe and a small bottle of Riofactol laid out on a metallic rectangular tray.

'I just want to make sure you cooperate, Dr Willington!' Paulo smiled wickedly at him. His expression changed, 'Do it!' he ordered Garcia as he took a gun from his holster and pointed it at Bill. 'Do not resist. If you do, I will kill you!'

Bill did not openly resist but fought mentally to retain control of his mind, as he prayed that the antidote would work for him in the way he hoped it would. He sat on the sofa as his eyes suddenly watered and the room swam before him. After Garcia and Paulo were finished with him, he closed his eyes and went to sleep on the sofa, as Garcia had instructed him to do.

The room was dark when Bill woke up and he had a dull headache. Garcia had overdosed him slightly, but apart from that he felt fine! Normally, the subjects had no memory of the hypnosis or the injection. It was a good sign. Bill ran through the chain of events up to his being injected and everything, including the instructions Garcia had given him was clear in his mind. It had worked! Now he was certain that he could maintain control of himself.

Paulo had ordered him to cooperate and attempted to make him believe that he and Garcia were his friends. Bill knew he would be forced to go along with that or risk death. They would not keep him alive if they thought he could not be made to do as they wished.

He had to get out of this somehow, but how? He was deep in an underground fortress with no one to help him escape.

Taking a deep breath, Bill walked out of his room after finding that his door had been left unlocked and open. He heard Paulo's loud laughter and headed in the general direction of the sound. He found his captor in a large stone room where Paulo had directed him to meet with himself and Garcia, 'For a social get together as soon as he awoke,' he had ordered. Bill hoped his act was convincing.

He was not interested in socialising with his captors but pretended to be so in order to avoid suspicion.

The sound of laughter greeted him as he walked into the makeshift bar. The two men sat at a table, their glasses half filled with beer. One of them called to him.

'Bill, my friend; come sit with us! Have a drink!'

'Yes, do have a drink,' Garcia insisted, hardly able to contain his smug satisfaction at his handiwork.

Stan smiled back as sincerely as possible; he hoped it would fool them as he greeted them cheerfully, 'Thanks Paulo. I think I will!'

The two men roared with laughter.

Dr Elio Garcia looked across at Paulo, 'You see! It works. Now we wait for our little messenger to come home!'

Bill looked on, smiling with great difficulty but enough, he hoped, to fool his captors as he took a drink from his glass. You bastards, he thought to himself, I'll get the better of you yet... you don't know everything!

Decker returned to the desert hideout two days after Bill had learned of his own part in the bombings. More stolen weapons were transported via Nixon Freight by Neko's brother-in-law. The aircraft flew first to Sana'a, where the deadly cargo was unloaded and then reloaded straight onto another boat at night. Customs officials were bribed to look the other way. They knew that Paulo's friend always made it worth their while and they knew better than to make an enemy of the man.

The men then shipped their haul around the Gulf of Aden to Rakhyut in Oman as they had done several times before. Some of the sailors on board were in Paulo's employment. They knew without doubt that they would be killed if they talked so no-one ever did, especially as their main motivation to keep silent increased their meagre income quite substantially.

It was always risky unloading the weapons by small boat to the shore, but the sailors always chose the darkest night when the waves were not too rough. They bribed anyone they needed to or threatened death so encountered no opposition from any quarter. The guns, ammunition and explosives were safely stored in a hideout close to the shore until the trucks arrived to take them to Paulo's hideout. None of the sailors knew where that was and they did not care as long as they were paid.

Decker sat in his private quarters, drinking beer with Paulo. A tall man sat quietly behind them, speaking to no-one. His fair hair was damp with sweat and his eyes stared straight ahead as if he were blind.

Paulo looked at the quiet man then at Decker expectantly. 'Well?'

'It worked perfectly. I think he could do it on his own now

so you can send him back if you want to. There was no trouble. Not for us anyway...'

Paulo smiled, totally satisfied. 'Good, Elio will work on the others. Now we will never need to use our own men. That lessens the risk of discovery. We can now begin our campaign! Soon we will be richer than we dreamed possible! Our contacts in Afghanistan and Iraq have already announced their interest in our most recent acquisition. Of course I will not sell him, but I will continue to set up bombs for them as long as they continue to pay me. These stupid Americans, they will not know what hit them!' He raised his glass, 'To success!' he roared, feeling in incredibly good spirits. The trial run was over, time to begin in earnest!

'Success!' replied Decker raising his glass. All he had to do was baby-sit and pick up his share of the money. That was all that mattered.

CHAPTER EIGHTEEN

The Return

Four days later, another bomb blast rocked San Diego. Kassar and his men were kept busy investigating the previous attack and were unprepared for the next one, which devastated an area near the Sun Sport Centre, a shopping and leisure complex next to the harbour.

The strange thing about the bombing was that it happened in the middle of the large car park outside of the centre itself. Kassar was one of the first on the scene.

All the cars around the blast were wrecked and burnt when the fuel tanks caught fire. Some cars had shattered windscreens and burnt or bubbled paintwork and tyres. The fires were out by the time the medical trucks had departed with the victims, who were mostly suffering from slight burns and injuries from flying glass.

Only one victim died at the scene. The partially burned torso of a man was found at the heart of the explosion. He had died instantly. His hands and lower legs had been blown off and were found by a shocked police officer between twenty and forty metres away under some of the cars. The coroner had the body and limbs moved immediately to the local pathology lab.

Ben Harrington had just arrived on duty when the body bag was wheeled into the lab. The hands and legs had been placed in separate polythene bags then bundled together in the large black bag. A label with a number written on it in waterproof ink, which corresponded to the case number, was tied to the clothing that remained on the man's torso.

He scrutinised the map of the incident and read the notes accompanying the body, his eyes taking in the state of the burned flesh around the neck and chin. The eyes of the corpse were half-open, and the mouth was closed. The upper arms and forehead was not so badly affected but the hair had been burned off at the forehead. The flesh on the lower half of the torso from the waist down was very badly torn and scorched. The torn stumps of the legs were also very badly burned where that end of the torso had lain, and been captured on one of the photographs taken at the scene, near a burning car.

The man had caught the effects of the blast from about thigh level. Ben turned his attention to the legs and hands. They were intact except for the impact area. At least he could get some prints from the fingers. That would help with identifying the man.

He called Patty, his assistant, and asked her to take some fingerprints from the hands. She was experienced in the lab but had never been confronted by detached limbs before. She looked in horror at the hands that Ben had placed on the stainless steel tray on the bench.

'Go on. They won't grab you!' he laughed. 'I need a complete set of prints. When you have finished ask Kassar to arrange for one of his men to run them through ICID. Tell him I want the results quickly because I need at least two foolproof sources of identity before I can ask the precinct counselling staff to contact relatives. If ICID doesn't come up with anything, ask him to check the military records, this guy looks pretty fit. He could easily have been a soldier with that tattoo.' He pointed to the remains of a shield emblem tattooed on the upper arm. It was half obscured by burnt flesh.

Feeling decidedly nauseous, Patty picked up the tray of hands with her own gloved ones and did as she was asked. It was a great relief to bag them and put them away. She gave the envelope with its labelled fingerprints inside to a courier. The police precinct was only five minutes away by car. When the courier arrived, the envelope and orders were delivered to Kassar's office.

Mike drove to the address on Harbour Drive that Hibbot had given to him. He rang the doorbell and waited around for five minutes. The bell was unanswered. He looked through the opaque window in the door but here were no signs of anyone being at home so he drove to the Pasadena Village Hotel. It was one o-clock and the bar would be open. Maybe Sheree was working. After parking his car, he took off his tie and opened his shirt collar. It would not do for him to look too much like a cop in case he scared her off, which would be decidedly unhelpful. He wanted Decker and he wanted him fast!

The hotel was quite respectable but the basement bar was noisy. He could hear and feel the loud music pumping its vibrations up the metal staircase as he walked down it. Trade was quite busy but the large room was not overcrowded. A blonde barmaid approached him and took Mike's order, as he took a seat at the long bar Her perfume wafted pleasantly into his nostrils. Turning her back to Mike, her hips swayed provocatively as she pressed a tumbler to one of the optics.

Smiling as she placed the drink on the bar in front of him, the young woman looked him up and down with appreciation. 'We don't often get a good-looking guy like you in here. It's mostly kids.'

'Thanks, I'm flattered.' said Mike, returning her smile. 'I was hoping to see Sheree today. Is she in?'

'I'm Sheree. Who are you?' she asked. 'I've never seen you here before. How do you know me?'

'I'm Mike, a friend of a friend of yours.' He replied.

'Hi, Mike, and who might my friend be?' she responded. 'I know most of my friends' friends and I still haven't seen you before!'

'Decker. You know, long white hair, blue eyes.' he stared unflinchingly at her. 'Nice body.'

'Nice body?' she laughed. 'Do you know him well then?'

Embarrassed, Mike laughed; he had meant to say athletic body. It was a Freudian slip. His mind was appreciating her body and his mouth did the rest.

'Not that well, but I know you do!' Red faced, he picked up his glass and took a sip.

'So what?' she said defensively, 'He doesn't own me. I see him sometimes when he's around.'

'Is he around today?'

'No.' Sheree leaned closer, her breasts almost resting on the bar between her elbows as she moved further toward him. 'Does that make it easier for you and me?'

'Well… it could,' Mike replied, somewhat taken aback by her blatant approach. What time do you finish?'

'At three o-clock.' She wrote a number on a scrap of paper. 'Call me after three thirty?'

'Thanks. I'll do that.' He smiled. That was easy!

At three thirty five as he had promised, Mike contacted Sheree and arranged to meet her. Half an hour later, having removed his jacket, he was sitting on her sofa. After finishing work, Sheree had hurriedly showered and changed into a skimpy top and a pair of tight fitting leggings that complimented her slim body.

In broad daylight, Mike estimated her age at around forty-five. She was pretty without doubt but her blonde hair was not her natural colour. He could see short red hair roots that were probably hidden in the reflections from the coloured lighting in the bar.

She poured a glass of white wine from a green bottle. 'You want some too?' she asked.

'Yes, thanks.' he replied.

Handing him his glass she sat down close beside him and patted the top of his thigh. 'Boy, you are solid!' she observed as she felt the taut muscles below the fabric of his trousers.

'Thanks. I work on it.' he replied. 'Do you think you should be doing that? What if Decker comes back?' He removed her hand gently He was fishing.

'He won't.' Sheree said cynically, placing her hand again on his leg. She knew what she was doing. If he were around she wouldn't dare be seen with any other man. Decker was a jealous man and she had felt the weight of his fist before. He was away and she liked the look of Mike.

'How do you know?' Mike insisted, feeling like a boa

constrictor's dinner. It was not his intention to get involved with her, he just wanted some information. A man would have to be blind to think anything other than that she was a very attractive woman to look at. However, she was clearly not the sort of woman he would be proud to introduce to his uncle and aunt. They would think he had taken leave of his senses. It was clear that she had no feelings of loyalty to Decker and was making her desire for him very clear.

Sheree sighed. 'He's out of the country.'

'Where? How do you know?' He was determined to find Decker and he would do whatever it took.

'I don't know where he is. He said he was going to Washington.' Unperturbed, Sheree removed her hand and unbuttoned her top, placing his hand on her uncovered breast.

Mike was not at all interested in Sheree, despite her attractions but her way of communicating seemed to be pretty clear. It was lamb-to-slaughter time.

Later in the afternoon Mike lay completely relaxed in a hot bath. He preferred a shower, but Sheree claimed priority. His body glowed with the aftermath of their encounter. The woman in question had already showered and had changed into her working clothes. She was due back at work at six and was now running a little late, but she cared little about that!

Swinging her car keys in her hand, she walked happily into the bathroom. 'I've got to go now, I'm late. Don't get up!' She laughed, amused by the thought, 'Are we going to meet again? I won't tell Decker if you don't.'

'How can I refuse?' he smiled back falsely, feeling dreadfully guilty. 'Why don't I give you a call again tomorrow?'

He would not see her again unless he absolutely had to. Having sex with the woman was one thing. His job was something else. Taking a bath was a useful delaying tactic to ensure the woman was out of the house before him.

'Okay.' Sheree made her way to her car, calling, 'Lock the door when you leave!'

After she left, Mike hurriedly dried and dressed himself. Neatly and methodically, he spent two hours going through every drawer, cupboard and shelf looking for signs of Decker's whereabouts. There were some articles of men's clothes in a wardrobe in one room, including a tan leather jacket. If it belonged to Decker, wherever he was he obviously didn't need it with him. Frustrated, Mike found nothing to indicate where the man could be found. He was good. He was too damn good.

Back at his hotel, Mike picked up a message that Kassar had left for him at the desk. He had switched off his mobile before visiting Sheree. The inspector was still at the precinct when he called him. The man's voice reflected anxiety.

'Mike... thanks for calling back. I need you here right now. Come over to the precinct right away! I'll explain when you're here. Something important has come up and I think you will be interested to know about it.'

Mike did not waste any time asking questions. Within twenty minutes he joined the inspector in his office. Kassar handed him a coffee as soon as he walked in the door.

'What has happened? Have you found Decker?' he asked.

'No. Worse than that.' Kassar handed him a data sheet printout, complete with a photograph. He had printed it off after a search of the military database. 'We found him! This is your bomber. He was killed when the bomb detonated prematurely according to the autopsy, but I guess you don't need the report to tell you that.'

Mike read the information on the sheet and looked in amazement at the photograph. The face was not a particularly clear image but it was recognisable. Shaking his head in disbelief, he cried, 'This can't be possible! It just isn't possible!' He could not believe what he was seeing.

Kassar shook his head. 'It's true. The records are accurate. His fingerprints and dental records all check out. We'll know about his blood sometime tomorrow. Samples have been sent to the local lab for testing. This man has been identified as a soldier, Gerd Schumacher, from Orlando.'

'Gerd Schumacher? Jesus Christ!' He just could not accept it. 'I know... knew Gerd! He could never have planted bombs in America even if we wanted him to!' Mike was astounded. He pointed at the face on the photograph. 'This soldier vanished last year in a military aircraft over the Indian Ocean!'

'I read about that and your guys told me that when I rang them earlier.' Kassar was astonished, 'Are you sure we are talking about the same man?'

Mike nodded. 'Yes. I knew him well before I joined ASIU. I know his face as well as my own. This is definitely the Gerd Schumacher that I knew.'

Kassar was adamant. 'Then how can he be turning up here, dead? If he were loyal to the Peacekeeping forces why would he be planting bombs in San Diego? Why would he not just go home to his family? They would be happy to have him home! It doesn't make sense!'

Mike was wondering the same thing. 'It certainly doesn't. I need to talk to a colleague in Washington.' The whole thing was inconceivable. 'Don't do anything about this until you hear from me. There is something not quite right about this! In the meantime, ask the military records office to double check their personnel records and if you get anything further from the forensic examination I can be reached on this agency address.' Mike wrote down his email address. 'Let me know immediately!'

The two men left the precinct, Kassar heading for home and Mike to his hotel, despite his mood, to eat a light supper. His activity that afternoon had given him a very hearty appetite but his meeting with Kassar had somewhat diminished it.

Gerd a bomber? No way! Mike was certain.

CHAPTER NINETEEN

The Link

Smiling, JP welcomed Mike back to the agency the following day. He had waited at the reception desk after signing the papers for Mike's new security pass which had just been made. JP handed him his pass card.

'Hi Mike. Are you continuing your investigations here now?' Mike had emailed his boss in advance of his return to Washington. He had not given JP a reason for his return.

'No. I have something to tell you which I know you will not believe!' Mike still did not believe it himself.

JP's smile faded as he looked into Mike's face and saw the seriousness of his expression. 'Not bad news I hope. Willington isn't dead is he?'

'No. This is nothing to do with the doctor. This is something entirely different.'

Minutes later they were on the eighth floor, sitting at the meeting table in JP's office.

JP was puzzled. 'What's all this about then?'

'At this point, I'm not sure,' Mike confessed, running his hand through his hair, hardly knowing how to start because it all seemed so unbelievable. 'I'm not sure what it means but we need to discuss this latest bombing event in San Diego.'

He sat down at the table and accepted the coffee JP handed to him. Handing him a copy of Kassar's printout from the military database, Mike began, 'Yesterday, the body of a soldier was found after a bomb blast in San Diego. He was one of ours. What makes this situation even worse is that he was one of the soldiers aboard the aircraft that went missing across the Indian Ocean. A police inspector in San Diego had his fingerprints and dental records checked and confirmed against the military staff database. He has asked them to check their records again. To add to the accuracy of identity of the body, he also arranged for a blood test so they could check his DNA with a family member. I know how hard it is to believe that he is one of ours but we must consider the possibility. From the photo, I believe that it is Gerd Schumacher but nothing on this earth will convince me that he is a terrorist.

The result from the blood test is due back today. Kassar is busy tracing his sister who lives in Fort Lauderdale. A police officer called at her home last night but she was not at home. They will be trying to contact her again as I speak. He will call me as soon as the body has been officially identified.'

'What?' JP could hardly believe his ears. 'Are you saying that our own soldiers are bombing our cities? Why would they want to do that?'

Mike shook his head, 'I'm not saying anything of the sort. It could be that there was a mix up over the identification given to Kassar. His sister will confirm either that he is the man we believe him to be or that an error in identification has taken place. We should know one way or the other by later today, or tomorrow latest. I have to say that from the photo I saw, this is a bad situation. I recognised the man but I don't understand how this can be.'

JP was shocked, but thoughtful, 'If he turns out to be one

of our soldiers, where does that leave us?' He frowned then answered his own question. 'With another public enquiry I expect. If one missing soldier suddenly turns up dead, really dead, it does leave us wondering what happened to the others! If this gets out, all the other relatives will converge upon Washington asking to know where they are. I had better inform the President. He ought to know about this.' He headed towards the video conferencing screen on his desk. 'I'll speak with you later and let you know what he advises.'

Mike left the office as expected during JP's conversation with the President. He waited in his personal assistant's office. To his surprise, Don handed him an email printout. 'I think you had better see this sir.'

'Thanks.' Mike read it anxiously.

'You can contact him from here if you need to, sir.' The younger man offered.

Kassar asked him to contact him immediately he received the message. Mike dialed Kassar's direct line into the telephone.

'Kassar here.' a deep voice responded. He sounded tired.

'You asked me to call you?' Mike smiled his thanks as Don passed him his coffee, which he had brought out of the office with him.

'Hi Mike. Thanks for getting back to me so quickly.'

'That's ok. What have you got for me?'

'I don't know yet. The blood test result came back with some notes from the biopsy of a section of the man's brain. There was an unidentified chemical present in the bloodstream and there was some irregularity around the frontal lobe of the brain. Neither the pathologist nor the scientists at the lab could identify it so I have had a sample sent to one of the foremost specialists in California, Dr Marsha Kepler. Officers from one of the Fort Lauderdale precincts are on their way right now to see the victim's sister, Lene Schumacher. I will keep in touch and inform you when either Professor Kepler contacts me or after the body has been formally identified.'

'Marsha Kepler? I know that name well.' Mike replied. 'Thanks for the information, Al.'

Kassar disconnected.

JP called Mike back into his office and he briefed JP on the blood test and biopsy anomalies.

'I can't believe that Schumacher could do such a terrible thing.' It was so unlike the man. Why? I just don't understand it. Ever since they all disappeared, the whole business has been keeping me awake some nights. Even though one of them has appeared in these circumstances, if they are all alive, why aren't they contacting us?'

JP was as mystified as he was. 'I don't think they can be alive. As you said, one of them at least would have contacted their family. Maybe this body in San Diego just looks like him and the records are messed up. The photograph is not very clear.'

Mike was not satisfied. It was clear enough for his eyes to recognise the man.

CHAPTER TWENTY

Fort Lauderdale, Florida

Lene Schumacher listened to the news as she made breakfast. Out of habit she still rose early even when not working at her office job at the bank in the city centre. She was a small, neat woman and quite pretty, but her crowning glory was her beautiful fair hair. It was braided and tied up on top of her head, just like her grandmother did when she was her age. She was forty years old, a widow and childless. Her husband, Ludwig Von Heinckel, had been killed whilst on a tour of duty in the marines. No one else had taken her husband's place and she doubted that she would ever marry again.

After her brother Gerd had so mysteriously disappeared, Lene was all alone in Florida. Gerd had owned an apartment in Orlando when he was alive. It was still full of his belongings. Disposing of them and selling the apartment was the worst task, which she had put off because she could not bear to think she would never see him again. It was hard to believe that he was gone.

The pot of coffee was made and she waited only for the breakfast rolls to warm up in the oven. Loudly, drowning the voice of the radio newsreader, her doorbell chimed.

Pulling her wrap tightly around her shoulders Lene headed toward the door and peered through the security peephole. She could see two women police officers and a third standing by a car, unmarked except for the portable orange light that flashed silently and resolutely on the top of its metal roof.

Opening the door a little nervously, she said. 'Hello. What do you want?' Her German accent was soft but discernible. She still spoke in her mother tongue to her cousins in Hamburg so she had not lost her roots entirely after moving to Florida.

A young, fair-haired officer smiled gently and asked, 'Mrs Von Heinckel? Please may we come inside?'

'Why? Who are you?'

The young officer pulled her badge out of her breast pocket to reassure the woman and after scrutinising it carefully, Lene opened the door. 'Come in,' she offered.

The two officers followed the woman into her spacious sitting room. It was immaculate. Two comfortable sofas faced each other with a small coffee table between them. The furnishings around the room were old but cared for and the porcelain objet d'art sprinkled around the room were bright and shiny.

'I am Officer Kinsey, Ma'am. My colleague here is Officer Blundell. We are following up on an enquiry about your brother. We are not sure at this stage, but we think we may have found him.'

Tears sprung into Lene's eyes at the mention of her beloved Gerd. 'Is he alive? Is he hurt? Where is he?' She had found it unimaginably hard to believe that he was dead.

Officer Kinsey gently took her hand, 'I'm sorry to tell you Ma'am, we have recovered what we believe to be his body and want to ask you if you would be prepared to identify him.'

Lene covered her face with her hands and began to weep softly. The officers sat quietly to allow her time for the news to sink in. It was heartbreaking to watch the woman's grief.

'How did he die?' She did not want to know just for the sake of it, but if she knew how he had died she could share his last moments in her mind to bring him closer to her.

Officer Blundell looked away, not willing to be the one to tell her, 'I'm not sure Ma'am. You will need to talk to Detective Inspector Kassar in San Diego. He is in charge of the case. We will arrange your transport to San Diego and someone will pick you up at the airport. Do you have someone to go with you?'

Lene thought for a moment, and after several attempts to stem her flow of tears said, 'No, there is no one to go with me but I will go. We only had each other in this country, you see. I must know for sure. I must see for myself that he is really dead and say goodbye to him.'

Some hours later, in San Diego, DI Kassar welcomed Lene into his office. After taking the time to prepare the woman for what she was about to see, he accompanied her to the pathology lab morgue. To make it easier on Lene, Ben Harrington pulled the sheeted body drawer out only part of the way so she could not see the gap where the man's legs should be. The dead man's face was covered by a small square of white cotton fabric. Ben removed it and Patty put her arm around Lene just before the sheet was removed. The poor woman almost fainted when she saw the state of Gerd's face even though she had been warned to expect burns to his features.

'Mein Gott!' she whispered in distress. Turning to Kassar she confirmed, 'Y...yes. That is Gerd. Th...that is my brother.' Tears flowed freely down Lene's face as she crossed herself, kissed her right forefinger and placed it gently on Gerd's lips. 'Gerd, Gerd, my dear brother. May God bless you!' she wept, 'God bless you!'

Patty led her gently back to the relatives' room. Once she had recovered some composure she was taken to the medical room where she allowed the precinct doctor to extract a blood sample. This would not have been necessary had Gerd not already been officially declared dead. JP wanted to make absolutely sure that there was no mistake in the identity of the body. A whole lot of work, not to mention the uncertainty about the fate of the other soldiers, rested upon the outcome of the DNA test.

Lene did not believe Kassar when, because she insisted, he told her how her brother had died. After a cup of coffee and her chat to him, she walked out to the police car where Officer Carter, who had picked her up at San Diego airport, was waiting for her. During the journey back to the airport, Lene voiced her sadness to the officer that Gerd's body would not be released until the mystery of his involvement in the bombing had been resolved. The young police officer held back her tears as she took her grieving passenger back to the departure lounge where she waited with Lene until she boarded the plane for her flight home. They fell as she watched the departing plane rise into the sky. Sometimes the job was just awful!

CHAPTER TWENTY ONE

A Mystery

The two men sat at the table drinking coffee. They were both deep in thought with their own interpretation on how Gerd Schumacher's body, if it was his, could turn up blown to bits in the middle of San Diego when he was supposed to have disappeared into the Indian Ocean in a aircraft. Could he have been responsible for the disappearance of Flight 198? Was he a traitor? Did he hijack the aircraft? Mike would not believe that.

Eventually Mike asked JP, 'Do you want to tell me what the President recommended?' It was a difficult situation for anyone to accept and one which opened up a complicated can of worms in terms of military security on Diego Garcia.

JP was pragmatic. 'Simply this... if this body does turn out to be Gerd Schumacher then the inquiry is to be reopened but not made public. Not yet anyway. Not until we are sure that we know what happened and are in a position to inform the relatives. The President has stipulated very firmly that this is to be kept between as few people as possible. We don't want a riot and we don't want relatives complicating things by speculation. You've seen the headlines before.' He grimaced at the memory of the press's accusations of 'Government Plot' at incidents in the past. They were wrong of course; he could have told them that from the start but rumours are very hard to kill.

There was a light tap on the door and Don stepped into

the large room. He walked over to the two men and handed JP an email, 'From Professor Kepler, sir.' He left the room, closing the door softly behind him.

JP read the email out loud to Mike. "I have examined the blood sample sent to me by Detective Inspector Kassar from San Diego and must report that I have found a serious irregularity. If you are free at this time, I consider it essential that you contact me as soon as you read this to discuss my findings."

'Well, that is rather brief for a report.' Mike said humourlessly. His grief for his comrades had returned to haunt him. Part of him hoped that the body was not that of the missing soldier. If it was, it opened up the whole gut wrenching business again. It was not uncommon for one man to look like another with their shaven heads and muscular physique, but no matter how much he wanted to doubt it, he was so sure he had recognised Gerd.

Hastily, JP made a connection to Professor Kepler's video-link on his computer. Her mature, bespectacled face appeared on the screen of his computer.

'Hello Professor.' JP greeted her. 'Thank you for your email. What can you tell us?'

Anxiety showed in the professor's eyes. For a few seconds, her right hand was visible as she pushed a stray wisp of hair away from her face, 'I am alarmed, very alarmed. The unthinkable has happened. You are aware that Dr Willington and I were investigating the effects of the new rehabilitation drug, Riofactol. Do you recall that we had experimented with volunteer prisoners but our trials were called off after some prisoners suffered serious side effects? Dr Willington was working in his research lab at the university in England to try to find an antidote.'

'Yes. I remember.' JP replied, not knowing what to expect.

'The blood sample I was sent by Ben, the pathologist in San Diego, contained Riofactol in it. So did the samples of brain tissue. He would not have known what it was because the samples of the drug were tightly controlled by members of our team. The drug does not degrade through the normal processes in a corpse.'

JP asked, 'What does this mean? How can he have these traces of the drug in his body? The military were not using it were they?'

'No, definitely not, but someone is using it! It should not be hard to find out who the culprit is. Not too many people had access to the drug. As I said, it was rigidly controlled. I will email you a list of the project team members and the staff employed during the trials.' The professor was clearly concerned about the apparent breach of security.

'Find whoever is doing this fast, JP. Riofactol is a potentially dangerous drug until an antidote is available. God alone knows what could happen if it has fallen into the wrong hands. With the disappearance of Dr Willington and his research now on hold, the likelihood of an antidote is a long way off!'

'Thank you for your help, professor.' JP's voice reflected his deep concern. 'I will contact you again when I need to. I am not sure what to think at this stage but I will be discussing this with my colleagues today. Goodbye.' he pressed the button to cut his link.

Professor Kepler's anxious face disappeared.

Two minutes after JP's conversation with the professor, Mike's phone pinged as he received a text message from Kassar confirming that the bomber had been identified by his sister and was indeed Gerd Schumacher. JP wanted to be sure and would not believe it until the DNA test confirmed it.

After Professor Kepler's comments, Mike had become even more concerned. How was it possible?

CHAPTER TWENTY TWO

Sheree

With a large payoff from Paulo, Decker returned to San Diego two weeks after the bombings in San Diego. He took a cab to Sheree's home just as she was showering at the end of her shift.

'Hi sugar!' he called as he opened the front door. He was looking forward to the next few hours.

Sheree walked into the sitting room draped in a towel. Her hair was tied up to keep it dry. Throwing her arms around him, she kissed him long and hard, putting her hand in his pockets to find the small polythene bag he usually gave her as a present whenever he came to see her. 'Where is it, where is it?'

'It's in my bag,' he laughed. He grabbed her hair, yanked the towel away and nipped her neck playfully with his teeth. 'I don't plan on staying long so you'd better make the most of me while I'm here!' he joked as he stripped off his clothes and headed for the shower.

Later, in the aftermath of their drugged lovemaking Sheree snuggled sleepily up to Decker and, suddenly remembering something she had to tell him, slurred, 'Oh, I forgot to mention, I met a friend of yours.' The effects of the drug were not yet at their height.

Decker stirred, saying sleepily, 'Who?'

'A guy called Mike.'

'Mike who?'

'I dunno, he didn't tell me his other name.'

'Where did you meet him?' he said guardedly.

'In the bar. He came asking for me; he seemed to know you quite well.' She was gradually drifting into a drugged stupor.

Abruptly, Decker sat up, not quite awake. He shook Sheree roughly, dragging the woman out of her comfortable mood. 'Just who is this Mike? I don't know anyone called Mike!'

Sheree's glistening eyes widened in fear. With a clear head she knew what to expect when he got angry. In her drugged state she had no control, so could not recognise the warning signs.

'I don't know… I don't know. He just turned up at the bar asking for me by name. I swear I don't know him.' Although her brain was foggy, she was afraid. 'I never said anything, honest. I didn't tell him about the stuff…'

Angrily, Decker got out of the bed and dressed as quick as his fuzzy head would allow, muttering, 'Only one man in the whole of San Diego knew about you and me!'

He turned on her; 'Did you screw him too!'

'Who?' Sheree cried. The drug was working.

'That conniving bastard, Hibbot! Did you screw him? You can't do without it, can you? Did you screw the other one too, this … this Mike?'

Sheree cried out as he slapped her hard across the face. Desperately, she held her crossed arms over her face to ward off the blows. 'No! No! No, I didn't. I don't even know him!'

'Lying bitch!' he grabbed her by her neck and pushed her

up against the wall at the top of the bed. 'What did you tell him about me? What did you say to him about me?'

'Stop it! You're hurting me.' Sheree was terrified by the evil glint in his eyes. She had only seen it once before when she thought he was going to kill her. All she had done, and it wasn't even that bad, was to ask a neighbour's husband to fix a dripping tap for her when Decker was out of the city. He only got to hear of it when the neighbour's wife, who was aware of her husband's kind act, asked him if the tap was working properly. For that he had beaten Sheree until she was so bruised she had to take a week off work. She did not leave him because she had nowhere to go. She had no family. He paid all her bills and he was often away so she felt safe most of the time. It was better than being on the streets.

Decker squeezed her neck tighter until she started to choke. 'Not until you tell me what you told him!'

Tears fell down Sheree's face as she realised he had really lost it this time. 'I never said a...a... w...w...word,' she choked, hardly able to get the words out. 'H...honest, b...baby, I n...nev...er said ..a ..w...word.' The room was spinning as he shook her violently, and her body dropped like a heavy sack onto the bed as she momentarily lost consciousness. Decker let go of her throat and moved back to his side of the bed.

When she came to, Sheree lay weeping, hoping he would go out of the room, like he had the last time after he had finished with her but he didn't. He stayed; his threatening presence was uncomfortably close to her.

Decker's anger was momentarily spent and his voice was almost composed. 'So what did you talk about then, with this

135

Mike?' he asked, almost apologetically.

'Just about my job at the club, about me,' she whimpered, 'He didn't ask about you.'

'About you? About your job? So how is it that he says he knows me?' His anger boiled up again. 'How can he say he knows me if he didn't ask about me?'

'How do I know? You must know him! Maybe he came to see me to find you!' Confused thoughts flitted through the woman's mind. If only she could remember what he had said!

'And you talked about you?' Decker didn't believe a word.

'Yes!' she shouted angrily, wishing he would go away and leave her alone.

'Oh, so you talked about you to a man who came to see me? Is that it?' he sneered as he leaned aggressively toward her. 'And all he talks about is you! A likely story!'

Sheree jumped and shook with fear as he raised his fist again. His mood became even darker. 'Yes... No..., I don't know why he wanted to see you! He hadn't come to see me! Honest. I didn't know him!' she shouted. 'I hadn't met him before that day and I haven't seen him since!' Frantically she sat up, trying to get away from him. She could see it coming. 'No more, please, baby! No more! No more!' she sobbed.

Once more, he hit her full across the face, this time with his fist.

Out of control, she fell backwards and cried out as her head crunched on the corner of the cabinet by her bed then she bounced sideways and slid to the floor. Decker grabbed her again and threw her on the bed.

'Bitch! You're lying!' He grabbed her by her hair. It was

wet. Blood was seeping onto the pillow from a deep wound in the back of her head. Finally, Decker let go of her hair and shoved her head sideways. The red patch under her head was growing wider, and wetter.

'Sheree!'

She didn't answer but lay unmoving, her breath coming in short gasps.

'Sheree?' he held the edge of her chin and shook it roughly, but still she didn't answer. He hadn't planned this but he knew she would forgive him. She always did.

Eventually, Decker's patience wore out and he shouted at her. 'Sheree, stop screwing around!'

Sheree's eyes were closed but her mouth was moving as if trying to say something. He couldn't hear her. 'What are you saying?' he asked as he put his ear to her mouth.

Opening her eyes, she half smiled, kissed his ear and said softly. 'This stuff's good, I can't feel any...thing.'

'What?' Decker only heard half of her sentence. 'What's that?'

Sheree's eye's closed as a soft sigh escaped her lips and she lay still. There was no reply. Irritated, but seeing that Sheree was not moving, Decker felt for the pulse in her neck.

There was none. She was dead.

A cold feeling crawled across his stomach. He had never killed a woman before.

'Oh God! This is all I need!' he growled to himself. He had to leave now, before anyone saw him.

He picked up the telephone and tapped out a number.

The line buzzed twice and a man's voice answered.

'Yes?'

Restraining his anger, Decker commanded, 'Pick me up in the K Mart car park in half an hour!'

'Okay.' The line clicked off.

After his encounter with Sheree, Mike had asked Peter Grainger to monitor her activity and communications. His men were instructed to keep himself and Kassar informed of any visitors or unusual calls. Up until now, nothing much had taken place and no strange communications had been picked up. She was keeping a low profile. The only event had been the arrival of a tall, white haired man, who was just leaving the apartment. Finding that Mike's mobile was switched off Grainger rang Kassar immediately. He was at home.

Startled by the noise of the telephone in the quiet of the night, Kassar rubbed his tired eyes. His fingers fumbled with the switch on his bedside lamp. At that time of night it had better be important.

'Kassar here. What's going down?'

'We've just monitored a call made to Nixon's by a visitor to the woman's apartment. It's a private air freight business on the other side of town. He's on his way to the K Mart car park to meet someone. Actually, he is jogging, for Christ's sake, at this time of night! We don't yet know who he is. Do you want us to pick them up when they meet?'

'No... not yet. Take your videocam with you. Get some footage of anyone he meets. Only pick him up if he looks like he's going to run. Whatever happens, keep me informed. I'm coming over.' He sighed as he got out of bed. One of these days he was going to get a full night's sleep.

Fifteen minutes later he was in the back of an unmarked police vehicle and heading for the K Mart car park. Switching off the lights before they reached Grainger's surveillance van, the driver pulled up behind it. Using the side door, Kassar slipped quickly into the vehicle.

'Well, what's happening?' he asked Grainger.

'Nothing yet... just one parked car.'

Kassar watched as Grainger looked through the darkened windscreen with the videocam lens into the car park below the embankment. A car, which he assumed to belong to the man the white haired man had called, was parked in a dark corner behind the service entrance. Grainger handed the videocam to Kassar, who zoomed up to someone approaching the car. He's got some nerve, he thought.

A man, jogging around the roadside, suddenly swerved into the car park and headed down the side of the building to the car. The door opened, the man got in and the car sped away.

'Follow him. Not too close, but don't let him get away!' Kassar ordered.

The van driver obeyed. He knew what to do. After five minutes it was obvious to Kassar that the car was headed for one of the freight terminals near the back of the local airport. As they followed, he emailed the duty sergeant at the precinct and asked him to process the electronic file of the jogger, which he had downloaded from the videocam into the satellite computer terminal in the van. He emailed the photo to the clerk in the precinct. By the time he returned to his office, a

139

printout from the electronic picture would have been produced and they would have the means to identify the man.

Kassar jumped into the police car, which had followed the van and they returned to the precinct.

The first thing Kassar did was to ask the clerk for the printout of the photo. It was not a great shot but it was all he had. He viewed the photo and scanned it into the ICID. It came up a blank. The face was not known. That meant that no charges had ever been brought, so the man did not have a record. That was a blow to Kassar. He had hoped it would have been easier, that this new man on the scene would have given him something for Mike. Feeling tired, he made a coffee and took out the ginger crunch cookies.

CHAPTER TWENTY THREE

Rosa

Mike returned to JP's office after lunch to be greeted by Don. 'An email for you, Commander Forde; this one is from DI Kassar.' He handed the printout to Mike.

Mike read it, passed it silently to JP and shook his head in despair. He could not believe it. The email confirmed that the body had been that of Gerd Schumacher. The DNA tests confirmed it.

JP read the email and was equally astonished. Quietly he said, 'This is bad news indeed. We must make some sense of this. There are several ways we could view this situation. One, that however unlikely it may seem, Gerd Schumacher is a traitor, possibly he may even be responsible or involved with the hijack of the missing aircraft. We know without doubt that he was responsible for the bomb in San Diego. Two, he is a deserter who was never on the aircraft that left Diego Garcia, or three, he could be an infiltrator who used his experience in the peacekeeping force to gain and use intelligence for the enemy.'

'All three explanations sound feasible but I'm sorry, JP, I just can't believe it. Gerd was a good soldier; he was dedicated and good at his job. He had several commendations and a very good future. I don't believe he would have thrown that away. It all meant something to him!' Mike interrupted, hardly able to contain his disbelief that JP would consider Gerd a hostile.

Abruptly, he stood up and walked over to the office window, not seeing the busy street scene below.

'So why was he blown up setting up a bomb?' asked JP, exasperated. It seemed fairly clear to him. The man was a bomber. All the evidence was there to see.

Mike walked back to his seat and sat down. 'There is more to this than just a bomb. Look at Professor Kepler's findings. Gerd had traces of Riofactol in his blood and brain tissue. Is it not possible he was used against his will? We both know what it was used for, JP. You were on the committee that decided it would be tested in San Quentin. How can you decide he is guilty before you know the full circumstances?' Mike was furious and trying to keep it under control. He knew Gerd and he felt that he was a good judge of character. He refused to believe he could be so wrong.

'He could have been injected with the drug to make us believe he was used by the enemy.' JP looked at Mike. 'Would you accept that possibility? Those tactics have been used before. Not with the rehabilitation drug specifically, but with other drugs used by the military to inoculate soldiers against local health hazards. Some of them leave residual evidence in the body. In South Africa the enemy tried to convince us that our soldiers were doing something they weren't. It's not new. Some of those factions will go to any lengths to discredit the service. I just don't know how they could get hold of a drug that was not used by the military.'

Mike was adamant. 'With all due respect JP, I cannot agree with you on this occasion.'

JP looked uncomfortable and he stood up, indicating that

Mike should leave. 'I will contact the President. He must be informed of this development. We will talk again later.'

Mike returned to Craig's home, where he had stayed the previous night and related his discussion with JP.

'You gave him a hard time!' Craig grinned as he handed Mike a mug of coffee. Much against habit, Mike refused Craig's offer of a malt whisky. He was bristling with anger and wanted to keep a clear head.

'I know. I meant to.' Mike frowned; he was furious with JP. 'Gerd Schumacher is not an enemy of this country. He was a good soldier!'

'You could be wrong, you know.' Craig responded.

'I'm not. I just know I'm not!' Uncompromising to the extreme about this, Mike would not even entertain the idea of Gerd willingly agreeing to commit an act of depraved destruction. He had too much respect for human life and too much pride in his country, even if his roots were foreign.

Half an hour later, Don sent a text to Mike with a list of the members of the project team involved with the trials of Riofactol at San Quentin prison. Professor Kepler had emailed it as she had promised earlier. Mike contacted two of his agents to arrange the investigation into the current location of the project team members.

By the end of the day, Don sent another text to Mike saying that the President had ordered an emergency, but necessarily confidential, inquiry into the appearance of Gerd Schumacher's body, and it was to be held two days later.

Two days later the inquiry ended at two o-clock, five hours

143

after it had begun. The members of the board could not reach a unanimous agreement on how Schumacher could have appeared from nowhere and the eventual conclusion was drawn that he was a traitor who had never boarded the aircraft with his colleagues. Riofactol was not even mentioned. Mike was devastated as he was forced to accept the conclusion. The President was non-committal and made it clear to JP that he expected him to tidy up the situation without any adverse publicity.

At lunch Mike found himself seated next to the woman in the grey suit. He remembered her from the original meeting in Washington. His eyes ran over her slim, shapely body. Her hair had grown longer but she was all the prettier for that. Suddenly, he was aware that she was addressing him.

'Please would you pass me the water?'

Mike hurriedly reached over for the pitcher of iced water, almost knocking it over in his haste.

'Uh huh, nearly!' He managed to prevent it from tipping over by leaning over the table and grabbing at the spout, causing water to splash up his cuffs. He handed the pitcher to her as droplets of water dripped onto the table from his soggy cuff. As he reached for his napkin to dry his hands, it fell on the floor. Mike groaned inwardly as he leaned down to retrieve it; he was making a real ass of himself!

The woman laughed. 'Well caught!' as she took the pitcher from him and poured some water into her glass.

Mike saw the laughter in her sparkling brown eyes, which had suddenly come to life in a way that he had not seen in the meeting room. She had a beautiful smile.

'I'm Mike, Mike Forde.' He offered his hand.

She took it and shook it briefly.

'Yes, I know, Commander... Mike. May I call you Mike? I'm Rosa. Rosa Fernandez.'

'Yes, please do. Nice to know you, Rosa, it's a nice name.' He couldn't think of anything else to say. What was wrong with him? It was unusual for him to be lost for words.

Rosa looked expectantly at him. 'It was my mother's name. She was Spanish. Do you live in Washington?'

'No.' His mouth had gone dry. He reached for his drink and took a sip. 'Do you? Live in Washington, I mean?'

'No. I live in Newport Beach, California, when I'm not working in Washington.'

'That's a coincidence; I live in Laguna Beach. That's good isn't it? I mean... I'm not too far away from you.'

Mike was beginning to feel rather good. This was the best thing that had happened in a long time even if it was turning him into a clumsy, incoherent imbecile!

As they ate, they talked about the food, the wine and how much they both loved to travel. Mike said nothing about his feelings about Gerd Schumacher's activities. He was inwardly furious with the outcome of the inquiry. Thankfully, Rosa's presence kept his temper in check. He was enjoying her company very much.

After they had eaten he poured coffee for them both from the pot on the table saying, 'When are you returning home?'

Rosa smiled, 'Tomorrow afternoon. Why?'

'I was wondering,' Mike was out of practise when it came to arranging dates and he found himself stumbling over his words, 'if you .. er, might like to come out to dinner with me, that is .. er, tonight? There's a Mexican restaurant, and it's reputed to be very good, not too far away from here.'

He could feel his face burning. What an ass! He hadn't had problems with other women. Why was he so embarrassed with this woman? What would he do if she turned him down? The thought of it turned his face red.

Seeing the heat of his embarrassment, Rosa thoughtfully fanned herself with her hand. 'It's hot in here isn't it?' then she smiled and said, 'Yes. I'd like to, thank you. What time?'

'About seven? We could have a drink first. I could meet you at your hotel?' Mike's could feel himself relaxing. She had accepted!

'Fine. I'm at the Sherfield Tower, a block away. I can meet you in the lobby.'

Lunch was over and Mike saw JP leaving his seat further down the table.

'It looks like I must leave now. My colleague and I have a meeting at three o-clock. We'll meet up in the lobby at seven then. I'll see you later.' Mike smiled, rose to his feet and picked up his briefcase from where he had left it next to the wall behind his seat.

Rosa smiled back at him. 'I look forward to it.'

Mike left for his meeting with JP, and after it was over he took a cab to Craig's home. Again, they sat in Craig's study drinking coffee while Maddy busied herself elsewhere. They discussed Gerd Schumacher yet again and Mike impressed upon Craig that he felt there was more to his death than just a bomb blast.

146

'Gerd was one of the most dedicated soldiers ever to have served with me. He was a bit of a joker, but he never gave less than his best. His record was outstanding. Nothing stopped him. He made friends easily and he took no risks. He was one of the best in his field when it came to setting explosives. I can't believe he could blow himself up.'

'Men aren't perfect, they sometimes make mistakes.' Craig countered sympathetically, ever the devil's advocate.

'Not Gerd!' Mike's eyes flashed in anger. 'It must have been the drug. Maybe it was forcibly injected. Maybe he was made to plant the bomb.'

Craig did not believe it but he had never seen Mike so fixated in his opinion. 'Why?'

'I don't know, but as far as I am concerned this is unfinished business and I'm going to finish it! I won't rest until I find out why Gerd is dead.'

They talked for the remainder of the afternoon, again exploring theories about how Gerd Schumacher could have found himself in the situation causing his death. Nothing seemed to fit, except that he had been under the influence of the drug. But who had administered it? Neither of them could offer any answer to that question.

Eventually, Mike went to his room to change into suitable clothing for his evening date, leaving Craig in his study not totally convinced but thinking that maybe Mike had a point.

Gerd remained in his thoughts as he showered and dressed in preparation for his evening with Rosa.

A cab delivered him to her hotel and he was delighted to see that she was waiting for him in the lobby when he arrived.

147

She looked stunning in a royal blue suit, cream top and smart, blue heeled shoes and carrying a matching handbag. Her hair was held back with a gold clasp at the back of her head.

'I'm glad to see you aren't one of those women who feel it necessary to be ten minutes late.' he greeted her. 'Thanks!'

'Likewise... I don't like to be kept waiting either. Do so at your peril!' she parried, laughing back at him.

They teased each other as they walked the two blocks away from her hotel until they found the restaurant Mike had spoken of earlier. The food was good, the atmosphere quiet and romantic, and the service efficient without being intrusive.

Throughout the meal they talked of their experiences in the line of their respective professions and then about their childhood. At the end of the evening they found they had quite a lot in common. Both of them liked swimming, walking and the same type of music.

Mike was so pleased to be with someone he could talk to. Rosa made it unintentionally clear throughout the conversation with Mike that like him, her work with ASIU was just as important to her. She was a well-qualified communications specialist with senior management responsibility for the international communications department managing all of the programming and tracking of American satellites from all over the world. She understood Mike's obsession with his job and she was just as obsessed with her own. Mike was the first man in years to have been seriously able to get her attention for longer than a conversation at dinner.

Rosa thought Mike was very attractive and she was quite taken with him. His conversation was interesting, he was not the pushy type and he had the most gorgeous brown eyes. When they arrived back at her hotel and Mike offered to walk her back to the room she did not refuse him. Her desire to be alone with him quite surprised her. It had been some time since she had found a man so attractive.

When they arrived at her room, ever the independent woman, Rosa unlocked the door with her card.

Mike stood in the doorway as she walked inside. 'I guess I'd better be going now.' he said quietly. He didn't really want to go yet.

It was clear to him that Rosa had enjoyed the evening but she had given nothing away about her feelings toward him. She would have to be blind to have ignored the level of his interest. She fascinated him and he was aware that he had found it very difficult to hide his feelings It surprised him greatly that he had not once thought about Lisa since seeing Rosa again in the meeting room.

Rosa turned around to face him, floundering in her own emotional confusion. She didn't want him to go. How could she keep him there a little longer without seeming too obvious? She had to say something, or lose him!

Standing beside him at the door, she held out her hand to invite him into her room, saying softly, 'I'd like it if you would stay awhile. I've rarely enjoyed such a lovely evening with anyone and it may be some time before we get the chance to meet again.'

Saddened by her last comment, but relieved and delighted by her invitation, Mike stepped into the dimly lit room and closed the door. They stood for a moment looking at each other before they both stepped forward and embraced. The outcome was inevitable.

Sometime later, an elated Mike caressed Rosa's cheek, concerned because she was so quiet. She was awake but her eyes were closed.

'Are you ok?' He thought she might have regretted their beautiful union.

'Rosa opened her eyes. 'Yes, yes, I'm fine. I was just relaxing and thinking how wonderful this evening has been. It's been a long time.' She smiled up at him, ran her hand through his thick, dark hair and said softly, 'Where do we go from here, Commander?' Her heart was almost bursting with joy.

Relieved, Mike smiled and kissed her gently on her soft, full lips, put his arms around her, and gently drew her close to him. 'Anywhere you want!'

CHAPTER TWENTY FOUR
The Search

Believing Bill to be under the influence of the genbriotic hypnotherapy, Paulo and Neko allowed him to move about more freely. Bill explored more of the cave's depths at every opportunity. He found that it was made up of many narrow corridors with rooms leading off to other rooms, all having a sandstone ceiling. Some of the rooms he explored were impassable where the ceiling had collapsed and tons of sand and sandstone rubble lay on the floor. The cave complex was strange and fascinating to him. He had never seen anything like it. It was a marvel of nature.

On one of his trips he found another occupied cave with four beds inside it. Cautiously he had unbolted the door and looked inside. The room was in semi darkness as the only available light was that which shone through the grille in the door. The men lying on the beds appeared to be all sound asleep. It was too dark to tell who they were. All were hidden underneath thick blankets. Not one of them stirred as he closed and bolted the door as quietly as he had opened it.

Returning part of the way he had come, Bill hoped he would not be discovered as he walked along one of the other passageways. Several times he was forced to hide behind a wall as he heard and saw men passing in front of him less than ten metres away.

He made several trips out when he thought it was safe and found another two more caves which also each housed four men. The doors were both bolted but as before, he could see through the grille in the doors that the men were sleeping.

Climbing another flight of steps he could hear muffled voices coming from a small hole in one of the walls. He strained to hear what they were saying but the hole was too small and the voices were not clear enough to hear. The only clear words he could hear were 'I will make they pay! ... plant so many bombs they ... we will send ... home ...' The voices were those of Paulo and Garcia; he also heard a voice he had not heard before and all three were laughing.

The bastards are planning more evil, he thought sadly.

The following evening Bill stood listening from his hiding place above the room. He heard Garcia laughing. He was heartily delighted with himself for the success of his work He had found the captive soldiers aggressive and uncooperative at first but once they were injected their attitude became whatever he wanted it to be. It delighted him that he now had their cooperation after using the treatment to convince eight of the soldiers that they were members of Paulo's army. He was proud of his work and happy to work with the brothers when they paid so well.

Triumphantly he sat drinking whisky with Paulo and his brother Neko, who had announced when he arrived that he would be staying only one week. That had been three weeks ago and just after Decker had returned to the US with Schumacher. Neko had delayed his departure and now intended to return to the US the following day. This was their last evening together and they were all very drunk and loud.

Paulo was beside himself with laughter. 'The fools! The

soldiers think that they are working for the government and that Brent is their CIC. He is doing a good job of controlling them. He had them marching up and down the old riverbed on the lower levels yesterday! The rehabilitation certainly works well. Willington can sure be proud of his achievement!'

'Are they all done now?' Paulo asked.

'No, not all, we need more Riofactol. It was a shame about that woman, what was her name…? Lorna, Laura…. oh, yes, Lana. I'm afraid she reacted very badly. I can't bring her around. She appears to be comatose.' Garcia had seen it before during the project but he did not know how to deal with it.

'What have you done with her?' Neko was curious; he was in the room as Garcia had drugged the woman and watched as she slipped into a catatonic state within twenty minutes. He found the whole process fascinating as he had never seen genbriotic hypnosis before.

'I left her in a cell on the edge of the dormitories. I suppose she might have some use. Maybe the men might find one. She could be a reward for their services to our cause!' Wildly drunk, Garcia laughed lasciviously. 'Can you imagine how good this drug would be in a brothel?' He drank more of the whisky, almost choking with laughter at the thought.

Paulo had volunteered Lana as a guinea pig for somewhat dubious reasons. Garcia's demonstrations on the hijacked soldiers had astonished him. Apart from the stewardess, Fatima, who was his woman, there were no other women in the hideout except for Lana and he had been hoping to make full use of her. The state she was now in made her useless to him unless he got desperate. He had become bored with

153

Fatima. She had served her purpose on the aircraft before his men hijacked the plane. No-one suspected her. She might have been less inclined to be helpful if she had known Paulo planned to replace her, permanently. A week after she returned to the hideout Paulo had her corpse buried deep in the sand a mile away from the entrance to the cave.

In his hiding place above the room, Bill was furious. When the room was empty the night before, he had spent some time grinding at the hole he had discovered a few days earlier with the sharp edges of a newly cracked rock. The hole was not a lot larger but the result of his work enabled him to place his ear nearer so that he could hear the conversations that took place between Paulo, Neko and Garcia. He was horrified by what he heard, particularly about the woman. It was obvious what Paulo had planned for Lana.

How could he stop them without being caught? That was the problem. If he could find out where the woman was being held he might be able to help her.

Quietly he retreated and returned to his quarters.

For two days he searched the caves, crawling though jagged holes and cracks in some of the walls. He theorised from the state of some of the rooms that the hideout was some sort of buried city which had lain undiscovered for hundreds, if not thousands of years. There were huge broken rocks holding up some of the smaller sandstone rocks. They had eroded in some places and cracked in others, causing holes to form in the walls and making it possible to walk from room to room. Some of the passageways had been physically hacked out of already cracked rock; other larger rooms had been made even bigger by explosives either accidently or deliberately. In some of the many rooms he searched, the ceilings had collapsed sometimes making it almost impossible for him to pass through and he was forced to find an alternative route.

Unobtrusively, Bill marked the walls in numerical order as he passed safely through them to enable him to find his way back. The oil lamp he found in one of the unused rooms, although old, still worked. He felt like a child who had discovered a treasure when he unearthed it along with a very old pitcher of oil. Discreetly he made the wicks from bits of old string that he found in the corners of his lab or coarse cloth torn from the inside fabric of his sofa when the string ran out. It was crude but welcome in the dark caves.

On the third day Bill found the woman lying on a bed covered by a thin sheet in a small and stuffy unlit room.

The wooden door was locked on the outside by a bolt and like his old cell he had to step down into the room. He pushed the door closed hoping no one would pass and notice that the bolt was not in place.

Lana made no sound except for her breathing which, although much slower than normal, was regular. At least she was still alive. Bill listened carefully at the door but could not hear any sounds from along the dimly lit passageway.

He shook the woman gently. Her eyes, wide and watering constantly, were open and she stared straight ahead. 'Miss… Lana…, Lana.' He had not heard her surname from his hiding place, only her forename. The woman did not stir from her position and continued to stare straight ahead. He was horrified by Garcia's cruelty, they could have at least closed her eyes to keep the insects out.

In despair, Bill realised he would have to make a return journey later that evening or the following day. He still had some pills in the hem of his coat but he had no water. She would choke if he tried to force a pill down her throat.

Paulo was expecting him to join himself and Garcia, no doubt to play his sickening game of comrades at arms. It was hard to play the part and equally difficult for him to extricate himself from the group without arousing suspicion.

Reluctantly he locked the woman in her cell. It did not take him long to return to his lab. Following his hidden directions made his return much quicker than his search to find her.

Garcia had ordered Bill to make more of the drug and fresh supplies of chemicals and equipment were due to be delivered to the camp any day. He hoped he would be able to help the woman before he became too tied up in his work.

CHAPTER TWENTY FIVE

San Diego

Kassar was frustrated after unsuccessfully trying to call Mike at Craig's home in Washington. He contacted Craig once more. Craig explained that Mike was not with him, he was out somewhere. Dammit! Where the hell was he? He needed him to check out the new man in the situation. His men were still parked outside of Nixon's Air Freight terminal. The owner, Bart Nixon, and the man were still in there but for how much longer he had no idea.

At midnight Kassar called Craig again.

Craig answered sleepily, 'Baxter.'

'Have you any news of Mike? I really need him down here!' The DI was becoming impatient.

'No. Sorry. He is still out. Will it wait?' Craig enquired.

'No. I don't think so. I really need to speak with him. Do you know where he is? I must get in touch with him.'

Craig smiled to himself. Mike had told him of his date with Rosa. There was only one place he could be.

'I think I may be able to find him,' he said to Kassar, 'If so, I'll ask him to call you. If I can't I'll call you back within fifteen minutes. Is that OK with you?'

'Thanks.' Kassar disconnected.

Following Craig's phone call, Mike rang Kassar twenty minutes later. He was slightly embarrassed to be tracked down in Rosa's hotel bedroom but Craig made light of it. He had done the same thing in his youth. The woman must be special. At least he was letting Lisa go, and that was a good thing.

Mike dressed and left Rosa in bed promising to contact her again tomorrow. He used the guest's office facilities to contact Kassar via. video-link

Kassar's face appeared on the screen in front of him.

'What is it? Has something new turned up?'

'Yes, we have a new man on the scene. He turned up at the Nixon's today. He's still in there. I have a photograph of him. Can I send it to you?'

'Yes.' Mike gave the inspector the fax machine address at the hotel.

Moments later, a digitised image appeared and spilled out of the machine. Mike picked it up, startled by the man's face in front of him. It was Decker. It had to be, the image matched Hibbot's description although the photo was quite dark. He returned to the screen where Kassar waited.

'Keep him there. Don't let him go. Arrest him if you have to but don't let him go. This is Decker, the man I'm looking for. I'm on my way. Get confirmation of his identity from Hibbot.' Mike disconnected.

Kassar called out to Tad Vickers. 'Get Hibbot out of bed! I want him in interview room four.'

Hibbot was in the interview room seconds before Kassar walked in holding the printout in his hand.

'I need you to identify this man. Who is he?' The DI thrust the paper in front of the scared prisoner.

Hibbot glanced at the face of the man staring back at him; his heart sank. He would have to tell them. He was a dead man

158

for sure! 'It's Decker.'

'What's his forename?' Vickers demanded.

'I don't know. I only know him as Decker.' Hibbot shook, seeing a mental image of Decker pointing a gun to his head at point blank range when he found out he had ratted on him. 'Honest. I sweat!' Only if Kassar put Decker behind bars, preferably with a death sentence would Hibbot feel safe. He wished he knew more about the man, he'd have told them everything!

Vickers and Kassar reluctantly accepted that Hibbot was telling the truth and he was taken back to his cell.

Kassar contacted the men in the surveillance van. 'Keep watch. Make sure the new guy doesn't fly away. His name is Decker. He is on the wanted list. Arrest him only if you think he is about to bolt and you have no information on where he is going. Leave him until then. Keep watch. Commander Forde will take over when he arrives in a few hours.'

Arriving back at San Diego airport, Mike cursed the inconvenient timing of Kassar's communication. He was disappointed at having to leave Rosa halfway through the night. She had smiled and asked, 'Work?' and he wondered how he would have reacted if the situation had been reversed.

'I'm afraid so, but it's very important and I must go. I'll contact you when I can.' He had kissed her then left for the taxi waiting to take him to the airport.

Eager to talk to Mike, Kassar picked him up at San Diego airport then drove straight to the vicinity of Nixon's airfield. They talked about Decker and the likelihood of his part in the

159

shooting of the driver in the UK. They also theorised on how the bullets found at the kidnap scene and inside the driver in England, came to match the one found in the skull of the dead driver in San Diego. They could not quite tie them smoothly together. What was the link?

'I do have one break. I can arrest Decker on suspicion of murder.'

'Murder? Who's dead?' Mike was surprised.

'His girlfriend failed to turn up for work yesterday and one of her friends got the janitor at the apartments to unlock her door. They found her dead in her bedroom. She'd suffered a severe blow of some sort to her head. A neighbour described a man fitting Decker's description entering her apartment the same day she died. As you already know, Hibbot confirmed Decker's relationship with her.'

Mike was sorry that Sheree was dead, she was too young and pretty to have died in such a horrific way. He also realised that her neighbours could also have seen him at her house, and if they appeared at Decker's trial they might recognise him in the witness box.

Mike sighed inwardly. Now was as good a time as any; 'I need to tell you something,' he looked at Kassar, 'before somebody else tells you.'

'What's that?' The Detective Inspector's thick, black eyebrows curved upwards.

'I screwed Decker's girlfriend.' He shook his head, embarrassed, 'or should I say, she screwed me.'

The man threw back his head and gave a long, raucous laugh. 'Is that all? Hell man, that dame has screwed half the city. You'd better get yourself checked out at the clinic!'

Mike groaned, caught off guard. What would he say to Rosa if he'd caught something? Without thinking he said, 'Oh God – I screwed up that time didn't I?'

Kassar laughed again. 'Yeah, that's what causes these problems!'

Mike looked out of the window, thoroughly mortified. They were approaching the block next to Nixon's. 'Just keep it to yourself if you can.'

'You can count on it, Mike. I know you didn't kill the woman so let's concentrate on Decker. Do you want me to pick him up now?' Kassar's strong voice brought Mike's attention back to the job in hand.

'No, don't arrest him yet. His girlfriend is dead and you have a witness, we can arrest him anytime. We must let him go. I don't think he was acting alone and we need to get to the other people involved in the kidnap. I don't intend to lose him. I want to see where he goes. We need to find Doctor Willington. Decker must know where he is. He's the best lead we've got so far. The English driver was unable to identify his face because the gunmen all wore masks but the name fits and Hibbot confirmed that Decker was in England at the time of the kidnap.'

They reached the surveillance van and discreetly climbed inside.

The attention of the ASIU agents, Peter Grainger and Piers Henneman, was glued to their receivers. Kassar had arranged for one of his undercover men posing as an exporter's agent to visit Nixon's where, after Bart Nixon invited him into his office to discuss freight costs, he had discreetly hidden a listening device.

'He's going to fly,' Grainger announced, holding on to the ear-piece against his ear, watching Kassar and Mike as he listened attentively to the conversation taking place between Nixon and their quarry. 'Decker's just phoned again and asked Nixon to get him an airline ticket to Sana'a in Yemen.'

'Yemen? Why on earth would he go to Yemen of all places?' This assignment was becoming even more complicated. Mike turned to Kassar, 'Find out which flight. I'm going to follow him. I'll arrange to be in Sana'a before him if one of your men can get me a ticket on the flight before his, if there is one. I'll also want one of the agents on the aircraft with him in case he gets off before he should. Even though he is booking a ticket, he may change it at the airport and not take a direct flight. I don't want to be on the same flight in case he spots me following him when he gets off. There is a chance he may see me on the plane and recognise me. That could be disastrous. If I have to arrest him, I may never find out about his connection with Dr Willington's kidnap.'

Piers volunteered to fly out with Decker.

Kassar emailed Patrick Mckay, the desk sergeant, asking him to check which flight number Nixon had booked for Decker, then to set up two tickets to Sana'a. He managed to get one on the same flight as Decker for Piers, and one on an earlier flight for Mike.

Mike was pleased, Piers was a tall, strong man of Swedish origin whom women would describe as very good looking. Younger than Mike, he was broad shouldered, of slim but muscular build, and with his blonde curly hair and square jaw he looked every inch like one of Michaelangelo's magnificent statues. He could definitely be relied upon in a scrap if it came to it. Some of his past escapades made pretty impressive reading. He was a martial arts champion who had fought many men to a bitter end and had few visible scars to show for it. He was the best of the best in his category.

Mike was also well experienced with Ju Jitsu and was confident he could handle Decker alone if need be, but he knew it was unlikely that the man was going to Yemen to be on his own. There might be some of Decker's accomplices to take care of at some stage. Having Piers around would definitely be useful. 'If we arrest him he won't come quietly, and in all probability, if there is a group of associates we may need to call upon the local police to assist us.'

'I'll keep an eye on him.' his colleague promised.

'Thanks. Don't try to apprehend him. Just keep in touch with me. I want to know as soon as you touch down. Just send me a text. I'll be waiting at the airport to follow Decker; you should follow me in case I need you but don't get too close, he mustn't see either of us.'

Piers laughed. 'Don't worry, he won't see me.'

Mike believed him but he was desperate to find Bill Willington and wanted nothing to go wrong. To Kassar he said, 'Let's get going.'

Twenty minutes later they returned to the precinct. Mike thanked the desk sergeant for his fast work and he and Piers signed for their airline tickets.

Kassar received an email re-routed to Mike from JP, who

had received it from Professor Kepler. Dr Elio Garcia was two months overdue and should have returned to the lab at the university. No-one knew where he was and he was not responding to texts or emails. Mike explained to Kassar that Garcia was a member of the project team at the prison during the experiments with Riofactol. He was the only missing team member. Agents from ASIU checked his credit card records and discovered that he had made his eighth trip to Yemen this year, and again around the time he went missing.

'Garcia travels frequently to Yemen; Decker is going to Yemen. Maybe there's a link somewhere and we're missing it!' puzzled, Mike said to Kassar, 'What would Garcia have to do with Decker? What business would Decker have in Yemen?'

'Maybe it's drugs.' Kassar shrugged his shoulders. 'There were some drugs in Sheree's apartment. There was only a small bag but it could indicate that he may have been a distributor, possibly for a Middle Eastern contact.'

Mike nodded, 'Possibly.'

Realising he would need money, transport and some weapons, which he did not have, Mike contacted JP and asked him to arrange for a contact to meet him and Piers at the airport in Yemen with transport, weapons and appropriate clothes for himself and his colleague.

Mike and Piers headed out to the airport in separate taxis half an hour apart. It would be wiser not to risk being seen arriving together.

CHAPTER TWENTY SIX

The desert hideout

Bill was fraught with concern for Lana. Eventually he decided that he would attempt to revive her. He knew it was risky but he was convinced it would work. He would face the problem later of what to do with her if it didn't.

When he knew that Paulo and his friends had gone to bed drunk as usual, Bill made his way cautiously through the caverns to the woman's cell.

He took with him a blanket and a small polythene bag holding two Tintomin pills. In a cloth bag tied to his belt he carried a two litre plastic bottle full of drinking water.

Warily, Bill walked through the darkness, feeling his way at first then when he was sure he was away from the main part of the underground area that was inhabited, he lit his oil lamp. Several times he stopped and listened to ensure that he was not being followed.

In a shorter time than it had taken the first time to find her, Bill reached Lana's cell. The woman lay just as he had left her. He knew that if he were caught, Paulo would kill him. His presence in Lana's cell would indicate his disloyalty and deception. There was no way he could justify his presence there. As far as Paulo knew, the doctor was under his influence. To be caught with Lana would prove beyond doubt that he was not.

Bill held the lamp up to Lana's eyes, which were closed

and did not open when he touched her face to flick away an insect that had settled itself on her eyebrow. He held the lamp to her face and opened her eyelids. She did not blink in the unaccustomed brightness.

He sat down on the floor next to her. Struggling because she was a dead weight, the doctor lifted the woman up until he could prop her against himself. He tilted her head back and poured some water down her throat to help clear any dust or insects that might have crawled inside her mouth. When he was sure the water had gone down her throat naturally, he crushed the two pills into powder inside a polythene bag, using a small rock.

Tipping her head back, he dropped some of the powder down her throat and poured water down after it, trusting her body's reflex actions to cause her to swallow. It worked, although she coughed twice, instinctively. He lifted her head up again ensuring that her back was straight and in a sitting position as he supported her upturned chin, making her head face forward and look up toward the ceiling. This ensured that it did not slump down onto her chest. He did not want her to choke.

Bill repeated the exercise several more times until all of the powder was gone, checking her airway after each time to ensure that she was breathing naturally. When he was as sure as it was possible to be that the last of the drugs had been delivered to her stomach, with great difficulty he stood the woman up to allow her inner biology to do its work and then waited. After some time he sat her down again, resting her shoulder against his chest to keep the upper part of her body raised up as much as possible. She was cold and her breathing was still shallow.

He dozed for a while, waking up involuntarily because of the cold. Trying to stay warm, he had wrapped the blanket around them both as well as he could but he was in a sitting position and Lana had slipped down into a lying position next to him. The blanket had slipped down with her so it didn't cover them both completely. Eventually he lay down next to her to share his warmth, covered them both with the blanket and fell asleep.

Some hours must have passed because the lamp began to sputter as the oil level dropped. It had been full when he left his lab. Bill began to be afraid of being caught. Lana continued to sleep, with no sign of consciousness. Eventually, with no way of telling the time except by the use of oil in the lamp, he realised that he had little option but to go. It was very much against his better judgement but there was no other way of lessening the risk of discovery. He had to leave the woman but he was uncertain whether he should lock the door or leave it open.

If the door was left open and she recovered and no one else was there, it was possible that she could wander off and come to some harm in the dark if she fell. The only advantage of someone finding her would be that they would assume that her recovery was spontaneous. It was a risk he felt unable to take. The woman would be none the wiser. She would have no memory of her treatment by Bill and would be unable to explain her presence anywhere other than where she was found. A truth spoken with confusion is often more plausible

167

than a clear-headed lie, he thought. Alternatively, if he locked the door she might not recover but at least he would know where she was and he could continue trying to bring her around. It was better that she should stay where she was for now.

Before leaving, Bill left no trace of his presence in the cell. With great misgivings he even removed the blanket he had used to keep them both warm. He closed the door intending to lock it but was horrified to hear the murmuring of a conversation and the sound of footsteps approaching. There was not enough time, and the bolt would have made a noise if he slid it into place. He fled along the passageway in terror of discovery and hid behind a fallen rock. Two men stood not too far away from Lana's cell. They would see him if he returned to lock the door. After ten minutes the men showed no sign of moving. Bill had to leave. If all was well, he planned to go back to Lana's cell and lock it the next time his captors slept.

The next morning, back in the small room next to the lab, Garcia shook Bill who lay sound asleep and fully clothed on his bed. 'Come, wake up my friend. We have some work to do.'

'W... what..?' the Doctor yawned; he had only just closed his eyes, or so it seemed. He was so tired and his body ached with climbing through the half-blocked passageway to Lana's cell.

Garcia watched Bill carefully. He was not sure whether he had measured the dosage right when he had injected the doctor. During the trials, either Kepler or Willington had administered precise amounts based upon the weight of the prisoners who had volunteered to be guinea pigs. He had no such data about Willington and there were no scales in the hideout with which to measure the weight of a man. The only scales that were available in the camp were those that Paulo's men used to measure the materials needed to the make bombs, but they were too small for any other purpose.

'Work? What work?' he said sleepily. Bill had hoped that his contact with Paulo and Garcia would be minimal. They had got what they wanted. The bombs had gone off. He desperately wanted to check on Lana.

Garcia laughed. He could hardly contain his amazement at his genius! Willington's kidnap had been his idea. Here before him stood a testament to his greatness as a hypnotherapist. The man responsible for the creation of the remarkable drug he used was his to command!

'We are out of Riofactol. You need to make some more.' he ordered Bill.

Paulo had promised to pay Garcia as soon as he received the last half of the payment for the guns that had just been delivered by one of Paulo's friends, which were to be sold to a dealer representing one of the middle-eastern terrorist networks. Paulo had paid for the guns to be stolen for him with the money he was paid to set off the bombs in America for the terrorist group in Iraq. A few more jobs like this and he would soon be able to retire! He had his eye on a beautiful house in Barcelona.

'But I have no materials!' Inwardly, Bill was shocked. Why did he have to make some more? He was sickened by what he had done to help Paulo and had hoped it was over after he had delivered the first batch he had made. Now he was being asked to make more! How could he possibly not do it? How could he maintain his credibility as a 'friend' of his captors if he refused? Bill's mind screamed silently in torment. He could not do it. He could not send the innocent victims of Garcia and Paulo's warped ambitions home to America to kill and maim other innocent civilians! There had to be a way of stopping them. But how could he do it? How?

His mind raced to think of something… anything, but he was too stressed to focus. With superhuman effort to shrug off his despair and disgust and affect a jovial presence of mind, he forced himself to smile agreeably back at Garcia, who stood opposite him, grinning like an evil demon. 'Do you know, I believe that we might be able to get better results if I make a slight change to the production process of the drug? I've been giving a great deal of thought to another method of refinement which might speed up the reaction time.'

Paulo had been so seriously annoyed that the process of the first batch had taken so long and that Bill had made such a small quantity that he would welcome any means to speed up the process.

Bill continued, 'Perhaps I should go with the driver to the supplier to obtain the new equipment I need? We could save at least two weeks' production time per batch!' After all, he was one of them now, wasn't he?

Garcia eyed the doctor with suspicion and his grin disappeared. Stupid fool, what did Willington think they were... a bunch of amateurs?

'There is no need for you to go out.' With an air of superiority he replied, 'A new consignment based upon the list you made when you came here was delivered this morning. We have everything you need.' Bill's heart sank as the man went on, 'I will mention the suggestion you made to me about speeding up the process, though. Paulo will be pleased to know that. We need a large batch to be ready very soon, a much larger batch than the last. Come… let us go into the lab.' Garcia did not explain why he needed a large batch of the drug and he said no more but beckoned the captive to follow him.

Bill was gutted as he followed Garcia into the lab. Boxes, sacks and crates were piled high by the benches. Paulo's men had indeed delivered a larger load of the chemicals and equipment he required to make more of the drug, than the previous load. The new equipment, all of it boxed separately, was particularly necessary because sterilising the old glass equipment in the cave environment was almost impossible. It had to be disposable, except for the metal holders for the pipettes and the distilling and siphoning tubes. There was so little ventilation in the cave complex that fine dust, caused by the natural erosion of the sand and limestone ceiling, fell everywhere.

Realising that Paulo would now expect to find him in the lab from now on, he knew it would be too risky for him to visit Lana for a while. Sick at heart, his stomach churning with disappointment he said calmly. 'Good. This is excellent. I will begin right after I have eaten.' God knows how I will be able to keep food down, he thought, but his desire to remain healthy made him accept that he would have to eat something.

171

He was of no use to anyone if he was sick.

Garcia left the doctor to sort through the boxes. Bill stood looking at them, not believing he had just agreed to do it all again. His throat was parched with the dust of the passageways from his visit to Lana. He had not had anything to drink since before he had slept. Feeling decidedly sick, he walked along to the cave that served as a kitchen and made some coffee. He was desperately tired and needed something to keep himself awake. Once made, he sat at the table drinking the brown liquid from a white mug, all the time thinking of ways around his predicament. Garcia had said that he had to make a large batch, why?

A large batch? In a flash of inspiration, a germ of an idea began to grow in his mind as he thought of the effects of the drug he had invented. There might just be a way he could foil Paulo's plans and stop some of the soldiers from being sent away.

Involuntarily, he gave a short laugh. 'Why didn't I think of this before?' he said softly to himself.

CHAPTER TWENTY SEVEN

Sana'a

Mike was to be met at Sana'a airport by Geordie Masters, an English Arab agent working for ASIU in Yemen.

Before Geordie was born, both of his parents had worked with the Red Crescent, tending to the wounded during several of the intermittent Arabian wars over ownership of the border territory. His father, a British army soldier from Tyneside in the north east of England, had married a woman from a Bedouin tribe who found him, almost breathing his last when her tribe was moving through the desert to a new site. She saved his life. While exploring the desert he had been badly wounded during a skirmish with a group of bandits who had robbed him of his belongings leaving him for dead in the hot sun. After Geordie was born, his parents spent most of their time in Arabia. He had happy memories of his childhood, which had been spent wandering the Rub' al Khali, or the 'Empty Quarter', which is a vast desert on the Arabian Gulf, with his grandparents and their Bedouin family.

As far back as he could remember, his grandmother had spoken to him in her native tongue. His fluency in Arabic and his naturally dark skin tone, which he had inherited from his grandmother, meant that he could legitimately claim to be an Arab when the need arose. This background was his greatest asset as an ASIU agent.

His father was dead and his mother still wandered the

desert with her family.

The Rub' al Khali is a hot and deadly environment, inhabited in turn throughout time, by bandits and oil wells, but Geordie loved the area, preferring not to return to his father's English roots after he died. Instead, he married Amina, an educated, enlightened woman who was attracted by his penetrating gaze during a visit to Al Baleed in Salalah, the southern capital of Oman. He was there on an ASIU assignment to monitor the activities of a visiting Colombian drug dealing gang. Now he was back in Sana'a.

Leaving Sana'a airport entrance, Mike spotted his contact sitting in a Land Rover 'Desert Storm'. It was a vehicle specially adapted to cross the desert with its high sand dunes, some of which rose to five hundred metres. Manoeuvring the relatively flatter, but rocky stone-covered part of the vast desert with its mixture of sand dunes and stony wastes would be a piece of cake.

The two men shook hands, each aware of their importance to the other. Mike needed Geordie's help to follow Decker, and Geordie needed the money the assignment would raise for his own and his wife's relatives. They walked together to the Land Rover.

Mike gave Geordie's vehicle an appreciative whistle. The Desert Storm was the latest model. JP had ordered Geordie to provide the best available transport for his man.

'A DS? They give you the best don't they?' He was impressed.

Geordie shrugged his shoulders, 'It's better than the older

174

model for hiking the dunes. I can work with it but I prefer my camels actually, they are slower but much better, you don't have to keep stopping to get the sand out of their exhaust.'

It was too hot in American clothing in the early afternoon sun. Mike took the bundle that Geordie gave to him and hiding behind the DS, which was parked next to a deserted alleyway, he changed quickly into traditional Arab robes. He had discovered their value when he was a member of the Peacekeeping Force in the Sudan. The first time he had put on the robes he felt like a transvestite, until he found out how much cooler they were in the scorching heat, in which he had been obliged to spend a considerable amount of time.

They sat together, talking and drinking lemonade in the restaurant at the airport, awaiting the arrival of Piers and Decker. Mike briefed Geordie on their joint assignment, which was to follow Decker and, if and when appropriate, apprehend him and return him to the US as a suspect in his girlfriend's murder, among other crimes. He also explained to him that his main interest was to interrogate the man about Dr Willington's kidnap as soon as he could.

Two hours later, Decker's aircraft landed. Piers sent a text to Mike to announce his arrival. Unseen and from a safe distance the two agents watched the passengers as they passed through the immigration gates. Within seconds of Decker walking past Mike, followed by a porter with his luggage on a trolley, he saw Piers following at a discreet distance.

'Time to go,' he said to Geordie.

For the first time, Mike saw Decker in daylight. He was tall and tanned and wearing a sleeveless shirt that exposed his muscular arms; he was clearly a strong man who had built up his muscular frame either in a gym or by a very active lifestyle. However, it seemed incongruous that a man of his stature would grow his hair so long, much less wear it combed back from his brow and tied with a black band at the nape of his neck. He wore a cream shirt over cream linen trousers and matching cream sport-shoes. His stride was relaxed and slow, like a tourist as he made his way through groups of people, heading for the exit to the airport car park.

Piers followed Decker, watching his every move as he left the airport and walked over to a large truck parked at the far end of the road. There was only one man waiting to greet him, the driver, who dropped several coins into the hand of the porter who had delivered Decker's luggage to him. Geordie and Mike followed Piers, until Decker was driven away.

All three ASIU agents then boarded their air conditioned vehicle and watched as the truck headed south to Aden, approximately two hundred miles away, stopping only to refuel and eat. Piers managed to purchase some sandwiches without being seen from a shop near the restaurant where Decker and his driver ate their meal quickly then returned to the truck. When they resumed their journey, Geordie kept a respectful distance between themselves and their quarry, and almost missed them altogether when they turned into Aden airport.

When Decker went to the ticket desk Geordie followed close behind and was able to hear him when he booked a flight to Al Ghaydah near the border between the Yemen and Oman, for the following day. Eventually, the driver dropped the man off at a back-street hotel on the edge of the city.

'The hotel isn't up to much but that is probably why he chose it.' Geordie remarked to Mike as he looked through his binoculars at the hotel entrance. They had parked out of sight of the hotel near a shop selling fruit and vegetables.

'One of us will need to travel with Decker to Al Gaydah.' Piers remarked. 'He may have seen me on the plane so it can't be me.'

'It can't be me either,' Mike turned to Geordie, 'It will have to be you.'

'OK, fine with me. That means you two will need to get to Al Gaydah ahead of us. I will arrange for the car to be returned to Sana'a, and for another DS to be waiting for you when you land.'

Mike and Piers returned with Geordie to the airport.

Geordie booked a ticket to Al Ghaydah for himself for the following day on the same flight as Decker, and two tickets for Mike and Piers on the next flight out, which was within the hour.

Phew... no rest for the wicked, he thought.

Three quarters of an hour later, Mike and Piers were in the air; both mystified by Decker's change of direction. What was waiting in Al Ghaydah for him?

'Where's this guy going?' Piers wondered aloud, sipping on an orange juice. There was no alcohol on the flight.

'Search me.' Mike replied, 'We're going to look pretty stupid if he's going on a sightseeing trip! I hope he stays in one place when he gets off at the next stop; I'm beginning to dry out.' The lemonade he had chosen to drink was distinctly unpalatable because of its sickly sweetness. His taste buds were

177

being severely insulted!

Unhappily for Geordie, he spent the early part of the evening watching Decker drink himself to sleep through the window of an adjoining building. He had bribed a young boy to find out which room Decker had been allocated in the grubby back-street hotel. It was easy for the boy to earn his reward because his uncle owned the hotel. Obviously the man wasn't looking for publicity. However, Geordie was glad not to be running around the streets following his quarry. If he kept to his room it was a lot easier on his feet.

The agent only managed to get five hours' sleep before the taxi arrived to take him to the airport. Geordie had to be on board and in his seat before Decker, to be sure that he did not suspect that he was being followed.

To Geordie's surprise, Decker was not alone when he took his seat on the aircraft. Another man was with him. He was almost as tall as Decker, with a thin, elegantly clothed frame. He was dark skinned, with deep brown eyes, a thin nose and short, well styled hair. He was Arabian, but looked like a western businessman. They were talking, and Geordie wished he could hear their conversation. This was an unexpected turn of events. The stranger must have joined Decker after he left the hotel that morning or he would have seen them together.

Decker and his friend's seats were one row in front of the aircraft door, behind Geordie's window seat. To hear any of their conversation he would have to move. Half an hour into the flight, he walked to the service area of the aircraft and spoke with one of the flight attendants, a young, black haired woman who was busily unpacking the food trays.

'Excuse me, Miss.' he rubbed his stomach as if in pain. 'I seem to be having a problem with my stomach, something bad in my dinner last night, I think. Do you think you could swap my seat for one nearer the er...?' he indicated the rest room door. It was the best he could do.

Keeping a watchful eye on it, Geordie had ascertained that the only spare seat near the rest room was one of the two next to the aircraft door, which backed onto Decker and his friend's seats but faced in the opposite direction. That would place him back-to-back with Decker. Perfect!

The young woman expressed her concern in her expression. 'Yes, I'll do what I can. Wait here a moment.' After checking the passenger list against the seating plan, she returned to Geordie, and pointed to the spare seat by the door, 'Here... you can sit here.'

Geordie sat on the seat next to an elderly woman who was engrossed in a novel, and took out his pocket radio. 'Thanks for your help.' he smiled at the attendant.

'Let me know if you need anything else,' she returned his smile as she resumed her task.

Pushing the earplugs of his radio into his ears, Geordie turned up the volume so that he could pick up some of the conversation between the two men behind him. The radio wasn't really a radio. It was an ultra-sensitive hearing device with a built-in digital recorder. He would be able to play the conversation back to Mike and Piers when he reached Al Ghayah. As long as the background noise wasn't too bad he could be lucky enough to pick up something useful. He settled into his seat and closed his eyes to help him focus on the conversation behind him. It also ensured that the woman in the next seat wouldn't disturb him.

CHAPTER TWENTY EIGHT

The Chase

Decker and Geordie's flight landed in Al Ghaydah at three o-clock in the afternoon. Mike and Piers sat in the newly delivered DS, waiting for their colleague as arranged. They were as surprised as Geordie had been to see that Decker had a travelling companion. They were even more surprised when Geordie walked directly to their vehicle, leaving the two men to get away from him.

'What are you doing? They're getting away!' Piers said urgently as Geordie climbed into the DS.

'No, they aren't. I know where they are going!' Geordie said confidently. 'They are meeting some mates of theirs at Rakhyut. Apparently they are expecting some goods being delivered by boat from Djibouti, and from the conversation, I would say that those goods are being smuggled into Oman. What they are is anyone's guess, they never said, but my guess is its probably drugs or weapons. As you know, there are more than a few terrorist organisations operating throughout the Middle East as well as drug gangs. I know they operate here too, I've chased after them often enough, though I don't recognise Decker's mate.'

'Why didn't they just fly to Salalah and drive south to Rakhyut? That would have been a lot easier for them.' Mike asked.

'That is the interesting part.' Geordie laughed. 'Decker's

mate is afraid of being picked up in Oman. I didn't get his name, they're a cautious pair; neither of them referred to the other by name. That means they might also be using false passports, otherwise his mate might not have been allowed on the flight at Sana'a either. Either that or he is only wanted for something in Oman and not in Yemen. Maybe they have his face in their computerised checking system at the airport.'

'You say you know where they're going?' asked Mike.

'Yes.' They are headed along the coast road to Damqawt; a small boat is taking him at night to Rakhyut to rendezvous with Decker, who's going to drive himself there. That is the plan to get our mystery man into Oman without being spotted. He must have been hiding in Aden, waiting for Decker to join him.' Geordie showed Mike the listening device. 'It's all here if you want to listen.'

'Thanks, I'll listen on the way. Let's get going. We're all fuelled up.'

During the almost seventy kilometre trip to Damqawt, Mike listened to the recorded conversation between Decker and his mate. The sound of the aircraft's engines could be heard in the background but the quality of the recording was quite good. He could hear practically every word spoken. Once the goods arrived in Rakhyut, a truck would be used to transport them by main road to Mudhai, then onto the quieter road that would meet the main Shisur/Fasad road and a right turn back towards Shisur. One man said that it would be too dangerous to travel on the Salalah/Dauka trunk road because of the police patrols. There was also some talk of a helicopter. The men had dropped their voices even lower at this point, and he could only just make out one of the voices saying that using a helicopter would be risky because of a .... something, nearby. Mike listened turning the sound to its highest level but still could not make out the word.

He asked Geordie to listen to that part of the recording because the word sounded foreign to his ears.

'An encampment, that's what the word means.' Geordie confirmed. 'There may be a tribe in a temporary encampment nearby and they won't want to be seen or heard if they are doing something illegal, because the people in the camp will either shop them or ask for a share of the goods or profits, not to. Some of the people in the desert are not true Bedouin and are a shifty lot. Not all by any means, but there are some people in some camps who are not quite civilised. They help the terrorist organisations to ship arms and drugs around the desert regions. Some of the police won't go near them for fear of being shot.'

But what has this to do with Dr Bill Willington, Mike wondered? It was so far away from England and America. What if this is a wild goose chase and Decker's trip has nothing to do with the doctor? If they did pick him up he is hardly likely to want to grant favours and tell them where he is, assuming he knows of course. If Decker were free to go where he liked, someone else might have the doctor. He could be anywhere! The thought was not a good one so Mike pushed it to the back of his mind. He had to trust his instinct, which was telling him that Decker knew where Bill was.

The car that Decker and his friend were in was driven by a much older driver and he drove at a reasonable speed, indicating that the occupants had no idea that they were being pursued by anyone. As before, Geordie kept a safe distance, swiftly dodging out of sight behind a house when Decker's driver pulled up at the side of a small white building in Damqawt. They watched as Decker and the new man on the scene got out, picked up their luggage from the trunk of the car and disappeared into the building.

Later that day the DS was parked behind a large white building that might have been habitable if it had a roof. The agents watched for half an hour, hidden from the view of the four men who were loading wooden crates onto a large truck parked at the entrance to a narrow lane nearby. When the truck was fully loaded, the boxes were covered by brown tarpaulin spattered with sandy markings then secured with rope.

Two figures slipped surreptitiously through one of the house doors that led out into the lane. It was Decker and the new man. The truck driver and the car driver got into the truck and Decker and his friend got into the car.

It was a great relief to the three agents that the four burly loaders did not accompany the men when they drove away. The last thing Mike wanted was a set-to if they were discovered. Any distraction from their purpose would be unwelcome.

For three hours Mike and Piers slept in the cool DS as Geordie followed the two vehicles. He kept a good half kilometre between his vehicle and the truck. There was only one road through the desert once they passed the turning to Oafa. Unless the truck or the car stopped or slowed down, or they both stayed where they were for any length of time, the agents were unlikely either to lose or meet up with the occupants of the two vehicles unexpectedly. The undulating but straight road was half covered in sand in some places, and before darkness overtook them, the shimmering heat haze kept the DS well hidden from the range of a rear view mirror.

As the sun disappeared below the horizon the two drivers in front, and Geordie, were forced to switch on their headlights. When the road emptied in the late evening, Geordie pulled further back from the truck in front of him, so that his lights would be only a distant glow but he could still see the truck's rear lights. He had heard the dark-haired man say that the truck would pull off the road near the latest excavations at Ubar, north of Shisur, for the night. They would be easy enough to find.

Two hours later and fifteen miles north-west of Shisur, they parked at the back of an excavation site. Several hidden cities had been found in that area and this was the latest to be excavated. The DS was dwarfed behind a compound surrounded by a two-metre high fence. The three men left the DS, stooping low in the shadows as they crept around the perimeter to see if the truck and Decker's car were there. They were.

Both vehicles were well hidden and out of sight of the road. Two of the men were asleep in the cab. Likewise, Decker and his friend were also asleep, sprawled across the two seats of the car, which was only a couple of yards away from the truck. The car windows were only slightly open.

At four o-clock in the morning Mike woke to the sound of the truck's engines as it passed in front of the compound behind which they were hidden.

They watched as the truck sped on, heading north and then far away over the stony ground that bordered the high dunes. There was no sign of the car behind the truck, so Piers went to see where it was. It had gone.

'Probably one of the drivers drove off somewhere else in it. I expect their fingerprints were all over it. Best thing to do. That's what I would do to ensure it wasn't found where it shouldn't be.' Geordie said pragmatically. 'It's not in their interests to destroy it out here because that would attract attention. Have you any idea how many cars are being driven around the country after being used by terrorists? If you do something stupid in or to a car, you get noticed. If you just drive it around, nobody cares. Anyway, it would never have made it over the dunes. I expect Decker and his friend are in the truck.' He waited but did not switch on the ignition of the DS for a full half-hour.

'We'll have to box clever here. It would not be wise to follow them further in this vehicle, they will probably have to stop or refuel from the cans they are carrying, and they will be able to see us at the peaks of the dunes. They can't move fast, even with the wide tyres on the truck. The dunes are too steep and the load they are carrying is quite full and heavy I shouldn't wonder, so it will leave deep marks behind it. It would be better to follow on foot. If we move fast we can reach my tribe; they are camped about eight kilometres north-west of here, near Fasad. That's not far away in this,' he patted the steering wheel of the DS, 'which I can leave with my people. They will provide us with camels. We will still be able to find their tracks before the sun is completely up. They won't be blown away because the air is so still at the moment, which is lucky for us.'

Geordie reversed the DS and turned back toward the road, crossed it and headed north-west toward Fasad and found his mother's family, who were camped near the edge of the dunes. Geordie's mother was sleeping so he did not wake her to introduce Mike. There would be time for that later perhaps. The DS was left at the camp and covered with a sheet made up of several pieces of black canvas, tied down with rope, to protect it in case a harsh wind should blow flying sand into the engine parts.

They left the camp with four camels, one heavily loaded up with supplies and the precious water-barrels. Mike wondered how the beast could move with such a heavy load.

Two hours later, based upon years of experience in traversing the desert, and having judged the speed and distance the truck would have travelled since it left the excavation site, the three men travelled due east.

'Gotcha!' With a low cry of triumph, Geordie found the tracks left by the truck which, as they saw five minutes later, was rolling slowly onwards halfway across the ridge of a large sand dune. With Geordie dashing ahead every ten minutes to check on the truck's progress, they followed twenty minutes behind until the land started to flatten out again. They watched, hidden below the horizon of the dune, as the truck moved very slowly away from them over the stony ground.

Clearly they were protecting the packages loaded into the back of it. Mike wondered what else they had in the truck... the driver was nursing it like a baby.

In the distance was another expanse of dunes lower than those they had just left and the truck seemed to be headed toward them.

Mike had travelled on camels before but he was not enjoying the ride. It was too slow; a helicopter would have been better but would also have been too easy to see and hear. Piers seemed to cope quite well for the first few hours but he did throw up when they stopped for a while for lunch and to drink from the water barrel.

'I suffer from seasickness too,' he apologised to his companions. 'This camel is worse than a boat!'

During lunch, Geordie introduced the fourth camel as 'Matey', whom he had raised from birth after its mother died.

'He has a habit of trying to nibble my ears off.' he explained. 'The silly so'n-so!' He gave the camel an affectionate pat, which incited a smelly nuzzle of affection. 'Gerroff, you little horror!' he rebuked him.

Matey turned his head away and spat in disgust before regurgitating some undigested food with a low growl, showing his long, filthy teeth. The men laughed.

Giving Mike and Piers a small bag of salt to eat to prevent dehydration, Geordie reminded them not to go without water for too long, especially in the daytime.

The truck and the camels continued resolutely to clamber over the lower dunes, taking a rest every hour before heading for the high dunes. The light began to fade as evening set in and the heat had diminished slightly but it was still quite warm. It would become much colder later but they were well prepared for that. There were additional items of clothing and blankets loaded onto Matey.

Amina had loaded dried meat, cheese made from camel's milk and several flat, stone baked loaves of bread into the baskets carried by Matey. Geordie had procured three long-range radios that could be picked up by JP via the nearest NSA satellite, as long as they were in a favourable area of reception. They also had a GPS beacon.

Geordie signalled the men to stop. Sand blew lightly into their faces and they were forced to put on the linen hats and wrap long cloths around their faces, leaving only their eyes uncovered. Amina had packed them into the baskets on Geordie's instruction because he knew how suddenly a sandstorm could blow up in the desert.

Gradually, the sky darkened and the truck stopped. The driver, Decker and his friend settled down for the night at the side of the truck. The three agents huddled together by the camels.

They started out again at sun up, watching the dust flying behind the wheels of the truck in the distance as it manoeuvred the stony wasteland.

The riders again kept their distance as the truck started its ascent of the first of the higher dunes. For twenty minutes it climbed slowly upwards, then the wide tyres eventually hauled it over the top and the three men on camels started their ascent.

For two hours they followed slowly behind the truck. Eventually, they were so close that they could hear the low throb of its engine. Wondering why it had stopped, they dismounted and crawled carefully to the ridge of the dune separating them and peered cautiously over the top.

Below them in the well of the very steep slope of the dune he saw an opening about fifteen metres wide and five metres high. Made of solid sandstone, it was overlain with tightly packed sand which, when the wind blew hard, tumbled continuously downward onto several four metre wide canopies below it. The canopies were made from sand coloured fabric and were suspended over the opening in the rock, on a framework of metal rods, driven into the sand. Two men in desert fatigues stood with automatic weapons hanging by straps over their shoulders, talking to the truck driver. Two other men stood beside the newcomers. One of them shook Decker's hand, while the other greeted the man whose name they did not know, with some enthusiasm as if he knew him very well.

The three onlookers gasped in disbelief! They had never seen anything like it. A cave of solid rock and in the middle the desert!

CHAPTER TWENTY NINE

Rub' al Khali

So this is where he hides! Using his field glasses, Mike scanned the faces below. He recognised Decker but not the others. It was obvious that there was no way of getting past the guards and into the opening without being seen, even in the dark. They would shoot him immediately he climbed down the dune, and there was no angle of approach that would give him the element of surprise.

They would have to find another way in.

'Hell's teeth!' Geordie said softly. 'In all the time I've spent in the desert, I've never come across this place before... what are they doing in there?'

All three men were amazed. 'It could be anything. Guns, drugs, white slavery. Your guess is as good as mine.' Piers commented.

Mike was determined to find a way into the cave. 'We've got to get inside that place somehow. They need air. Perhaps there's a ventilator shaft nearby.'

They returned to the camels, which they had left nearby. Normally noisy creatures, they were unusually quiet.

'From the look of that reddening sky,' Geordie warned, 'there's a sandstorm heading this way. It'll have the skin off your face in no time! We'd better get some shelter... fast!'

'Bloody hell! That's all we need!' Piers complained, holding on to the rein of his camel.

'You should welcome this shamal wind, my friend. This sandstorm will hide our tracks and prevent our discovery.' Geordie was serious. 'Quickly, we must seek some shelter because it will be with us very soon.'

Geordie was right; the wind was rising and the animals were becoming restless. As fast as they could, the men and camels walked in single file over four smaller dunes until they chanced upon a small outcrop of sandstone.

'This is a good place,' Geordie announced. 'We can take shelter here.' He persuaded the first of his two camels to sit down and covered its head with a blanket, which he tied as tight as he safely could around its neck to avoid choking the animal. When he tried to do the same to Matey, the animal protested wilfully, snorting his disapproval and trying to bite the fabric. Piers laughed at his efforts. 'C'mon you silly bugger, stand still and stop struggling.' But as fast as Geordie tried to tie up the cloth, Matey shook his head defiantly and it fell off.

Eventually he gave up, saying to Mike, 'He's like this every time, he just won't have his face covered.' He sat beside Piers who had already unpacked a blanket with which to protect himself, and he scowled at Matey. 'Sod you, you stubborn devil. I hope you get a mouthful of sand and your nose drops off!'

Matey didn't care. He pulled his head down until it was level with the top of his single hump and, flashing his long lashes at the two men, spat out a dollop of masticated yellow gunge into the sand beside them, then closed his eyes.

Piers looked at the disgusting mess and retched as he threw a handful of sand over it. Geordie laughed, saying, 'He's a soft old thing really! He wouldn't hurt a fly.' He tugged at the camel's reins, 'Would you Matey?'

Matey ignored him.

Taking a swig from his water bottle and wiping his mouth Piers said sardonically, 'Oh, really?' He didn't fancy his chances with the animal. For some strange reason, he could never quite get along with animals. Even his girlfriend's dog had taken a dislike to him.

The wind was becoming stronger, blowing the sand around their faces and up into the air like mini whirlwinds.

Mike covered the head of his camel, which meekly obliged by not struggling, then sat on the ground beside Piers. All three men wrapped themselves up in their blankets and prepared to sit out the storm. For a while all they could feel was a slight patting as the wind blew the edges of the blanket against their bodies. Over the next twenty minutes its strength increased, becoming so much stronger that it seemed to claw at their blankets. At first, Piers and Mike felt protected by their covering, but it soon became a losing battle. They were partially sheltered by the rocks, but the whirling sand found its way into every fold, stinging their faces and hands. Eventually, they found themselves wrestling with their blankets just to keep them around their bodies. Geordie was expertly enveloped by his, curled up into as small a shape as he could manage, still holding onto Matey's reins.

The howling of the wind grew louder, rising higher until it screamed like a banshee, making even a shouted conversation impossible. The wild sand pulverised their covered bodies and flew against the rocks around them. Mike's face felt as if it was being scrubbed by unseen, glass-spiked fingers as the wind threw sand at him from every direction. Eventually, even Geordie had difficulty keeping his blanket wrapped around his body.

Following Geordie's example, they crouched down with their faces almost in the sand beneath them, and tried to stop their blankets from blowing away by kneeling on the edge of it.

It seemed as if the storm lasted for hours but it eventually blew away from them. They found it hard to move at first because they were almost buried by the sand that had blown against their bodies. Uncovering themselves, they stood up and started to shake the fine grains out of their blankets, hair, clothes and boots.

Above them, the sun eventually burnt its way through the red, dusty haze and shone relentlessly once more, scorching the sand beneath their feet.

With the exception of Matey, whose reins Geordie had resolutely kept secured around his own wrists despite the animal's attempts to pull them away, they found that the other three camels, which had been tied together, had wandered off.

Mike and Piers groaned. They would be gone by now! Both men did not relish the idea of walking on the hot sand.

'I'm glad Matey didn't get away. We'd be dead without the water.' remarked Piers as he took a drink from his refilled water bottle to lubricate his dry throat.

'We'd better find them. We won't get far without them. This heat will wear you down in no time if you try to walk.' Geordie warned.

The two men did not doubt it. It was baking hot already

and despite the Arab dress both he and Piers were wearing, they were beginning to feel like a Sunday roast.

Geordie, cool, unruffled and completely at home in the environment, listened carefully. The contrast between the howling gale and the silence that now prevailed was almost deafening. It was broken only by the rasping sound made by some small creature hidden among the nearby rocks.

They walked on for half an hour. Suddenly, Geordie, still listening intently, heard something and pointed behind one of the dunes. 'Over that way!'

The three men scrambled up the dune and rolled down the other side. At its base, partly covered by sand was an almost circular group of smooth, thin sandstone rocks, about one and a half metres tall, like fingers pointing upwards to the sky. They had been worn away long ago, covered by sand again and then been exposed by the wind that drove the sandstorm. The camels stood patiently beside the rocks as if they had been there all the time. The blankets that had covered their eyes now hung around their necks.

Piers tried to persuade them to go with him, by pulling at their reins, but one of the animals seemed to have trapped its foot among a pile of rocks. The Swede held on to the unfortunate animal as Geordie tied the other two camels to Matey. Patiently, Geordie pulled away the larger interlocking rocks that had trapped the hoof.

Suddenly the sand gave way, one of the larger rocks tumbled over, the camel stepped back, and the surprised man fell about two metres down into a hole. He held his hands over his head as some of the smaller rocks and sand started

195

collapsing into the hole around him, covering his feet.

When the subsidence stopped, Mike jumped down into the hole. Geordie had managed to free his feet and suffered only a minor scrape to his ankle. The two men found themselves in a small, cone shaped cave, which was just big enough to hold four men standing together. A large number of rounded rocks lay half buried in the sand below their feet.

Piers' hoisted Geordie out of the hole.

Suddenly, Mike stooped low and started to shove some of the sand away from the base of the rock. He had spotted a small opening, partly obscured by a larger flat rock about two and a half metres tall. It was covered at its base by several smaller rocks and sand at the back of the hole. Picking up the half-buried, bleached bone of a long dead camel that had fallen into the hole when it collapsed, Mike stepped carefully over the smaller rocks until he could lean against the obstruction. Holding onto the bone, he pushed it through the opening behind the rock and discovered that there was enough space to turn its full length anti-clockwise in a three hundred and sixty-degree circle. Pulling the bone back out of the opening, Mike threw it out of the hole. It landed next to Piers who, with one bare foot on the ground, was shaking sand out of his sock. Mike then picked up a rounded stone about fifteen centimetres in diameter and threw it, with only a little difficulty, through the hole. All three men heard it clatter and bounce a few times. And there was an echo!

'There's something behind this large rock!' Mike exclaimed. 'Maybe it's a way into the cave if we can move this obstruction out of the way.' The hole wasn't large enough for a man to climb through.

Geordie jumped down to join Mike in the hole.

'Help me dig this out,' Mike asked him. 'We've got to move that large rock at the back of this pile.'

The two men dug at the sand with their hands and threw some of the smaller rocks into the entrance to the hole, hearing them rattle downwards.

Piers called down, 'Need some help?' His sock was back on his foot and he was lacing up his boot.

'No, there isn't enough room down here for the three of us to work effectively. Just hang onto the animals and keep a look out for unwelcome visitors!' Mike warned him.

For almost half an hour, stopping only to rest and to eat and drink, the three men took it in turns to dig away at loose sand, removing the smaller rocks until they were in a position to move the larger rocks. Eventually only the largest rock stood in the way. It was too big for one man to move without help.

'That's going to take some moving!' Piers was exhausted. His fair hair was soaked with sweat from his brow.

'We can do it. The camels can help us.' Geordie said as he climbed out of the hole.

He dragged two of the animals down the incline they had made and, after visually estimating the distance between the camels and the stone he tied two makeshift rope harnesses around them. Carefully, he wound a blanket around the rope to prevent it from cutting into the camels' skin then threw the ends of the ropes to Mike and Piers.

'Tie the ropes tight around the top of the rock. I'll get the

197

camels to pull it over. It's quite a narrow rock and the base is thinner than the top. If you dig out more of the sand and climb up here, the camels can do the rest.'

Geordie was right. The rock was narrower at the base. Obligingly, with their bare hands Mike and Piers pulled away more of the sand from the base of the large rock. The ends of their fingers ached with the effort. After clearing away as much sand as they dared without bringing the rock down on top of themselves, the two men tied the ropes around the top part of the rock then climbed out of the hole.

Pulling hard with the reins, Geordie turned the animals' heads until they were facing away from the rock then he urged them forward. The camels strained and pulled as much as they could.

Piers watched the rock for any sign of movement from a vantage point at the top of the hole.

'It's moving, just a bit more... just a bit more!'

Geordie urged the camels to move forward once more. Suddenly, the rock crashed forward and the camels lurched forward awkwardly as the ropes slid off the top of it and the tension was released. The sand slid backwards and down, seeping like an avalanche through the huge space that appeared behind the stone. It poured relentlessly over the thousands of stones, rocks and boulders that formed the downward slope into a huge, dark cavern.

CHAPTER THIRTY

Den of Despair

Lana's head was spinning, and lights danced in her brain as if she had a migraine but without the pain. She was lying on her back on a very hard, cold bed and something was crawling across her face. She brushed her cheek and the sensation ended as the unidentified beetle fell onto the stone floor and scuttled away. Before her open eyes was only blackness. Was she blind? Panicked, she opened her eyes even wider and wiped away the sticky substance that had accumulated around her upper and lower lids. The room was still black even after it was all gone. An involuntary, frightened croak escaped her lips; she could not see! Her tongue was dry and her mouth felt as if it were filled with flour. She tried to spit it out, but she had no saliva.

Where am I? Lana was confused. Struggling, she tried to sit up. Why was she so stiff? Gradually, moving very slowly, she managed to get onto her feet, swaying unsteadily at first as she put one foot in front of the other and with both arms held straight out in front of her, she walked forward, only to come to a stop at an ice-cold wall. Feeling her way around it, she reached a wooden frame and found a door. It took her a few moments to find a handle, which she opened cautiously. Thankfully, it was not locked. Instinctively, she was afraid. Something was not quite right.

I shouldn't be here, she thought, but where do I go? She

turned left out of the door. Five minutes later, to her joyous relief, she realised that she was not blind; she could see some light ahead. Cautiously she headed toward it, passing the entrance to two other passages on the way.

As she got nearer the light, voices came out of the darkness. Foreign voices. She could not understand what they were saying. Instantly, instinctively, she was filled with terror and she backed away and took one of the other passages. There were no lights and she was terribly afraid but something inside her head told her that the foreign voices meant danger.

There were more black passages ahead, and not knowing where she was going, the frightened woman continued to walk on. She saw no more lights. Eventually after walking until she was nearly falling down with the effort, she was forced to stop. Finding that she could not touch both sides of the passageway at once, as she had been able to do earlier, she realised that she was in an open space and that she could be heading for a precipice. Instinctively, knowing it would be safer she crawled on her knees until she found a space among some rocks. She was shaking uncontrollably in the cold, musty air, and terrified by the all pervasive darkness, exhausted and desperate for a drink, she closed her eyes and fell into a deep sleep.

Bill worked in his lab making the new batch of Riofactol. He laughed to himself. He felt energised. There was hope. Now more than ever he was pleased that Garcia did not realise that the list he had provided to his men to purchase the supplies for the first batch also meant that he could make more of the antidote. No one visited him except Paulo's soldiers who looked in on him from time to time. He had a plan. A brilliant plan... if it worked.

For the whole of the day, he worked without stopping. By the time the next meal was served, Bill was anxious to get back to Lana but he dared not leave the group too early. Paulo, Neko, Garcia and Decker drank more as time passed and, without much success, the doctor tried to avoid drinking the alcohol that was constantly being poured into his glass but he had no choice but to drink it. There was nowhere for him to discreetly dispose of it. He was supposed to be their friend, so he could not justify a refusal to be sociable. He kept up the pretence for another three hours.

Garcia eventually passed out in his seat. He was not normally a heavy drinker, Bill had noted, and although he drank with the brothers, sometimes glass for glass, he could not take it as well as they could.

Bill feigned a great tiredness, which was depressingly near the truth. He was not looking forward to another sleepless night. Remembering how cold he had been, he reminded himself that he needed to pick up a second blanket before his walk.

'I'm off now, my friends. I need to sleep.' He yawned. 'That was a fine bottle of whisky! Goodnight.' Yawning again, he got up from his seat and staggered toward the door.

Bill understood why the men were laughing as he left. They thought they had him under control. Turning his back on them as he walked out of the room, he allowed himself to smile at having deceived them so far. He also now had an inkling of the time. His watch had not been returned to him, but he had managed to see Garcia's. The watch face was exposed when the man's wrist was draped over the side of the sofa as he lay in a drunken stupor. It was twelve o-clock. They had eaten a large meal together, so he estimated that it must be midnight. It was some time since he had been to the mouth of the cave as he was not allowed to go there without Paulo being present. This meant that he had no basis for his estimate of time, which seemed to slip by relentlessly.

Packing another two pills and a fresh supply of water into his bag, the doctor returned to Lana's cell. It was empty. Anguished, he ran his hands over his face. Oh, God, no! Please don't let her be harmed, he prayed. Desperate to find her, the doctor made his way further onwards, through rooms that he had never seen before until he came to a large cavern with severely cracked walls. The ceiling was, he estimated, around ten metres high. The floor of the cavern formed an irregularly deep but fairly linear dip at its centre, which looked as if it might have been the bed of an underground river that had dried up years ago. He continued through banks of large and small rocks, tearing his overall as it caught on a jagged piece of newly cracked rock but Bill walked purposely onward, praying that the ceiling wouldn't collapse on top of him.

The light from his lamp was bright enough for him to see by, but it cast dark shadows that flickered around the nearby rocks, sometimes making his heart leap with fear. The flickering shadows could so easily have been a man.

After what seemed like hours, Bill found that his lamp was dimming as the oil diminished and he dared not spend any more time looking for Lana. He might never find her. In despair, he prayed that she would be safe as he turned back to the lab. He had absolutely no idea where he was and the oil in his lamp would soon be gone. As he walked back to his lab, he thought about his plan to outwit Paulo and Garcia.

One week earlier the two men had taken him to a large cave in which eight men were imprisoned. He had listened to the men as they protested at being held against their will. Paulo told them that soon they would be joining his army, though he never said how that would be made possible.

'Never!' one of them had shouted back in disgust.

'Dream on!' said another.

'Just give me the chance to get my hands on you without your guards to protect you!' a third man had shouted angrily, 'You're a dead man!'

Bill had remained silent, as expected. He dared not speak. Then he had walked just as silently behind Paulo and Garcia when they left the cell together and Garcia had exclaimed, laughing back at the men, 'You will join us, my friends. You will see!'

'Go screw yourselves!' The men had replied scornfully.

The door to their cell was kept locked, but Bill was with Paulo when he collected the key from a desk drawer in one of the smaller caves nearby before they went into the men's cell. The men appeared to be using the smaller cell as an office. At the time, he had made a mental note of where the key was kept in case he was in a position to help the men escape.

Bill's silence whilst in the room with the men had been necessary. It would have been dangerous to risk exposing his position at the time, but now it was a necessary part of his plan. Fearing discovery, he hoped that Paulo had not planted a spy in with them or he would certainly be punished. They would not kill him of course, they needed him to make the drug, but they could inflict a serious amount of pain!

The most important part of his plan required Bill to free one of the eight men in that cell. He dared not free them all. The escape of one man could be accepted, but not eight. The doctor hoped that the man he freed would then be able to find a way out of the cave complex and bring back some help to free them all, though what that help would be he wasn't quite sure when he first thought up the plan. He had to try.

Still worried about Lana, the doctor returned to his cell. After checking that there were no guards around and that Paulo, his brother and their cohorts were still either drinking or sleeping, Bill walked quickly along the passageway that he knew led to the soldiers' cell.

One of the guards nearly caught sight of him as he turned into the small cave near the prisoners' cell, to collect the key. The man was passing across the junction of the passageway, a mere ten metres away and just in sight of the office, but to Bill's relief he was not looking in his direction. He slipped quietly into the office. There were three keys inside the box and they all looked the same. He would have to work fast.

Two of the eight men in the cell were awake when Bill, as quietly as he could, tried the first key in the lock. A face appeared at the grille of the door. Bill signalled the man to be quiet. The man eyed him suspiciously but said nothing as he stepped away from the door.

The second key fitted the lock and Bill dashed quickly into

the cell as soon as the door was unlocked, closing it behind him. The rasping creak of the door was enough to awaken the other men, who left their beds and stood beside their friends. Again Bill put his fingers to his lips urging them to be quiet, and they followed as he walked over to the darkest corner then sat down on the edge of the nearest bed. The men sat or stood where they could next to him.

One of the men asked, 'Who are you? What are you doing here? I think I've seen you before.'

Bill decided not to tell them the reason for his captivity. It would serve no purpose to risk arousing their hostility. He would not have blamed them for wanting to kill him if they found out his contribution to what Garcia had done to some of their friends. Right now, he needed their trust.

Instead he said, 'Yes, you are right, you have seen me before. However, my name is unimportant, if you do not know my name it cannot be forced out of you and make no mistake, these evil men can make you do or say anything! However, you can believe me when I say that I am here to help you. There is a reason why I appear to have the freedom to walk these caves and you don't, but I need you to trust me and not ask too many questions. That would only waste valuable time.'

Introducing themselves, the men nodded their understanding.

A deep voice said quietly, 'Jacques LeCroix.' Jacques was a bald-headed man about fifty and wearing round, gold-rimmed spectacles.

'Hi.' a fair-haired man around thirty smiled. 'I'm Andy Stillman,'

'Zak. Zak Rosenbaum.' a young, dark-haired man with a serious face said, 'Pleased to meet you.'

'Tex Kirkwall... likewise!' Standing just less than two metres tall, Tex spoke with a relaxed southern drawl. 'This is Joe Jameson standing next to me, and that's Hans Schmidt on your left, behind Andy. Joe is our resident chef and Hans is our newest recruit.' Dave and Sam are on your right.

'Thanks. You can't begin to know how good it is to find a few friends in here.' Bill went on, 'Do you all know each other well? I can't be sure that Paulo hasn't planted a spy among you. I need to know that I can trust you all before I say any more.'

'We've been together for three years. I trust all my friends here.' Jacques said.

'Me too.' four of the other five men agreed in chorus.

'Shit, if I can't trust you all, my wife is sure gonna give me a hell of a time when I get back!' Tex exclaimed, looking at the five soldiers' faces and laughing.

Bill laughed briefly, then said seriously, 'I know there are eight of you and you probably all want to escape, but I only want to help one of you escape. I would prefer to help you all to get out of here, but if I did that you could all die or be killed. Also, I can only provide enough food and water for one of you. You have no weapons, and I know that there are none nearby. I have been looking around these caves for some time. Wherever their weapons are kept, it is definitely not around here.'

'At least tell us why you are here and where we are.' one man asked.

Another asked, 'How did you come to be here?'

206

'I am also a prisoner here.' That was a true fact. 'This place is in a desert, I think. Apart from that, I really don't know. That is why you cannot all escape at once. You could all be escaping to certain death either in the desert or at the hands of Paulo and his men if you were caught. How did you men get here?'

'I don't know how many of us are here. Twenty five of us were flying home from our tour of duty from Diego Garcia, and when our flight landed someplace we were all taken prisoner. I believe our drinks were drugged because when we woke up on the aircraft, our eyes were blindfolded and we were brought here by helicopter. I haven't seen any of the other men who were with us on the flight.'

'What about the crew of the aircraft. Are they with you?' Bill asked.

One of the men responded, 'No, not in here, and I never saw them again after leaving the aircraft. I don't even know if they were responsible for our imprisonment.'

The men were very interested when Bill said, 'I have seen other men, some are locked away... some are not. Their clothes are like yours. I haven't seen anyone who looks like they might be crew, though.'

'So there could be more of us here?' Eager to hear more, Andy asked, 'Have you spoken with any of them?'

'No, not yet, and I won't for the moment.' He was reluctant to raise their hopes. 'I don't want to take the risk of being found out. You all need to agree who will be the one to go. It should be only one man who leaves here. If the other men in the caves are your friends, they are in danger the

207

moment Paulo discovers one of you is missing, unless I can make him think you are all here. One man could conceal himself more easily in the passageways and find a way out. Also, he could hide in a smaller place than eight of you would need, if his trail was picked up after he escaped. Remember, you don't have guns.'

'That's true,' Tex drawled. 'Without weapons, a bunch of men would be an easy target. The man's right.'

Sighing heavily because he was so tired, Bill said, 'I must go now, but when I return I will bring some supplies. In the meantime, decide between yourselves which one of you will go.' As quietly as he had come, the doctor left the soldiers in the room, locked it and returned the keys to the box in the office. There was a glimmer of hope of rescue and an end to his ordeal. Cautious optimism sat at the back of his mind as he returned to the lab.

CHAPTER THIRTY ONE

The Escape

Bill managed to obtain some bread, cheese and fruit from the kitchen area, along with two large bottles of water. He dared not take any more. After placing them all inside a cloth sack, he eventually returned to the men in the cell.

They had decided that Jameson would go. He was the shortest and thinnest of the eight men and would require least water and food. It would also be easier for him to find a hiding place if he needed to.

The men agreed some contingencies with Joe and revised desert survival tactics. They were hopeful but anxious when it actually came to saying goodbye to their friend. Tex and the other four men wished Joe luck and Bill gave him the bag of food, along with an oil lamp, some oil and a spare wick. After showing Joe some of the markings he had left at the bottom of the walls, and what they meant, the doctor walked the young man as far as he dared along the passageways, wished him good-luck and returned to his quarters.

Fearful of being discovered, Joe clambered over the rocks and around the limestone obstructions, checking every now and then for the markings that Bill had described to him. He followed the passageways until he found no more. Eventually, following another route, he found a large, natural crack in the rock. It was wide enough for a man to get through. The narrow path in the rock-face in front of him divided into other smaller passageways, all wide enough for him to pass through. He was undecided about which direction he should take. As he bent down low to leave a mark on the wall where it would not be easily seen, he froze!

Someone leant over him and dragged him into a standing position then he felt a hand go over his mouth. The sharp blade of a knife was pressed against his throat and he was held fast, unable to say anything. The lamp was dragged from his hand. In the struggle, it sputtered and died, enveloping him and his assailant in darkness. Joe was no match for the man who held him in a vice-like grip. His muscles were underused and weak. From behind him the man's voice snarled, 'One false move, one sound, and I will slit your throat!'

The hand was removed from his mouth. Joe did not move. He felt his hands being tied together and he was dragged down to the floor. His captor sat in front of him and a flashlight was switched on. He could not see a face because the light was shining directly into his eyes, but he could see the end of a gun.

'Who are you?' demanded the disembodied voice.

Joe did not know how to react. The voice was American but as he did not know where he was, he could not be sure he was safe. What if this person was one of the guards? How could he explain his presence?

'Who are you?' The voice demanded again, more aggressively.

He was angry with himself. Some rescuer he was! He hadn't even managed to get out of the cave! Knowing that he would have to say something, and with a look of defeat on his face, Joe said, 'OK, so you've got me. So take me back!'

Behind him the captive heard the noise of more heavy-booted feet approaching. Two men leant on the wall behind his interrogator. They had heard the questions being asked as they returned to their friend, and were scornful of the defeatist response from a man whom they assumed to be one of the guards.

'Some guard! He gave in easily; let's hope they are all like that!' One of them said scathingly. 'This'll be a pushover!'

Another American voice! Joe realised the men could not be working for Paulo or they would know who he was. Up to that minute, he had been feeling angry; now he dared to hope that he had been mistaken in his assumption. Lifting up his head, he asked, 'Who are you? You don't sound as if you work for Paulo.'

'Paulo? Who's Paulo?' a surprised American voice asked.

Mike could hardly believe his ears. He was expecting to find terrorists, a gang dealing in guns or drugs, and at worst, white slavery; anything but this man, an American in military fatigues. What in God's name was he doing here?

Looking down at the shaking man, he asked in amazement, 'Are you an American soldier?'

'Yes!' Leaning against the wall behind him, Joe stood up. No-one stopped him. 'Who are you?'

Mike spoke quietly, wondering if this man was who he said he was. 'Commander Mike Forde, ASIU.'

'Jesus – ASIU? What are you doing here? Have you come to rescue us?' Joe was amazed to think that someone had actually discovered where he and his friends were.

Mike laughed, 'No, I came here to find a man called

211

Decker. When I arrived here, I thought we'd end up in a fight with the guards we saw at the mouth of the cave, or terrorists, and instead we find you!'

Piers and Geordie left them to check out the passageways from which the newcomer had appeared. They did not want trouble if it could be avoided.

Mike looked at the eager young soldier as he untied his wrists. 'I need to ask you some questions.'

'Would you mind answering one or two for me, sir.' Anxiously, Joe asked, 'Where are we? I have been here for so long, and I don't even know where here is.'

Mike observed the confusion in the young man's face as he asked the question. 'They didn't tell you then?' He ran his hand through his hair to scratch some of sand out of it as he looked at Joe, wondering if he even knew what day it was. 'This underground cave complex is in a desert area in Arabia known as the 'Rub' al Khali' or 'the empty quarter', it is north of Yemen and Oman. I'm here because I followed a guy called Decker. We had to find another way in as the entrance he used is heavily guarded.'

Shock registered in Joe's face. 'We're in a desert?' Joe shook his head in disbelief. 'It's an awful long way from home.'

'It certainly is.' Mike could see that he was tired and must have walked a long way. 'Do you know how many guards this man Paulo has? Has he got guns? Is he a drug dealer?'

'I can't be of much help to you, sir. We were locked up most of the time and my pals are still imprisoned. As to how many men, well, I gather from the man who helped me to escape that there are many men here but I couldn't say how many. Guns? The man couldn't tell us much about guns either. He said that he hadn't seen any, but he did say that Paulo and his men are terrorists. I can't help about drugs either.' Joe felt useless.

'Who was the man who helped you to escape?' Mike was curious.

'He wouldn't say, sir.'

'You mentioned that you were with some other men. Can you take me to them?' Mike asked. 'Perhaps you could introduce me to the man who helped you to escape, too. I would like to meet him. We need a friend on our side.'

'I doubt my mates will have expected me to get back so soon; they are probably hoping I am far from here, but yes, I can take you back to them. I don't know about our friend yet, though. He may not go back to our cell now he has helped me to get away, or thought he had!' Joe remarked ruefully. 'I marked the way back on the walls of the caves just in case I was lucky enough to bring some help back.'

'Good. You have done well.'

'Thanks, sir.' Joe felt a little less useless than he had earlier.

The two men made their way along the passageway that Piers and Geordie had taken.

Leaving Mike in conversation with the young soldier, Piers and Geordie walked deeper into the caves. Cautiously, by torchlight they looked everywhere for the marks that Joe had said were on the bottom of the wall at the junctions of the passageways. Eventually, they found one. The passageway branched out into two, only one of which was marked. The two men took the marked route. They turned right at the next marked fork. Fifty metres further on they found another fork, and there were no marks on the wall.

'We've missed one, I think.' Piers kept his voice low.

Geordie agreed, 'Aye, but we'll not get lost. I've been marking the turnings on my arm as we've been going on.' He raised the ballpoint pen into Piers' line of vision and with his torch close to his arm showed him the marks on it. 'All part of the game,' he grinned.

'Good thinking.' Piers commented.

They turned right again. There were no lights, so it was clear that this part of the cave complex was deserted. Another ten minutes into their walk the passageway widened considerably. Piers shone his torch up to the high ceiling and swept the beam across the floor. Several huge boulders lay as if they had been casually strewn around the area by a gigantic hand. Some were in the middle of the passageway, some next to the wall. In the centre of the cave was a twenty metre wide channel, it looked like a riverbed but there was no water.

Geordie walked on, sweeping his torch into the spaces between the boulders, but giving them a wide berth in case there were any guards hiding there.

Piers almost jumped out of his skin when Geordie, alarmed, called 'Bloody hell, Piers... get yourself over here mate!'

'What is it?' asked Piers, as he approached him.

Indicating a spot at the back of the base of a large group of newly cracked boulders, he replied, 'Look... look at that! There's a body in there.'

CHAPTER THIRTY TWO

The Body

Piers looked down to where an astonished Geordie was pointing. Sprawled on the ground and lying on its side, was a body. It was thin and dressed in military fatigues that appeared to be oversized. The hair was short, unkempt and caked with sand and dust. The face was so dirty it was hard to tell if it was male or female or even if it was alive because there was no evidence of breathing or limb movement.

Piers walked over to the body and felt its skin. The forehead was ice-cold. There were no obvious signs of bruising or injury, except for a few scratches and grazes on the knuckles and palms, which were also caked with dust and sand. He placed two fingers expertly into the cold neck to feel for a pulse. 'Thank God! Quick Geordie, help me to stand him up. He's still alive. We need to get his circulation going. He must be half frozen after lying on the ground like that! It's cold down here.'

Geordie quickly went to his aid. He stood behind the man's body as Piers put his hands under the man's armpits, intending to lift him up for Geordie to get a better grip from behind. He was a dead weight. Bending over and placing his two arms around the man's chest just below the rib cage, Geordie bent down and lifted him off the ground until he was standing with his back directly in front of him. The man would have slipped from Geordie's grip when Piers let go of him, in order to place his arm around the back of his body, if Geordie had not grasped the man tighter around the top of his chest.

'Phew... thanks, I'll be glad when he's awake.' Piers said, as he wrapped his arm under the man's armpit to support his back and at the same time, held on to the waistband at the side of his trousers.

Standing stock still, Geordie could feel his face turning red with embarrassment. 'Er.... I think we've got it all wrong, mate.'

Piers looked at his friend as if he was mad. 'What do you mean? The only way to get the circulation going when someone is so cold is to make them move about, how could we have got it wrong?'

'This man's not a man. He's a woman.' Sheepishly, Geordie moved his arms to a more appropriate place around the woman's waist and under her right elbow.

'Are you sure?' Piers couldn't believe it.

'Of course I am! When I nearly dropped her, I grabbed on to her.... well, her, er... dammit... I grabbed her... tits!' Highly embarrassed and just to convey his meaning, Geordie gesticulated a breast with his left hand as best he could, and placed his right arm around the woman's waist.

The woman moved her head slightly, moaning quietly as she opened her eyes.

'Oh... oh!' Piers understood. Instinctively, he took his arms away and reached out to check for himself.

'Get your bloody hands off, you sex maniac.' Geordie complained as, morally affronted on the woman's behalf, he slapped Piers' hand away. 'Leave her alone!'

Piers suddenly realised the implication of what he was doing. 'Oh, sorry. I only meant to....'

'I know what you only meant to!' Geordie laughed, heartily amused. 'Hands off!'

The woman moved slightly, as she took part of her weight on her own legs. 'Wh... Where am I?'

'Somewhere you definitely don't want to be love, and we need to get you away from here, so you're going to need to do some of your own walking!' Hoisting her against his hip, Geordie moved forward a step. 'C'mon now, let's go for a walk.'

The woman stepped slowly forward.

'That's the way!' Piers, taking care where he put his hands, took her other arm. 'Well done...' he encouraged her.

They stopped every few minutes to allow the woman to stretch her knees and elbows to ease the stiffness in them.

'What's your name?' Piers realised they hadn't even asked. 'Where have you come from?'

A confused look appeared on the woman's face. 'My name is... my name is...' She stopped, totally shocked. 'I don't know.' Frightened, she realised she could not remember her own name. 'I don't know who I am... Oh, God, I don't remember!' Her voice was hoarse and her mouth and throat were dry.

In an effort to comfort her, Piers put his arms around her shoulders, hugged her to him and said, 'Look, don't worry about that for now. You must have had some sort of shock or something. It'll come back to you.' He gave her his water bottle, 'You sound as if you could do with a drink.'

Without stopping, the woman drank the entire contents,

gasping with pleasure as she returned the empty bottle to Piers. 'Thanks.' The croak was still in her voice.

Geordie reminded Piers. 'I think it's time we got back.

They turned back to meet up with Mike and continued walking until they came to a fork that curved sharply to the right, where they met up with Mike and Joe.

'You're not alone then?' Mike asked as a third person rounded the corner, supported mostly by Geordie. Mike could see that the woman's face and the exposed parts of her limbs and clothing were incredibly dirty and spattered with dried blood in places.

'Lana!' exclaimed Joe. 'How did you get here?'

'Who are you?' she asked him, drawing back a little.

'I'm your friend. Don't you recognise me?' Joe was baffled.

'So you know this woman?' Piers asked Joe.

'Yes, I do.' Joe was amazed to see Lana.

'She's lost her memory; she doesn't know who she is. You say her name is Lana?' Mike looked at the woman, who was watching Joe with confusion in her eyes. 'Your name is Lana, apparently. Does it sound familiar?'

'No. It doesn't.' She was still cold and visibly shivering beside Piers and Geordie and she still did not seem to quite grasp where she was.

With Piers' help she cleaned up her face, which was emaciated and her eyes were red-rimmed, as if she had wept for a long time. It was impossible to do anything with her hair.

Piers placed his blanket protectively around Lana's shoulders in an attempt to help her to stop shivering. He gave her some bread and cheese and watched sympathetically as the hungry woman ate it as if she had not seen food in a long time.

Lana felt perturbed by her lack of control as she chewed the food but very quickly found that swallowing it was a little harder with such a dry throat. After a few more mouthfuls she gave up trying.

Mike joined Piers and Lana who were sitting on a pile of rocks. He needed to find out more about the woman. 'Do you know what you were doing here?' he asked Lana. He was surprised to find an American woman with a rusty southern drawl in the middle of an underground cavern.

'I can't remember. I keep trying but I feel like there is a big wall in the middle of my head. That man found me and brought me to you.' She nodded her head in Piers' direction.

'Piers Henneman, ma'am. My pleasure!' Piers smiled his dazzling smile.

Lana smiled weakly back at him.

The Swede looked at Mike. 'Which way should we go? We are two people up but no further forward in our search for Decker.' He looked at Joe and Lana. 'We need to get more men down here.'

Joe had an idea. 'What if I went back, as if I had never been away? I may not have been missed yet. If our friend returns, he can help me to get away again.' Then he said, 'As he is allowed to walk freely around the caves, he could try to find out how many men Paulo has, and perhaps where his weapons are stored. I can bring his information back to you and take your plan back to my friends in the cell.'

'Do you trust him?' Geordie asked.

Reflecting for a moment, Joe said thoughtfully, 'Yes, I do. There is something that is very genuine in his concern for us. I am sure we can trust him.'

Mike admired the young man's courage, it was not an easy offer to make and the information would certainly be useful. 'Ok, do it. Just ask your friend to find out about the number of soldiers. We will look for the weapons. This Paulo is unlikely to be suspicious about your friend walking around, but he will notice him looking for something he wants to keep hidden.'

'Right, I'll ask him if he comes back. Here, take this for Lana.' Joe handed Piers the bag of food and water. 'I won't need it now.'

Mike realised that Joe would need a way to contact them when he returned. 'If you can, bring your friend with you to us as soon as he has some information. We will also need to leave some sort of sign for you to find us. We won't always be in this particular spot, but we'll use it as a base. We will seek a hideout and mark the walls as you did, with a blocked numbered circle to indicate the distance in paces to the hideout. Look straight ahead as you look at the sign.'

'Ok, will do. Thanks. Good luck. 'The young soldier left to return to his cell.

'And to you...!' Piers called softly as watched him go. 'He's got nerve!' he said to Mike, admiringly. 'I doubt I'd be so keen to go back to a prison cell once I got out of it!'

Mike admired Joe because of his extraordinary offer, 'I agree, his decision can't have been easy. He's a brave man.'

Geordie agreed. 'Aye, it took a lot of courage, so we'd better not let him and his friends down.'

The three men and Lena walked cautiously along another passageway. The floor was covered in soft, dry sand and there were no footprints except those they left behind them as they moved through it There were many such passageways leading off larger caverns Some narrowed until they were impassable. Others led to smaller caverns with hard, dusty ground.

One of the largest caverns they discovered had a still lake of ice cold, clear water about thirty metres wide and a hundred and fifty metres long, trapped in it. The light from their lamps could possibly have been the first light ever to shine on it in hundreds or even thousands of years. Piers threw a handful of stones into the water. The impact sent glittering rings that reflected the beams of the men's torches, dissipating as they rippled across the surface. The sight was breathtaking in the dark, silent stillness.

They walked on until they saw a faint glimmer of light. Mike stopped. He switched off the lamp after motioning Piers and Geordie to take Lena out of sight. In the dark, he waited until he was sure no one was around and then moved forward again through the darkness. He saw a small patch of light reflected on the wall a short distance away. It came from a crack in the rock opposite. He peered through the crack into a room that was dimly lit by a string of very low wattage bulbs strung about two metres apart along a metal frame fixed around the walls.

The room was not large as far as he could make out. The view from the crack was quite good but he could not see all of the room. There were four people on beds next to the walls. Some lay at an angle that prevented him from seeing their faces, but two men were facing his direction. It was too dark to distinguish whether they were awake or asleep. They all wore uniforms. Mike could not see clearly but because they were pale faced he was sure they were westerners. He had to get inside the room.

After saying goodbye to Joe, Bill had made his way back to his quarters and collapsed onto the sofa. He was very tired. He decided he would immediately stop making the drug that he knew would successfully achieve Paulo's objectives. As there was even a slight hope of escape he was no longer afraid. He dozed fitfully, to be woken almost immediately or so it seemed, by one of Paulo's men. It was time to start work again.

Bill realised that it was important to make Paulo think that he was working. He prepared a special version of the drug. As Paulo had not thought to attach an experienced chemist to learn from him, probably because he was confident that his captive's fear of death would ensure his continued power over him, nothing that Bill did would appear to be unusual. Certainly Paulo would not know the purpose of the equipment that he had set up on the bench in the lab.

Hours later, when he was eating with the brothers, Garcia, and Decker, Bill asked suddenly, 'Are your soldiers mercenaries?' He had been present when Garcia injected a line of six soldiers, and he had ordered the doctor to assist him.

Decker looked at Neko and Neko looked at Paulo.

Garcia guffawed heartily.

Paulo did not laugh. Clouds of anger stormed in his eyes. 'Why do you ask?'

Bill realised he was flirting with danger but said, 'I just wondered. You must have a large army.'

Paulo was furious and shouted, 'That is none of your business!' Abruptly, he stood up sending his drink crashing to the ground as he walked threateningly towards Bill, 'Do you understand?'

Bill was taken aback by the anger in Paulo's voice but not surprised. Calmly he replied, 'Yes, I'm sorry.'

That seemed to satisfy Paulo because he sat down again and poured himself another drink in a fresh glass. It was not his first drink. He was incensed because most of his soldiers were now incapacitated. It was an unexpected event and he wasn't sure how it had happened. It was the doctor's fault. The drug had obviously confused him and he had made a mistake in the process. This setback was interfering with his plans.

Neko and Paulo talked about the men who had been the last to be treated with the latest batch of Riofactol. Neko reflected a few moments, 'Maybe, if you interfere with a man's brain you could destroy his intelligence or capabilities.' He also wondered why Garcia hadn't mentioned the potential damage the drug could do to Bill.

Paulo decided that as soon as Bill had another treatment, he was to be ordered to make more of the drug. In the meantime, he had ordered Garcia to destroy the latest batch. There had been something wrong with it and eight of the fifteen men who had been injected with the last batch were lying comatose on their beds. He had arranged for them to be moved to two separate cells. Garcia didn't dare inject any more men until he had a new batch of the drug. He was furious.

223

It was obvious to Bill after Paulo's violent response to his questions that he would learn nothing of the number of men in Paulo's army of mercenaries. However, he took comfort in the knowledge that Garcia would not be able to plant any more bombs for a while. It would take weeks to get new supplies delivered and to make more of the drug.

Inspired by the success of his plan and with the comfort of knowing that one of the captives had gone for help, Bill knew he was as safe as he could be for now. He could continue to produce the antidote in peace.

Paulo left his captive alone after that, he would not see him again until the next batch of the drug was produced. Bill dreaded seeing the man in case he vented his fury on him physically. Despite his fear, Bill sat eating and drinking as amiably as he could to avoid arousing his anger. As they often did, the brothers drank too much and he would sit quietly watching them but saying little. Decker just watched and listened and said nothing unless he had to.

Garcia, too drunk to control himself, drank whisky as if it were water, becoming groggier as the hours passed. No one cared, they were on 'home territory' and they were sure of their invulnerability. Bill sat wondering how far Joe had managed to escape to, as the four men continued to drink. He would have to be going soon. The brothers and Garcia broke into song in a mutually agreeable language. Decker lay nursing a bottle of Scotch. Bill closed his eyes and slouched across his seat appearing to be asleep. In a while he would take his leave. It was time he paid his friends another visit.

CHAPTER THIRTY THREE

Sleepers

Mike and Piers joined Geordie and the woman in their hideout. They had explored many of the caves around the underground lake and after marking a few of the rocks to make sure that Joe knew how to find them, Mike decided to make one of them their base. The cave was only an hours' walk from the room they had found earlier that housed four sleeping men and was not too far from the lake.

After first entering the cave they had stored their supplies behind large piles of rocks out of sight of the entrance. The camels were still outside of the cave, tied loosely together on a nine-metre rope which was looped over one of the finger shaped rocks. The rope would ensure that the animals did not stray. They would be safe for a while. While Lana slept, Mike, Geordie and Piers collected their hidden supplies and returned with them to their hideout by the lake.

Leaving Lana with Geordie, Mike led Piers to the room with the men in it. The Swede was surprised at their inactivity. 'Why are they not doing something? If they were soldiers, surely they would not be just lying around? That's no way to stay fit!'

Mike had other concerns. 'I don't know... what concerns me more is that they are wearing our uniforms. Where did they get them? Have they stolen them?' What happened to the others, he wondered? Are their bodies buried under the sand?

What happened to the aircraft? Joe had told him of the hijack but he did not know where all the other men were. Were they lost forever? So many questions and not enough answers!

The desert sands shifted constantly and could bury a huge ship or aircraft in an afternoon if the wind blew hard enough. The aircraft that had carried the men was tiny compared to the sand dunes, some of which were over eight hundred feet high.

The thought made Mike even more determined. 'We've got to get in there. I want to see who these men are. Perhaps we can creep in. They are all lying down; they won't see us if we keep low. I can just make out a door in the far corner. Perhaps this passageway will lead to it. Let's go!'

Piers followed close behind, hoping the men would wake up. It could be fun! He loved to fight and he was good at it.

After securing the silencer on his gun and with the safety catch in the off position, Mike moved into the darkness of the passageway heading he hoped, in the right direction to find the door to the room. Keeping their backs close to the wall, the two men hoped they would not meet anyone in the passageway. It was clear. For a fortress, that was unusual. The men holed up in the cave complex were probably so sure of their remoteness and that no one could penetrate the entrance he had seen that they did not feel it necessary to guard the inside. They can't have known anything about the hole through which he and his friends had accidentally penetrated their domain.

They reached the door to the room where the sleeping men lay. It was unlocked. Mike wrapped his left hand firmly around the handle ready to open it, and with his gun raised in front of him.

'Ready?' he whispered to Piers.

'Sure, go, I'm right behind you!' his colleague replied quietly. He was ready for anything.

Piers covered Mike as he opened the door with lightening speed. Arms locked straight out in front of him, legs bent slightly and with both hands gripping the gun shoulder high, he moved to the nearest bed. Pressing the point of the gun barrel roughly into a sleeping man's neck, with the intention of waking him, he said firmly, 'Stand up, with your hands in front of you where I can see them!'

Piers jumped into the room from behind him and standing beside the man on the opposite bed, growled in a low voice into the man's ear, 'Do as the man says! Now!' He pointed his gun at the man's head.

Not one of the men stirred.

Like a strange tableau, the men lay unmoved by the voice of their aggressors. Had it not actually happened, the two intruders would never have believed it. The scene before them was outside of their experience. It was totally unreal. Something was wrong. The men were too still, too quiet.

For a moment neither of them moved then Mike relaxed his stance but stayed warily alert. Piers shook his head as he looked at him and shrugged his shoulders in disbelief.

Keeping his pistol raised, Mike joined Piers at the bed of the first man nearest the door. He lay on his side, facing away from them. They turned his shoulder towards them. The man flopped over onto his back and lay with his eyes closed, without the slightest response.

227

The two men walked around the room, looking at the other soldiers. They were all the same, as if they were in a trance.

'Give me your torch,' Mike called to Piers, who left the soldier he was examining and quickly handed it to him.

Mike shone the light into the face of the soldier then went to the next bed, where he did the same. He walked around all of the beds, examining the faces of the other men.

He was speechless as he looked at Piers.

'What is it?' his colleague asked, worried by the expression of shock and amazement on his colleague's face.

Mike shook his head in disbelief, hardly able to believe his eyes.

'I know these men!' he half whispered, 'I was their CO before I joined ASIU!'

He pointed to one of them, 'That is Mat Sangell, next to him Jim Phelps. I know all of them. Brad, Pete, Gustav and the other three. These men are my friends. The missing soldiers! What have they done to them? Where are the others? What has happened to the others?' He was furious.

Piers was astonished. 'Are you saying what I think you are saying?' Piers knew about the missing aircraft. He had seen the news and read the articles. He had felt the loss, as had all the other peacekeeping soldiers.

'Yes. These bastards have done something to them! We've got to get them out of here!'

'No, we can't, there aren't enough of us. We'll never manage it. There are too many of them! We can't carry two each and they aren't fit to walk in the state they're in.' Piers was as staggered by the scenario as Mike. It was hard enough walking relatively unburdened around the stony surfaces, and dodging around chunks of rocks and boulders. Carrying a dead weight would be impossible. Spiriting the men away one at a time would be a huge risk to the unconscious soldiers who remained.

Mike stood with his back to the door, looking around at the men. 'Let's get back to Geordie. We need to get some sort of plan together.' How on earth were they ever going to move the men without discovery, he wondered?

Joe was greeted with dismay when he returned to the cell. His seven friends, who were all asleep and woke up when he crept into his bed, thought a guard had recaptured him. 'No, I came back from choice to give you some good news.' Joe smiled at them, 'I got the key and opened the cell. I've left it in the lock outside.

'So we can all get out then?' Andy asked hopefully.

'No! We've got to wait for our friend to return. We need his help. 'Joe explained. 'There are some men in the caves, American ASIU agents who are going to help us but to do so they need some intelligence about the enemy. There are only three of them and it would be stupid to walk in here if there are hundreds of soldiers with guns ready to shoot them down.'

'True, that would be pretty stupid,' Hans admitted, 'but if we could get hold of some guns, we could help them.'

'Yes, but the plan needs to be properly coordinated or we could end up shooting at each other, especially if we have no idea about what everyone else is doing. These passageways are too narrow to make assumptions about who is a friend and who is an enemy.' Joe warned. 'We wait. Ok?'

The other men agreed to wait until their friend showed up again.

It was time. Bill left his cell and made his way to the cave where the seven men waited. The doctor was excited but scared and knew he wouldn't feel totally at ease until he was away from this awful place. Before leaving, he had filled up three screw-top jars with about three hundred of the antidote pills to give to the men as a precaution against any treatment Garcia might inflict upon them. The pills should protect them for a while.

Surprised to find the key in the lock when he reached the cell, Bill removed it and put it back into the box, leaving the cell door unlocked. Once inside the room he was shocked to see Joe had not escaped.

'What are you doing back here? Did they catch you?' he asked, afraid that he was going to be implicated in the man's escape.

'No, I wasn't caught.' Joe explained how he had met Mike, Piers and Geordie and assured them all that Lana was safe. He had not mentioned it earlier.

'Thank God! I searched everywhere for her. I was afraid that she had wandered off and fallen into a chasm or worse!' Bill said, overjoyed.

'She's quite safe. Piers is looking out for her.' Joe smiled, remembering the look of compassion in the tall Swede's eyes when he looked at the woman. The man was obviously seeing something that interested him behind the dirt!

'So what is happening? How are they going to help us?' The doctor asked.

'That's the tricky bit. Mike needs some information and only you can get it for him, I'm afraid. If any of us go we could upset a good plan in the making.' Joe grimaced. 'Mike needs to know how many men Paulo has and if you can find out where the guns are kept without compromising yourself, then that would be great, but don't risk yourself. Mike said that he and his men would look for them. They must be somewhere. If and when you do find out, in particular about the number of men, come back here and let me know, then I can go back to Mike and we can formulate an escape plan. You can come with me.' He explained to Bill why they could not all go at once.

'I will try.' The Doctor produced the jars of antidote pills. 'I have brought something with me that will protect you. You must take these pills, two now, with water. Take two every day without fail. If you do not and Paulo forces me to inject you, you will be under his control and you will do as he says. Just believe me when I say that you would even shoot me if he asked you to! These pills are an antidote to the drug. On no account must any of Paulo's men see them or know what they are. If they find out about them, you and your friends will certainly never get out of here alive, and neither will I. They will not want the rest of the world knowing what they are doing or how they are doing it.'

In deep disappointment that their rescue was not imminent, Bill locked the men in their cell and returned to his quarters.

It was not easy for him to work and his stress level was high but Bill did his best when he was not in company with his captors, to find out how many men were in the caverns. The men he talked to did not seem to know or would not say. He had no luck at all in finding weapons. When Garcia visited him, he found the doctor half-asleep and slouched over the bench in his lab. He shook him awake. 'Come doctor, it is time for your injection.'

More treatment! Bill was alarmed. He hoped that the residue of antidote in his body was still effective. Hoping that he would soon be rescued he had not taken any pills that morning and it was impossible to do so with Garcia nearby.

Garcia walked behind the doctor to the cave they had used before as a treatment room and ordered him to lie on the table. Though he was nervous and his heart was pounding with fear in case he succumbed to the treatment, Bill did not flinch as Garcia injected him with the drug. He closed his eyes as his head spun and his legs turned to jelly.

Paulo walked in just as Garcia had injected their victim.

'That will stop him from asking questions, I hope?' he asked Garcia. 'My men told me that he was asking them questions he should not be asking. I did not expect him to be asking questions at all.' He was highly suspicious. 'Are you sure he is under our control?'

'It is unusual, but I have given him a higher dosage this time. He will only do as we ask him to. I will begin his therapy now. There is no need for you to stay.'

Paulo left the room and closed the door behind him.

Bill had heard the conversation but was not able to move

easily. The experience at the higher dosage was different to the first time he had been treated. That dose had also been more than necessary, but the antidote level in his body had been higher. Now the doctor's whole body felt incredibly heavy and he could hardly see the walls of the room around him.

Garcia's voice seemed far away but he could still distinguish his words. He was telling him to relax and listen to his voice. Trying to shut it out, Bill forced himself to think about his research. The lightness in his head alarmed him as the voice climbed in and out of his brain. He did not want to listen but it would not go away.

Fighting as hard as he could, he concentrated his thoughts on the events that had brought him to the situation he was now in. He pictured himself in the lab at the university and forced the image of the burners boiling the liquid in the flasks into his brain until he could almost feel the heat. In the background he could hear Garcia's voice, telling him he should inject the men who would be attending for treatment later. He could see Larry smiling at him in his office and Leo waiting by the car, then lying on the ground, bloodied and dead.

Garcia seemed to go on forever but Bill fought to stay in control. As if in answer to his prayers the voice finally ceased, saying, 'You can go now. Soon it will be time for lunch. We will begin our task after we have eaten.'

Relieved, Bill lay quietly until the man had left. Unbelievably, the pills he had taken for so long were still enough to counteract the Riofactol. Cautiously he raised himself, placing one foot on the floor then the other. He was still feeling light headed but he could walk. He returned to his lab feeling as if he was walking on air. The first thing he did was to swallow two of his pills with a glass of water. Within an hour his head cleared and he felt more in control of himself.

Knowing that Paulo and Garcia sensed that he might not be completely in their control, Bill knew that somehow he had to get away, but he was the only person who could help the soldiers so he stayed. His thoughts were confirmed when he found that Paulo had posted a guard outside of his door.

Alarmed, Bill realised that his movements would now be severely restricted and he needed to find a way to make the soldiers aware of this, but how?

CHAPTER THIRTY FOUR

The Beacon

After lunch Paulo ordered Bill to prepare some of the men who had not been treated with the Riofactol drug, for their injections. 'Six will be sufficient for now. We have some work they will be able to do for us.'

Garcia had, with confidence, assured Paulo that the doctor was under the influence of the drug therefore in their control as before. To remove any doubt Bill was not left to perform the task on his own. Garcia was to accompany him, and as a precaution against the men overpowering them, Paulo ordered them to take along an armed guard.

The doctor obediently went back to the lab and, closely supervised by the guard and Garcia, prepared a bag with six small corked phials of the drug, some hypodermic syringes, sterilising wipes and lint.

The guard said nothing, but accompanied Garcia and Bill as he made his way to the cell where his friends were imprisoned. Paulo had selected the men himself; they were strong and could quite easily unload the weapons consignment that was being flown into the camp by helicopter that night, allowing his men to sleep. Under the influence of the drug, they would assume that what they were doing was their allotted task as part of his company of soldiers. Garcia would perform the hypnotherapy himself as soon as the drug had taken effect.

None of the six prisoners gave any indication that they

knew Bill and subjected him to the same verbal abuse that they poured on Garcia and the guard. Garcia ignored their words and took them individually out of their cell and after they had been injected, under hypnosis he advised them of what they were to do. Then he returned them to the cell.

The guard stood inside the room as ordered, with his gun pointing to the men who stood at the far wall. Bill knew that Garcia would check for the telltale yellowed swelling around the puncture site, so the frustrated doctor could not avoid inflicting the injection on his friends. He dared not speak to them. He would find a way to do that later. Joe was the only one to risk a smile without being seen by the guard or Garcia.

'It will be over soon!' he mouthed then smiled as Bill's eyes lost their dejected look and reflected a measure of hope. Looking at the doctor, Joe reflected on how tired he looked, and how much inner strength he must have to cope so well in this devastating ordeal. He deserves a medal, he thought. Any man who risks his own life to save his friends from unconscious slavery to a tyrant is indeed a very brave man.

After their next meal, Paulo, Neko, Decker and Garcia left the cave together. Garcia had convinced Paulo that Bill was in their control and he removed his guard from the lab. He was no longer concerned about the men who had been treated that day as they were now under his control and transporting boxes from the truck which had recently arrived, to the cave in which they hid their weapons. When the job was done, they were again locked again in their cell. Armed guards accompanied them at all times and the men, who were unaffected by the

Riofactol because of Bill's antidote, and played along with their captors, were able to gain some intelligence about the structure of the cave, but they did not try to escape. There were too many of Paulo's men and they had no weapons, to take that risk. They knew their situation was about to change but they had been able to learn where the weapons were kept.

Bill was concerned when the four men left the room in which they would normally spend their evenings. This is most unusual, he thought. Why are they not drinking, like they normally do? He had to find out. As soon as he was sure they would be out of hearing, the doctor made his way along the darkened passageway to the room where he had first overheard the men in conversation. He was right; all four men sat talking. Bill stood with his ear to the hole he had made and listened to the voices within.

They talked about the bombings they had arranged in the past months and the payment they had received from their friends in Iraq. Decker spoke about the weapons he had stolen and had arrived that day at their hideout. The doctor wasn't particularly interested in what had already happened, but he was interested when a voice said, 'So... another wave?' It Neko's voice.

Shocked, Bill realised that they were planning to set off more bombs and that meant only one thing! One of the captives was to be used to implement them. Neko had a strong, clear voice that carried well as he continued to speak. For that, Bill was thankful. 'Yes. We will need four men. The day after tomorrow... they can go back with... pilots, to...'

Bill also recognised Paulo's arrogant voice. 'You shall have them, brother. I have had some men prepared...'

Suddenly Bill realised he had to leave quickly as Decker unexpectedly left the room. Afraid of being seen, he slipped quietly away to visit the prisoners in their cell.

As before, the route was clear and he quickly unlocked the door, returned the key to the box in the desk drawer, and joined his friends. They were glad to see him, believing that his return meant that he had something to tell them. It was not what they expected.

The first concern that Bill had was how they all were after the injection. 'Are you all OK?' he asked.

Zak spoke up first, 'Yeah, I'm fine. I'll pay them back for turning me into a bloody pincushion!'

He was relieved, the pills had worked. 'I'm glad you are all unaffected, but I'm afraid I have some bad news for you. I was listening to their conversation a short while ago. I think they're planning to send you to America to plant bombs.' he announced as they sat in the darkest corner of the cell, away from the door.

Tex responded first. 'Well, that's good. When we arrive in America, I can get away and tell everyone about this place.'

Bill shook his head. 'I don't think you'll be able to. From the conversation I have just heard, Neko and Decker will accompany you in a cargo plane. They are both dangerous men and they won't hesitate to kill you immediately if you don't do as they say. Also, if you do get away and alert the authorities, Paulo will cover his tracks and kill the soldiers who are still here. It would take only one text message or a phone call and he would make sure there were no witnesses,' he turned to Joe,

238

'I think you should speak with your friends from ASIU and get some help here quickly.'

The men agreed with Bill. Tex capitulated and although he was ready to fight, he agreed to wait until they received orders from Mike. Joe volunteered to return to the hideout where Mike, Lana and the other two men were waiting for news of Paulo's men.

'There's no time like the present!' Joe said to the doctor. 'I'd better go.'

'Now?' Bill replied.

'Now!' affirmed the young man.

'Ok, but don't get caught!' The doctor was terrified of the consequences of being caught out. He reminded the men to take another pill when they next woke up, and locked the cell door after Joe slipped out of the cave then he replaced the key to its rightful place. He waited a moment or two to ensure no one saw him then returned to his lab.

For twenty-five minutes Joe walked, looking out for and finding the distinctive signs at the bottom of the walls that led to Mike's hideout. He was cautious and always on the alert for any sign of discovery, and eventually found himself in the large cavern with the lake. Like the men he had come to find, he was amazed by its stillness. Still checking the bottom of the walls at the junctions, he found the two blocked white circles that Mike had mentioned and the number two hundred, indicating a two hundred paces walk straight ahead. He walked two hundred paces straight ahead but could see nothing.

Puzzled, Joe called out softly, 'Hello! Where are you?'

239

Piers was hidden behind a rock and watched as the man approached. As soon as he recognised Joe, he answered, 'Over here!'

The cave itself was only a short distance away from the edge of the lake and around the corner from the wall that rose above them to the ceiling of the cavern.

As soon as he arrived at the hiding place, Joe noticed that Mike looked angry and Piers was quiet. They needed help. One of them would have to take a risk and contact JP. Mike had brought with him a standard issue GPS beacon, which relied upon external contact with a satellite communication system. It was small but very effective. However, unless it was used outside the cave it would not work. They had not anticipated being underground.

'One of us needs to get out of here to make contact with ASIU. We need to get those men home somehow.' he said to Piers.

'What men?' Joe was curious.

'Mike explained his discovery and related the state of the men in the room. 'Those men are my soldiers and they look drugged! We need to get them away from this place, but we can't move them ourselves. There aren't enough of us. We need help.'

'We certainly do.' Joe replied. 'If we don't, some of us are going to be shipped back to America with a bomb strapped to our backs!'

'What do you mean?' Geordie asked, shocked.

Joe related what the doctor had told them about more bombs being planted and how they would get them there.

'Bastards!' Piers snarled. 'We can't let them do it. We've got to go in now!'

Joe also mentioned the boxes, which probably contained weapons of some description, which he and his friends had been moving for Paulo. Mike was disturbed to find out that the men had been drugged and wondered where the drug had come from. It had to be Riofactol. It fitted with the information gained during Gerd's autopsy. Joe explained the hypnotherapy he had undergone with Garcia, who thought he was drugged but he was unable to tell him the name of the man who had administered it. Mike had an idea, but he said nothing to Joe. It would wait until the men were freed.

After discussing the options open to them, Mike and his colleagues decided to send someone to the surface with Lana, who was in desperate need of sleep. It was obvious to them all that she could hardly keep her eyes open. She restricted their movements quite considerably.

Torn between his desire to protect Lana and his loyalty to Mike and after a verbal tussle with him, Piers agreed to take Lana out of the caves to signal JP and bring in some help from outside. He would rather have joined Mike in flushing out the terrorists.

'We need this help, Piers. There are men relying upon us. We can't risk letting them down. I know you can take care of Lana and yourself, and anyone who might try to stop you from doing it, should you meet anyone in the caves or outside. I need Geordie for his language skills and his knowledge of this area of the desert. Joe is not familiar with ASIU procedures and hasn't been on active service for a while. You are the only

241

one who can go.'

'OK. I understand... I'll go and take Lana. I know you are right.' Piers conceded. 'We'll go with you some of the way and then turn up to the surface if we find another way out.'

Mike agreed. Both men knew that there was nothing more they could do to get the soldiers out of the caves for the moment and Mike welcomed the opportunity to explore further.

'Let's take a look at our enemy!' Mike said firmly.

After ensuring that all their equipment was safely stowed in their packs, all five walked and climbed through many smaller caves and low, dark, and stony passageways. They found themselves walking, seemingly forever, along an endless narrow incline that led to a high bank of broken limestone and sandstone boulders, packed with smaller stones that led to the roof of a large cave.

'We'll need to climb up to the top and see if we can clear a way to get out. Maybe it leads to the outside.' Piers was optimistic.

Geordie stayed at the bottom with Lana and Joe, hidden in a recess behind a large boulder. 'Sleep now, lass.' he said softly. 'Get some sleep until they return.'

Gratefully, Lana wrapped herself in two blankets and lay down on the sand that thickly covered the stone floor, with her head resting on Geordie's pack. In moments she was asleep. Joe and Geordie conversed quietly so as not to wake her.

Cautiously, Mike and Piers began the climb up the treacherous slope. Stones slipped under their feet as they persevered, hoping the boulders and rocks that formed part of the pile would not crash down, carrying them with it.

Suddenly, Piers lost his footing. He rolled over and over back down the incline, and his body crashed heavily into the larger boulders at the bottom. Somewhat shocked, he sat with his back to a large rock, checking his head to see if he had done any serious damage. Apart from a small gash on his cheekbone and some bruising, which he would feel later no doubt, he appeared to be in one piece.

Mike climbed down as fast as he could, thinking that his colleague might have broken something. 'Are you okay?' he called.

Groaning, Piers gingerly stood up. 'Fine, I'll live... it serves me right for being so damned careless!' His left leg and hip had started to hurt but at least nothing was broken. He was lucky. 'Come on, let's try again.'

Mike and Piers again started the upward climb.

The second ascent was successful. However, after removing some of the larger rocks and stones from the top of the pile near the roof of the cavern, they both realised they would never be able to get into the next cavern from where they were, unless they abseiled. It was around a twenty metre sheer drop on the other side. That would be too dangerous. If they were spotted they were sitting ducks.

From above, they could see that the cave was occupied and it was huge. There were lights on the lower part of the walls and boxes were stored five pallets high, some almost to the ceiling. From his hiding place, Mike could see that the cavern curved right as if it were crescent shaped, and that they were at the very tip of one end of it. The curvature of the walls prevented the men from estimating the cavern's length. Surprisingly, the far end was very bright and through a gap in the boxes Mike could see that there were some large shadows on the walls, which did not belong to boxes.

I wonder what is causing them, he thought.

'What do you think is in the boxes?' Piers asked Mike.

'With any luck it will be weapons and explosives. Just what we need!' he grinned. 'If we could climb down we could take a look!'

Mike decided they should not attempt to climb down into the strange cave and the two men descended to where, Lana, who was still asleep, Geordie, and Joe were patiently waiting.

To Piers he said, 'You need to go now. Take Lana and find a way out of here. She should be rested enough to walk. Go back to where we came in if you have to, but get some help here, fast.' Mike asked Piers.

'Will do.' He shook Lana gently saying, 'Time to go.'

Lana felt better for her sleep. To Mike, Piers said, 'Good luck!' Then he left with Lana following closely behind him.

As Piers and Lana disappeared, Mike turned to the two men left with him. 'Geordie and I will go with you Joe, to find the men. We must try to get some more weapons and get the soldiers away from here as quickly as possible.'

Piers took Lana back along the path they had used to get to their hiding place, moving as quickly as she was able to. Their journey was uneventful except for a few stumbles over rocks. He was kind and patient, aware that the woman must have gone through a terrible ordeal although she never mentioned it. She was recovering well and after stopping for a five minute break along the way, she discovered that she could even remember her name, Lana Guilders. Her memory was returning.

In less than three hours they found their way back up to the hole through which they had entered the caverns. Outside, the air was still and cold. The sky was cloudless and dark and studded with millions of beautiful twinkling stars. Thankful to be out of the dry, dusty caverns, they both took a moment to enjoy the fresh, clean air. Piers had almost forgotten the smell of fresh air. The cave smelled of dust and the air was stale.

From his backpack, Piers pulled out his radio and entered the codes to transmit to the satellite that would unite the signal with ASIU. It took some time to get through. Quietly, and clearly, Piers explained the situation to his contact at ASIU and requested some urgent assistance, asking for troops, explosives and weapons. He also asked for some grenades in case they had to cut off pursuers in the passages. They would be more effective than guns alone.

Piers mentioned that he would leave the beacon as near as he could to the entrance if he was obliged to hide it. The GPS signal would enable the live link for the satellite to find them and tell ASIU where to direct the troops when they arrived.

After disconnecting, Piers set up the beacon and then they sat together, wrapped up in blankets in the hole in the sand. The temperature dropped very low in the desert at night.

'Do you remember how you got here?' he asked Lana.

'It's coming back to me. I think I was made to forget.' she shuddered, 'We were hijacked. A member of the crew forced the pilot, Glen Hawkes, to change course. He told me later that someone had given the hijackers the tracking code and he was forced to switch it off. I don't know what they did with the aircraft after they took us off. Maybe they flew it somewhere else, blew it up or buried it in the sand. I couldn't even guess. We were way off course so it could have all been done and over with long before any rescue operation was instigated. Glen told me about it when we were imprisoned in one of the caverns. They moved us around a few times. Most of us were sleeping when it started. We had been drinking, and the drinks had been drugged. Those who had drunk from cans were alright, but they were threatened with death if they attempted to regain control of the aircraft.'

'Was anyone hurt?'

'Wes Farlow was shot in the arm when he tried to tackle one of the hijackers. One of the medics patched him up. Sometimes the men took me out of the cave and... and..., ' she covered her face with her hands, ' It was awful!' She wept softly. It was all coming back to her.

Piers seethed with anger. He understood what she would not, could not say. It would have been better for her to forget.

'Can you remember which part of the caverns you and your friends were in?' Piers asked, gently. 'Are they still there?'

Lana brushed her tears away. 'No. I was blindfolded once the aircraft was hijacked and it stayed on from then until I was pushed into a cave with some other men, then they took it off. I have been in so many caves, I can't remember. The others may still be there for all I know. There was a woman who was a member of the crew but I have not seen her since we were

246

imprisoned in the cave. They took her away too. I hope she is ok. I can't remember how I got to where I was when you found me, but I'm glad you did.'

The confusion of the last few days had frightened Lana and she was very relieved that she was starting to feel more normal. The pills which Bill had given her, of which she had no recollection, had been remarkably effective. 'I'm tired now. Do you think I could sleep for a while?'

Piers smiled at her and wrapped his arm around her, drawing her close until her head rested on his chest. 'Sure. There's plenty of time for you to sleep.'

Mike, Joe and Geordie returned to the cave where his men were incarcerated. From behind a wall they listened to see if they could hear any guards outside the room. There were no noises of breathing or shuffling of feet. Mike took the lead, Geordie crept behind him, followed nervously by Joe who dashed into the office and took the key from the box.

In seconds the three men were in the room, to the astonishment of the other occupants.

'Commander Forde, what are you doing here?' Andy Stillman asked.

'I'm not quite sure actually, but I didn't expect to find you, knucklehead!' Mike laughed softly then seriously he said, 'I'm going to need your help with dealing with your captors and getting you guys away from here.'

'You've got it!' several voices chorused in a whisper.

'Aye, Sir!' Tex Kirkwall agreed, 'Lemme at 'em!'

Mike ordered the soldiers to place anything they could get

their hands on under the blankets to make it appear that they were still asleep in their beds. They needed all the time they could get. If all hell broke loose, Decker and his cohorts would not know the strength of the opposition, giving Mike and his men an advantage.

'What's the plan sir?' Jacques LeCroix asked. 'Are we leaving?'

'No... not yet. We need to get the others.' Mike replied, 'We also need to get some guns. Geordie and I will do that. In the meantime, find the means to arm yourselves but stay here until we come back for you. You know what to do. My friend Piers is arranging for some backup support.'

Pulling out his knife, he handed it to Jacques, who followed him. Gun in hand, Mike led the way out through the door, with Geordie taking the rear.

Turning left, they continued along the passageway, finding two other doors, both were locked so they were unable to look inside. Moving quietly on, they saw a patch of light further along. It was quite bright and as they drew nearer they heard the sound of conversation.

Cautiously, Mike looked through the gap where the door was not quite closed. Two men sat playing cards, talking and drinking. Two automatic rifles were within reach of them. Mike signalled to Geordie to move to one side of the doorframe to cover him, out of sight. With his back to the other side, he threw a handful of sand and gravel along the floor into the room.

CHAPTER THIRTY FIVE

Defences

The two men at the table heard the rattle of stones as they bounced on the stone floor. They looked up at the ceiling and at each other in surprise. The man on the left of the table stood up, looked around the room then walked toward the door. Opening it wider, he stuck his head into the passageway. Mike grabbed him tightly around the neck, and turned him quickly so that he faced back into the room and thrust his gun sharply into his back. Feeling the strength behind the grip, the captive had no opportunity to struggle as Mike forced him back into the room, holding the gun to his head. His friend's face registered confusion and a measure of fear.

With his arm in a tight stranglehold around the man's neck, Mike aimed his gun at the other man. His voice was low.

'Back up, against the wall. Not a sound or you're dead! Now!'

The confused man put his hands on his head and stood against the wall. He could see the silencer in front of his eyes and knew the intruder meant it. No one would hear the shot so there was no doubt that it would be foolish to resist.

Geordie followed Mike into the room and closed the door. They tied both men up, looping the rope binding their legs behind them to the rope around their necks, and gagging them with their own socks. To finish the job they taped their mouths up and bundled each of the two men into separate cupboards away from the door. He led them to believe that there would be a guard at the door who would shoot them if they tried to escape. The men believed him.

Mike picked up the rifles, along with four others which were stored in a third cupboard. He found four boxes of ammunition and handed them to Geordie. He also picked up several bunches of keys that hung in a small cupboard on the wall. They might come in useful.

By chance, Geordie found a single key hanging on a nail half buried in the wall. It fitted the padlock hanging on the door handle. He hooked the padlock into the bolt rings after bolting the door from the outside and locked the room after they left.

Lady luck appeared to be on their side. Two of the keys on the rings fitted the locked rooms they had found earlier. One of them was a storage cupboard for bedding and toiletries. The other door led to a much larger cell and Mike found four more sleeping men inside. To his intense relief he found that they were not drugged. He carefully woke one of the men, keeping his hand over his mouth. The soldier, Richard Baker, gasped in shock at seeing his old CO.

Mike asked him to quietly waken the others. When they were all awake, the soldiers pulled on their clothing and shoes as they greeted the two men with enthusiasm. They were aware of how dirty and dishevelled they looked, but they were all in reasonable shape compared to the men who were drugged. Like the men in the Joe's cave, they were amazed to think that someone had actually found them after such a long imprisonment. Questions poured from their excited lips.

Mike quickly silenced them and explained the situation to them. They nodded their heads as the enormity of their situation sank in. 'We need to account for every soldier on the flight and the crew. We will eventually leave here and take everyone we can, in one go. No-one gets left behind.'

'Yes sir.' They all said, keeping their voices low.

'OK. Follow me, but keep it quiet.'

Mike led the way as the men made a dash, two at a time, with Joe's guidance, back to his cell. Geordie brought up the rear, carrying the ammunition for the guns which they had seized from the two men they had locked in the cupboards. Mike distributed them to four of the soldiers.

The liberated men smiled as they greeted each other with quiet enthusiasm, glad to see their friends were still alive. Trapped in their caves they had feared for the safety of each other. Although the sound of their voices carried along the dark, narrow stone corridors, locked without stimulation in a room with each other for so long had stifled conversation as hope of freedom seemed to disappear, and the rooms had become progressively quieter with each passing month.

'There are still more men to find.' Mike said to Geordie; it would be a tragedy if Paulo were allowed to send some of the men to America to plant bombs, as Joe had said he intended to do the day after tomorrow. That meant they had less than forty-eight hours left.

Calling Geordie and two of the other men, Gary Jessop and Richard Baker, Mike motioned them to follow him. They made their way to the cave in which Mike had seen the drugged men, and slipped surreptitiously inside the door.

'Get some help and try to get these men out of here as fast as you can. Take them back to the cave we have just left,' Mike ordered, as he motioned with his hand to the sleeping men. 'Geordie and I will seek out the other men who are still in the caverns. Let the men know that I have sent for reinforcements but we are on our own until they get here. I don't know how long that will take or whether they will even get here in time.'

One of the men said, 'Sir, Lana Guilders was with us. Now she is gone. I don't know what they did with her.'

'Lana is fine. She is on her way out of here with another ASIU agent.' The two men's faces showed disbelief and disgust as Mike explained quickly about Lana. He did not mention Gerd Schumacher. The men knew him and he did not want to distract them. He would tell them the sad news when they were safely away.

'When we first came here I could hear some shouting going on down the passageway. Maybe there are more of us down there.' Richard said softly in his Aberdeen accent.

'Okay, so we look there.' Speaking to Geordie he said, 'Come with me and we'll check out the rooms further down the passageway, the one to the right.'

Mike found several of the doors locked and was thankful that they had picked up the keys from the guards' room. He unlocked them all, finding two more rooms each with two men lying on stone beds. The rooms stank of unwashed clothes and sweaty bodies. Mike groaned inwardly; God, they'd smell them a mile off! No surprise attack party from the men in this room!

The four men, all of whom had been drugged were comatose. The soldiers who were fit enough carried the

252

victims two at a time to the cave near Joe's, where they were placed onto beds.

The relatively small rooms were becoming excessively crowded and increasingly stuffy. If they did not move soon, they would all suffocate for lack of oxygen. Mike returned to his search for other captives. He had found twenty four soldiers, but where were the crew?

Soon afterwards, to add to the discomfort, Geordie returned with another two men, a pilot and a navigator, both of whom had clearly been severely beaten at some time earlier, as the not yet faded bruises around their eyes and lower faces more than adequately demonstrated. There was only one person missing from the plane's list of passengers and crew, the stewardess. She was nowhere to be found.

'I can't find anyone else,' Mike said to Geordie as he returned to the room. Careful to keep his voice low, he addressed the men in the room. 'Was anyone killed when you were brought here?'

'No, not that we know of,' came the reply from several directions.

'The pilot who flew the aircraft after the hijack was a new man. None of us had seen him before. He must have stowed away with the other hijackers.' The navigator reported. 'There were four and they were heavily armed.'

Mike was worried about how they would all get safely away. The men had helped him to search the rest of the rooms, but he found no more prisoners. The passageway eventually came to a dead end. He grew more concerned by the minute. Time was passing and he still had the drugged men

253

to transport to safety.

Mike realised there was no alternative but to leave. The prisoners were sure to be missed soon. He took Geordie aside and said, 'We must get some more weapons. It's getting dangerous to stay here for much longer but we can't get these men away yet without some weapons to protect them. I think we should try to find out where the weapons are, but the problem is that we can't leave the sleeping men without some sort of protection. We should leave most of the soldiers and guns here, but some should come with us. It's risky I know, but it's the most sensible thing to do. Some of the men need protection because they are unable to fight back.'

Geordie agreed with him and soon afterwards, along with five soldiers they made their way back along the narrow passageway the way they had arrived, intending to take one of the other unexplored routes.

On the way back, Mike checked the room in which he and Geordie had found the two men to see if they could find anything else of use. They did not. The cupboards were still locked and they could hear muffled moans and bumps coming from the trussed up prisoners within.

Geordie grinned at Mike, delighted with his handiwork as he addressed the two captives, 'Enjoy yourselves laddies, that'll teach you to meddle with my mates and me! You'll not get out of there so easily, will you now?' The men stopped moving and became silent once more.

Once again they locked the door and moved on. All was quiet until they rounded a corner and found a doorway within which they could hear a humming sound. It sounded like a generator. The humming noise grew louder as they moved closer to the source. Finally, with the noise so loud that it drowned their footsteps, the group of men walked further into the passageway and into a wide cavern. It had a high ceiling that curved away to the left, and it was filled almost to overflowing with wooden crates and boxes. Mike recognised the curvature of the walls and thought they were in the cave which they had seen earlier from the top of the high wall.

Some of the men broke open several boxes to find food and other homely items. As they opened more, they were astonished to find an arsenal of explosives, detonators, radios, and more importantly, automatic weapons with thousands of rounds of ammunition.

The soldiers each selected a weapon and several cartridges of ammunition, stuffing as much as they could into the waistband of their trousers. Expertly, they made them ready to use. Now they were armed and ready for action, but Mike advised silence and caution. No shooting unless absolutely necessary. They still did not know the extent of Paulo's defences.

Walking further into the cavern, they came upon the source of the humming, a large generator housed in a smaller cave which stank of combusted fuel.

There were several passageways leading off the cave but Mike continued to lead the men deeper into the curved cavern. Rounding the end of a vertical wall that stretched up to the ceiling and protruded halfway across the widening floor, the men stopped, looking at each other in amazement.

The cavern on the other side of the wall was enormous,

about the size of a warehouse. The high ceiling dipped like an arch to within fifteen metres of the floor, and piles of sand drifted up against the end walls. A refreshing, but hot breeze blew gently into the men's faces.

Near the edges of the external curve of the cavern, several trucks stood empty. He estimated that they were around a dozen men. Some of them were unpacking boxes onto small trolleys, but they were not what caught the astonished men's attention.

Incredibly like angels from heaven, sitting side by side in the middle of the cavern, were three small helicopters. Mike's surprise was so great that he almost choked in the dusty air. He looked at Geordie and said, 'So that is what those shadows were! Those three birds might come in handy. Go and check they are airworthy.' The helicopters were too small to take more than three passengers and the pilot.

Geordie laughed, 'As good as done, sir!'

CHAPTER THIRTY SIX

Discovery

Lana slept as Piers waited for the arrival of the help promised to him. He knew that ASIU would probably drop a band of reinforcements into the region some distance away rather then make a land based assault to the front of the cave. It took hours before he spotted the first few jumpers dropping silently as silhouettes against the dawn sky. The black shapes reached the ground, rolled up their 'chutes and buried them.

One of the first men to arrive greeted him with a quick shake of his hand as he introduced himself, 'Major John Winters. We're the nearest available help to you. How're you doing here? My men will be with us in just a couple of minutes. How many men are with you? There are twenty one of us, including me of course.' He smiled broadly.

Piers faced a tall, thin man with the biggest jaw full of teeth that he had ever seen. Despite the seriousness of the situation, he spontaneously wondered if the man was fond of nuts, and with great difficulty suppressed the grin that accompanied the thought.

'I don't know.' he replied, giving Lana a shake. 'We hadn't found them all when we left to climb to the surface.' Humour disappeared.

'What do you mean?'

'The men are, or were, imprisoned in the caverns below,' he pointed into to the hole behind him. 'We need to go in there to find them if they haven't been found already.' Piers shocked the major with his account of the drugged prisoners, and their identity.

'Bloody hell! Don't worry... sorry miss!' Winters nodded to Lana as she rose and stood beside Piers, 'We'll get them out if we have to blow the place apart!'

Ten minutes later, twenty-two men and one woman made their way down the hole and into the caverns below.

The five soldiers, Mike and Geordie returned almost an hour later to the captives' cave. Mike explained that he needed more men, especially helicopter pilots and asked for volunteers. Two of the men, LeCroix and navigator Schmidt offered their services along with three others, Kirkwall, Jameson and Stillman.

It took twenty minutes to find their way back to the crescent shaped cave. Once there, they concealed themselves behind some pallets. For a few minutes, they watched as Paulo's men continued to unpack the boxes.

'We'll have to take them on. Those helicopters must have got inside here somehow so they must also be able to get out.' Mike said grimly. 'If we can capture them, we may be able to use them to get to safe ground if we need to.' Pointing to LeCroix and Schmidt, he said, 'You two take the two bozos by the boxes, Geordie and the rest of us will clear the others.'

'Yes, Sir.' the two men acknowledged softly and crept on their way, keeping close to the boxes.

It wasn't until Mike and Geordie got closer to two of the other packers that they realised they were armed. Two sub machine guns were propped up within reach against the boxes.

Directly into Geordie's ear, Mike said, 'We need to distract them somehow to stop them picking up their weapons. If we try to jump them they'll shoot at us and raise the alarm. The crap will really hit the fan then and we can't let that happen until we get the men out.' He crawled back to the waiting soldiers behind the boxes and advised them of his strategy.

Five minutes later he returned to where Geordie was watching the progress of LeCroix and Schmidt, whom he had sent to deal with the two packers to their left.

They were good, very good! Keeping out of sight, the two soldiers crept behind the boxes to the right of the men until they were less than two metres away. Then they jumped at the men from behind and placed their hands over the struggling captives' mouths to stop them from shouting. In seconds the two packers were dragged quickly to the floor and each despatched with a swift twist of the neck. The other packers on the right of the boxes continued with their business, unaware that they had just lost two of their colleagues.

Working together, the two men quickly dragged the bodies behind some crates over by the wall of the cavern where they would not be seen, then returned to where Mike and Geordie watched as their two targets emptied the boxes they were unpacking. The other two soldiers were nowhere to be seen. Another of the former captives, who had crept up to the heavily laden trolley to move it from the other side, stepped out from behind it and gave the thumbs up to Mike. Suddenly, both packers raised their heads as they felt one of the trolleys move backwards. Instinctively, they both stepped forward to stop it.

At that moment, Geordie and Mike made a dash towards them, flung themselves at them and pulled them down to the ground. The men struggled, flailing out with both hands to protect themselves from the knives. The soldiers were too quick for them, delivering a quick and accurate thrust and twist into their hearts. It was all over in seconds.

Further around the curve of the cave there were two more men standing by the trucks, smoking and talking. There was an eight foot wall of boxes between them and the far end of the cavern where the rest of Paulo's men were working, which meant that that they could not see Mike's men, but they would be seen immediately they approached them. There was also no cover between the two men by the truck from where Mike was standing. The only way to get to the targets was to walk straight up to them.

Schmidt said quickly, 'I have an idea, sir.' and crawled over to where he and LeCroix had left the two dead men. He came back with one of their jackets and a cap.

'Good thinking, go do it!' Mike had every confidence in Schmidt, he was one of the best martial arts men in the unit, instructing and testing the men to their limit. He had the added advantage of being about the same build as the jacket's owner. It would have been too small to fit Mike and the jacket belonging to the other man wouldn't fit any of the soldiers. Its owner was built like a beanpole.

Schmidt put the jacket on and pulled the cap low over his eyebrows, confidence oozing from him. He stuffed his hands in his pockets and sauntered over toward the two men. They did not see his face until he was quite near because he appeared to be having some trouble with his boot laces, and leant down to pull at them as he drew near. By the time the surprised men realised he was a stranger, it was too late.

As the soldier looked up at the men confusion, then alarm flustered them both for a moment. It was just long enough for Schmidt to land a deadly karate chop across the jugular of one, and then to swing around, and with a backward kick, rammed his foot into the other man's face. He was so fast, neither had time to cry out. The first man fell to the ground, lifeless. The second man fell to the floor and Schmidt finished him off with a sharp sideways kick under the chin, snapping his neck like a dry twig.

Behind the pallets of boxes, Schmidt's colleagues had watched, fascinated as the instructor showed them a real live, cold-blooded execution.

The men dragged the bodies over to a stack of empty crates. To ensure they were not seen, the soldiers placed the corpses inside the lower ones, and put several of the empty crates on top and in front of the pile to hide them, then the men made their way back to Joe's cell to share out the weapons and ammunition they had taken from the boxes.

While Mike and his men were accumulating weapons, Bill could not sleep. After several hours he gave up and decided to visit the soldiers once more. Instinctively, he took his entire supply of the antidote with him. If he didn't return at least Paulo wouldn't get his hands on the pills. If he had access to a chemist the chemical composition could easily be identified.

261

That must never happen. It was his responsibility to ensure that it did not.

Joe was astonished but pleased to see him. The doctor was even more amazed by the sheer number of men, standing and sitting in such a small space.

'Where have they all come from?' he asked.

'The caves,' Joe replied. 'I'm glad you are here, we desperately need your help. Several of our men are sleeping and we can't wake them.'

For the first time, the doctor's face beamed with a wide, happy smile, 'Yes, I know, I expect you can't. The men are drugged, but they are not much use to Paulo as they are, are they?'

Puzzled, Joe asked, 'Why? What do you mean?'

'Garcia told me that he wanted my help to inject a lot of the men at the same time. His intention was to brainwash them into believing they were all in Paulo's regiment, on his side in fact. He planned some horrific act of terror. I altered the formula of the drug to ensure that they all suffered side effects. Some of these men are in varying degrees of an induced coma.' Bill seemed pleased as he spoke. The idea, such a simple idea, had come to him suddenly in a flash of inspiration. 'If the men were suffering side-effects, they wouldn't be able to be made to do anything for Paulo, would they?'

Joe was speechless. What a great idea!

The doctor went on. 'I had to do it to save lives, but don't worry, it's reversible. As you already know, I have the antidote and Paulo and Garcia know nothing about it. It was the only way to ensure that Paulo didn't send any more men to do his evil work. Garcia had already treated some men, and Paulo sent them to America. I don't know what happened to them or even if they returned. Now that some more of your friends are here, if they will help me I can bring the men back to full health. As soon as they are conscious we can get them out of here.'

Joe sat on his bed, amazed by Bill's explanation of how he had thwarted Garcia's plan to drug the men. 'Didn't he realise that you had outsmarted him?' he laughed.

Bill laughed. It was a genuinely hearty laugh, borne of relief. 'No. After the last injection, I heard Paulo ordering Garcia not to drug me anymore. He thinks that I may have made the drug incorrectly because of the effect of Garcia's hypnotherapy. Garcia is somewhat out of favour with Paulo at the moment. Neither Paulo nor Garcia have any idea that I was never under their influence at all.'

'Incredible!' The young man was impressed by Bill's ingenuity. 'Now what do we do to revive them?'

'I'm going to need water, lots of it, and some of the men to administer the dosage. They won't be able to swallow the pills themselves. They need help and it would take too long for me to do it all myself.'

Joe rounded up six men to help Bill. The soldiers were eager to help and grouped themselves around the doctor as he spent five minutes demonstrating the dosage and how it should be administered, using one of the comatose men. Then they each picked up the first dose of pills and a bottle of water for one of the victims, and went off to find something to crush

263

the pills into. An hour later, all the patients had been treated with the first of two doses. Now Bill and the volunteer medics had to wait for the pills to take effect.

'How long will it take?' Jimmy Cotter, who had been helping, asked the doctor.

'Hours, but it may be longer. I wasn't there when Lana recovered so I've no idea. I'm afraid we need to wait and see.' Anxious to get away from his captors, Bill hoped it would be soon.

'Lana? Do you mean Lana Guilders?' Jimmy asked. He had not been in the cave when Mike told the other soldiers about Lana. 'She's safe then?'

'Yes. She is.' Bill did not elaborate. He did not say, 'If it had not been for my drug we would all be out of here by now.' or that 'This might not have happened at all.'

The doctor hovered constantly over the men. He was not a free man however, and he was eventually forced to return to his quarters because he was expected to join their captors for the next meal. Bill was sociable during the meal and after yawning loudly several times during their conversation, left them to return to his quarters, declaring his need for sleep. He was able to return to Joe's cell four and a half hours later, before Paulo, Garcia and Neko again left with Decker to make plans for their next bombing campaign.

Some hours later, several of the drugged soldiers were beginning to show varying signs of awakening but their eyes were still closed. Their pupils were beginning to respond to light. That was a good sign. Sometimes a leg or a foot would

264

move, or an arm would be thrown above the man's head.

'They seem to be coming around, then.' Mike remarked to Karl Braun as he handed him a weapon. He had just returned after searching unsuccessfully, to find the stewardess. None of the men had seen her in any of their cells.

'We've got some help, sir.' The soldier pointed to the back of Bill's grubby white coat.

'Who is that?' Mike was curious.

Karl was apologetic. 'I don't know sir. He arrived some time ago and started giving us instructions on how to treat the men. I didn't catch his name, but I don't think he said who he was. Joe will tell you, he seems to know him.'

Wondering who the man could be, Mike walked over to Joe, and pulled him over to one side of the room. He pointed to the back of the man in the white coat. 'Who is that?' he asked.

'I don't know his name, sir, but that is the friend I told you about.' Joe explained.

Mike walked over to where the man was feeling the pulse of one of the sleeping men, and checking his eyes' reaction to light with a torch. He touched the man's shoulder and he turned around to face him.

'Hello.' Mike looked at the man's face. It seemed familiar. 'Good grief! I don't believe it!'

'Hello.' Bill replied; he was not very pleased to be interrupted. 'You are....?'

'You must be Doctor William Willington.' Introducing himself, Mike said, 'I am Commander Mike Forde from the American Special Intelligence Unit in America. I have been trying to find you ever since you were kidnapped!'

Bill managed to smile. 'I am pleased to meet you, Commander. Now if you will excuse me, I must see to these men. I am trying to forget about the kidnap. I lost a friend that day.' Bill was obsessed with the recovery of the victims of Paulo's cruelty. He was not in the mood for social chit-chat.

Mike was shocked. Incredible as it seemed to him, the sole purpose of his pursuit of Decker, the kidnapped doctor, was standing right in front of him! 'What do you mean, you lost a friend?' he asked quietly. 'Are you talking about your driver?'

Bill turned to him, having finished his check on the patient. 'Yes. I am. My friend Leo, the driver, was killed.' Sadness crept into his eyes as he remembered.

Mike spoke softly and placed his hand reassuringly on the man's shoulder. He didn't want to give the man too big of a shock. 'Bill... he didn't die. Leo Forrest is alive and recovering. I have spoken with him.'

Astonished, his face lighting up, the doctor replied, 'He's alive? Leo's really alive? Are you sure?'

'If I'm not, I've been speaking to a very lively ghost!' Mike laughed. 'Leo is in a wheelchair at the moment but I doubt he'll stay there for long, especially when we get you home.'

'Thank God, oh thank God!' Bill staggered and sat on the nearest bed as his legs gave way under him. 'Thank God... and thank you for telling me.' Then his face fell; he knew he had to tell Mike about the bombs.

Overwhelmed with guilt, Bill said, 'You must know by now about the bombs that have gone off recently in America. I saw it in the newspaper that Paulo showed me. It's all been my

266

fault!' As it had at the time when he looked at the photograph of the carnage in the newspaper, a wave of nausea welled up inside the doctor's stomach.

'Yes. I know,' he said, compassionately, 'Garcia drugged the men and told them what to do, and Paulo sent them to America to plant bombs.'

Tears welled unbidden in Bill's eyes; he rubbed them impatiently with his hands until they were dry. 'I never meant Riofactol to be used in that way. The drug was supposed to help people!' He was angry and exhausted. 'I will have to live with that for the rest of my life.'

Mike felt sorry for Bill. 'Justice will be served. However, we will need to talk about that later, when we get out of here. Right now we need to figure out how we are going to get away. I can't believe we haven't seen any guards yet,' he said, 'It can't be long now before they notice the absence of the workers.'

'If we don't go soon, those that are not sleeping are due to receive a meal after Paulo and his men eat. Paulo only feeds them twice a day. It would be a good idea to get these men away at the earliest opportunity.' Bill warned. 'That can't be far off now. Once they realise I'm not there they will send men out to look for me. If they get this far, they will find these soldiers in here and they will be killed.'

Mike again reassured him. 'We have weapons now. My men and I managed to find some in a large cave. How long will it take for these men to be recovered enough to move?' Impatient to get away, Mike was ready to brief the officers as soon as they were all in the same room and had sent Geordie to seek them out.

267

'Give them another half hour.' The doctor replied. 'If they are not recovered enough to walk, I will give them another dose of the antidote. Are you happy with that? After that, I need to go back to my lab. I need to destroy the remaining Riofactol supply.'

'Do what you need to, but don't take unnecessary risks.' Mike said. He was not happy to let the doctor go but he understood that the Riofactol had to be destroyed to prevent it ever being used again. He was going after Decker, Paulo and Neko. Bill left the men and headed for his lab. He now had a job which he was looking forward to taking care of.

Mike briefed the men who were clear-headed enough and able to take command in his absence, asking them to get ready to move the men who needed help to move. His plan was that Joe would guide the men out to the cave area by the underground lake, as soon as possible. The lake area was a good stronghold, and easy to protect if they were followed and shot at. There was a lot of cover among the large rocks if and when bullets started to fly. He hoped that by the time they reached the lake, reinforcements would have arrived. Joe felt sure that it would come soon. He too prayed that the help that Piers had requested from ASIU arrived soon. They were in dire need of it.

CHAPTER THIRTY SEVEN

Rescue

Garcia walked into the doctor's sleeping quarters. They had a busy time ahead. The men needed to be injected and programmed to set in motion the next wave of bombings. The targets were to be a building in Miami and an aircraft manufacturing plant in Philadelphia.

He needed the doctor to check on the condition of the men prior to the sessions. Paulo had ordered it because he had lost a man in one of the bombings in San Diego, after he blew himself up and he did not want it to happen again. His personnel resource for bombings was low, even with so many prisoners, compared to the plans he had for the campaign of terror he had been paid to implement by his friends in Iraq. Imperiously, Paulo had warned Garcia that he had to ensure the treatment worked properly and that his messengers returned alive, to strike again.

Garcia went to find their captive but Bill's quarters were empty. Irritated, he made his way through the archway to the lab. It was in darkness. Angrily, he stormed back to the treatment room, thinking he might have missed him. He was not there either! Like Paulo, Garcia had a very short fuse. Walking into Paulo's office, he asked abruptly, 'Where is Willington?'

Paulo looked up in surprise, 'He is supposed to be with you, is he not?'

269

Garcia looked at his nails impatiently. 'Does it look like it? Do you think I would be asking you if he were?' his voice was laced with sarcasm. Ever since the last treatment of the soldiers led to several of them becoming comatose, the relationship between the two men had deteriorated. Garcia did not care. He knew Paulo needed him, and he wanted the money the man paid for his services.

'So where is he?' Paulo's anger began to simmer. He did not like Garcia's attitude and although he needed the man, he was in charge, not that simpering fool! 'Find him!' he ordered.

Garcia left, furious at being spoken to with such disrespect.

Five minutes after Garcia left, one of Paulo's men walked into his office. He was terrified, knowing that what he was going to say was going to displease him. He stood in front of his boss, hardly knowing how to say it.

'Well?' demanded Paulo.

'We have a problem, sir,' the man looked at his feet, 'four of our men have been found dead and two are missing'.

'What? What has happened?' Paulo was enraged. 'Get some men, and follow me.'

Deep in the cold cavern Major Winters and the soldiers approached the lake where they gathered to hear Piers' instructions. It had taken a long time to guide so many men through the narrow stone passageways without excessive noise. Several times they were forced to slow down because of the difficulty of squeezing through the narrower stretches with their bulky backpacks, which were entirely unsuited to the cave environment. Piers, frustrated at the slow progress, eventually asked the men to abandon their packs near the lake, and carry only stretchers, ammunition and guns. They hid everything else in large cracks and behind rocks. To protect her, he left Lana with two armed men in one of the caverns further back.

One hour later, four men, led by Piers, finally reached the cave where the soldiers were caring for their comrades. The soldiers crowded around him as he told them that there was no more time. They were to work in twos and carry the drugged men to where Winters' men waited nearby. They had to leave now. They left the caves looking occupied by stuffing everything they could find under the top blanket of their beds.

As quietly as they could manage, the soldiers walked out of the cave, some carried their colleagues, who were only half conscious, between them. Mike, Geordie and five of the soldiers had already left for the large cave they had discovered earlier, with the intention of capturing the helicopters.

They filed along the passageways as quickly as they could, meeting up with Winter's men, who fastened the helpless men onto stretchers and carried them as carefully as they could over the stones and along the passageways. Piers was concerned about timing. The escape would be discovered soon enough and they needed to put as much distance as they could between themselves and their likely pursuers.

Paulo and his men reached the cells in which the prisoners were incarcerated. He looked through the grille of the door. He could see that the men were in their beds, still asleep. They did not move. He ordered Omar, one of his men, to go in and

271

check them. He did not trust Garcia. Omar unlocked the door and peered down at the sleeping man next to the door. Suddenly he savagely lifted the bed and turned everything onto the floor. He did the same with the other beds.

'They are gone... they are all gone!' he shouted.

Paulo roared, incensed beyond all reason, 'Find them, find them! They must not escape!' He led his men to a small cave where some weapons were stored in boxes. 'Arm yourselves!' he cried to his men. Eight of his men, including Omar, followed him carrying their guns and ammunition as they walked through the passageways to the dried up river bed. Ahead of them was darkness but Paulo's sharp eyes detected some faint traces of light ahead. They raced as fast as they could over the stones and boulders.

Joe, the Major and his men heard the echo of the commotion in the distance as Paulo and his men followed them.

'Take cover. Quick, get those men back to the lake,' the major ordered the stretcher bearers. Without a word, the men rushed forward as quickly as they could manage, onward through the passageways, heading for the large cavern with its calm lake.

Covering their departure, the major stationed several men behind boulders and in wider cracks in the walls, to take out their pursuers. Paulo's men arrived five minutes later. After fifteen minutes of intermittent gunfire exchange, in which two of Joe's friends were injured, but not seriously, the enemy became just another eight dead bodies. Joe saw one man running back into the passageway but by the time he dodged around the boulders and was in a position to shoot at him, he was too late to do anything but watch his target disappear into the darkness.

Breathless with his exertion, having managed to avoid being shot by Piers' men, Paulo ran to Neko's quarters. His brother, who had not heard the shooting, was lying on a sofa, ear-plugs in his ears, listening to music on his iPod. He quickly pulled them out as he saw Paulo's expression of anxiety, and that he was holding a Kalashnikov in his hand.

'The men have escaped... we must bring them back before they bring other people here!' Paulo cried, anxiously.

Neko leapt to his feet and opened a locker to collect his gun and ammunition. 'Where are they headed?' he asked.

Paulo was frantic, 'They have gone further into the caves past the old river bed. Eight of my men are dead. There are soldiers with them.' He had never seen them before. How had they had got past his guards?

'Then we had better get out of here while we still can.' Neko responded, calmly. He never panicked. 'Get to the helicopters. If there are soldiers in our hideout, more will come. Let's get our valuables and get out of here. Your men can fly us out of here. Get the doctor, we will need a hostage.'

'I don't know where he is,' Paulo replied. 'Garcia came to me asking if he was with me.'

Neko, older than Paulo, sighed angrily, 'Then for goodness sake, check the lab... just find him!'

Paulo had already checked the lab, but he went back there anyway, and pushed his way through the curtained archway.

273

The lights were on and Bill stood by the bench, dismantling the equipment. 'What are you doing?' he asked him.

Bill was afraid, but determined that nothing would stop him from destroying the Riofactol. 'I'm clearing this. It is contaminated,' he bluffed. The soldiers were all escaping. It was enough for him. He had done all he could to help them and now he was on his own with a madman.

'Stop what you are doing and come with me!' Paulo ordered.

Paulo's voice indicated that he was in no mood for delay. Bill picked up the flask holding the last of the drug. He had destroyed the small phials by crushing them with a rock at the back of his lab. Now they were just tiny fragments of glass.

'Give me the flask,' Paulo ordered, holding out his hand. It would come in useful at some time in the future.

Bill moved closer to Paulo and deliberately fell forward, dropping the flask. It shattered as it hit the floor and the precious fluid seeped quickly into the sand

'Oh God,' Bill exclaimed, 'I'm sorry!'

'You fool!' Paulo was beside himself with rage and struck Bill a cruel blow with the butt of his rifle. His precious commodity was gone, but he still had Willington. They would take him with them and he could make some more! He dragged his prisoner, bleeding profusely from his nose and mouth, back to Neko who was gathering several small bags of diamonds and currency into a sack. Bill was terrified. His situation was going from bad to worse!

CHAPTER THIRTY EIGHT

Retribution

In the crescent shaped cave, Geordie discreetly checked the fuel levels of the helicopters. If they could be flown out it would prevent any of Paulo's men using them to flee and they would also serve as a means of escape for himself and his friends as soon as their business was finished.

One of the soldiers, Stillman, had succeeded in reaching the outside edge of the cave, which was actually a solid roof of hard limestone. From the air it would have been inconspicuous against the surrounding expanse of dunes because of the curvature of the cave mouth. The curved shadow on the sand, caused by the ceiling of the natural 'hangar' would appear to be just another dune shadow. No-one flying above the area could have guessed its secret. It was a mystery how the stone came to be uplifted to form the cave, but no-one cared how the cave existed. It just did. It was a marvel that it existed at all. It was a shame that it would be destroyed. Mike had explained to his men that he would blow up the cave as soon as the helicopters were out, to ensure the weaponry within it would at least be temporarily neutralised. It could all be dug out later.

The soldier walked cautiously toward the two guards standing outside of the cave. They were looking for intruders approaching from outside, not inside and they were obviously not expecting company. Ready to do what needed to be done, Stillman knew he could handle them. He did, and left them lying lifeless behind a crate. The exit was clear. Almost time to go. He removed the silencer from Mike's gun and tucked them both back in his pocket.

Geordie confirmed to LeCroix and Schmidt that their helicopter was fuelled to the top and was ready to go. He crept up behind Kirkwall and Jameson and gave them the bad news. 'Sorry, your bird is out of fuel... she's not going anywhere I'm afraid, you'll have to take other one. Mike and I will find another way out' Kirkwall groaned. 'Damn!' He was hoping they would all get out together.

Crawling stealthily back to Mike, Geordie briefed him on the change of plan.

'We'd best blow it up, then, just to be on the safe side. I'll leave you with the pleasure of that. I need to go back to find Bill.' Mike left Geordie setting up the explosives.

Geordie had found some Semtex in one of the newly arrived crates which had not yet been unpacked, at the back of the cave. With great precision, he set up timed detonations around the packed up weapons, to prevent Paulo's men from using them against them. He would leave with Jameson and set off the charges remotely.

Piers felt relieved. Several times the soldiers and the major's men had to stop and manoeuvre the stretchers around sharp, narrow corners between the enormous fallen limestone boulders, but with determination and patience born of good training, they eventually reached the rocky ramp which Geordie's camel had found, leading upwards to freedom.

Major Winters contacted the captain of the ship as soon as

he reached the surface and arranged for Lana and the drugged men to be picked up and flown to a ship on stand-by in the Arabian Sea.

Soon after the Major's communication, they all had heard the faint sound of approaching helicopters. The sky was bright and the desert sun was blinding. The sand swirled up into the air as two Seahawks hovered in tandem just above the top of some sand dunes a hundred yards away. He watched with relief as the former prisoners walked in groups as fast as they could, carrying the stretchered men along the ridge of the dunes. Other, more able men sat on the dune, waiting their turn for rescue. In the distance, Piers could see another two waves of Seahawks approaching them. Soon all the soldiers would be safely away.

Turning to the major, who was watching the former prisoners enjoying the hot, but freshest air they had breathed in months, Piers said, 'Commander Forde is still in there. I need some of your men to come back with me to help him, and take down the men responsible for this atrocity. I was also wondering if you had seen Doctor Willington. He has not appeared yet and I'm rather worried about him.'

Major Winters did not know Bill but he was sure that the only men who had made it out of the cave system were soldiers. 'How many men do you need?' he asked.

'We need to be discreet, so I reckon three of your best should do. You should get back to the ship with the others and debrief the men.

After two more flights of Seahawks took away the last of the soldiers, Piers and three of Winter's men made their way

277

back inside the cave complex. They made straight for the caves in which the prisoners had been kept. Seeing the upturned beds was enough to tell the men that the escape had been discovered. Bill was nowhere to be seen. Stealthily the four men moved forward slowly, looking in every cave they came across but they were all empty. To cover more ground, the four men split up, arranging to meet up every fifteen minutes.

Piers found the cave in which Neko had been relaxing. Cupboards were open and drawers were pulled out. The room looked like it had been the object of a messy search.

Suddenly he found himself being pushed forward violently as someone grabbed his shoulder. He fell and a large man with white hair fell on top of him, trying to grab his neck, to choke him. The Swede kneed the man in the groin and using his weight against him, kicked him backwards, where he slammed against the hard rock of the wall. His head cracked violently and bounced forward again. Undeterred, the man again attacked Piers, who grabbed his leg as the man swung it out to kick him, and again he pushed the man backwards, twisting his foot around three hundred and sixty degrees. His assailant shouted in pain but he lost control of his balance and fell once more against the wall, but almost at ground level. The angle of his fall caused his neck to bend unnaturally as he met the ground, and Piers heard the crack as it broke. It did not take a genius to tell that the man was dead. His head was supported by the wall, his chin was on his chest and his long white ponytail curled around his shoulder. Decker was dead, but it was too late, they had no further interest in him. The doctor was missing once again and they had to find him.

Garcia picked up his gun. He had heard an exchange of fire in the distance and was unsure about what was happening. It was too early for Paulo to be on one of his wild, drunken cowboy jaunts with his gun. He walked around to the large crescent shaped cave. Someone there might know what was going on. He heard the sound of the helicopter engines starting up, and had just entered the cave when the rotors started to turn slowly as they taxied outside of the cave entrance and disappeared with a huge roar as they rose into the sky. One of the pilots saw Garcia and fired a shot at him as he passed. The bullet missed him but it hit one of the boxes and ricocheted into another box full of ammunition. Garcia ducked down behind the boxes. Seconds later the explosives set by Geordie detonated and Garcia was caught unawares. He just had time to register the wiring and the detonator at the base of the box he was hiding behind before he caught the full force of the blast.

Neko and Paulo, dragging Bill with them, were too far away to see the explosion in the crescent shaped cave, but they heard and felt it. The walls hummed with the vibration and several cracked, releasing large and small rocks, which fell through the ceilings of many of the caves in the immediate vicinity. Ammunition continued to crack unpredictably after the blast. When the three men eventually reached the cave they found that two of the helicopters were gone, the third was destroyed, and the trucks were being buried by sand, rendering them useless. Even if it had been possible to drive away a truck, the collapse of the ceiling had blocked their exit. They had no means of escape.

Mike heard the explosion from his hiding place in a small cave that was used for the storage of water barrels, from which various pipes fed out through holes in the walls.

He waited until the noise abated before venturing outside into the narrow passageway. The cave in which he had hidden was not too far away from the crescent shaped cave, and he could see that part of the roof had collapsed. The third helicopter was crushed beneath tonnes of rock and he could hear the hissing sound made by the sand as it poured relentlessly through a huge crack in the roof of the cave, burying the trucks, the debris from the explosion and pretty much everything else. Soon the cave would be entirely filled with sand as the desert reclaimed its depths. Sunlight streamed into the cave, lighting up the devastation.

Many of the men working at the other end of the cave were taken by surprise. They would never have escaped. Rock and sand ensured their burial but there were no words for divine mercy.

Fine dust hung in the air as Mike found his way deep into the heart of the caves. Walking through a wooden door and an archway, he found what he assumed to be the doctor's lab because there were many beakers, pipettes and tubing lying around on the bench. It was empty. A dirty white coat hung over one of the seats, but where was Bill?

CHAPTER THIRTY NINE

The King of the Moon

Paulo and Neko returned with their captive to the cave they had used to inject the men. It was intact. Paulo kept his accounts in a filing cabinet next to the back wall. He realised that he needed to destroy the paperwork and the laptop hard drive. Before doing so he printed out his lists of contacts and bank details, and picked up the delivery notes with the list of chemicals Willington required to make Riofactol then placed them in his sack.

Bill sat silently in the corner, under threat of being shot by Paulo. He had seen the devastation of the explosion and did not know what to expect next. Despite Paulo's threat to kill him, he was clearly still of value to the man or he would be dead by now. There was no escape. His captor was between himself and the door. To pass him he would have to fight him and he was no match for the man. His brother continued to push items into his bag. Bill was in despair. Was there no end to this misery? He wished the man had killed him... anything rather than remain their captive to be forced to be a pawn in their despicable game.

Neko left them alone and Paulo busied himself with shredding files. Without warning, the door burst open and Mike walked into the cave, pointing a gun in Paulo's direction.

'Drop the file. Hands up!' he shouted. 'Now, and I mean now, or you die!'

Quickly, instinctively, Paulo picked up his gun, which had been on the top of the filing cabinet and fired at Mike. He missed as the quick thinking agent dropped to the floor and returned his fire. Paulo cried out in pain as he grasped his right arm, watching the blood as it spurted from a wound just above the inside of his elbow. He was used to inflicting pain and found it hard to cope with it imposed upon him, but he bore it well. He would not let his enemy see him weakened.

Expertly, using the belt from Bill's lab coat, Mike tied a tourniquet on his arm, saying, 'I will kill you if you do anything stupid, make no mistake about that. I have seen what you have done.'

'And I am proud of it!' Paulo scowled, nursing his arm as Mike walked over to Bill. 'Are you ok?' he asked.

'Yes, thanks,' the doctor responded with relief in his voice. 'I am now, thanks.'

Mike passed his gun to Bill. 'Keep an eye on him. There is someone else I need to find. Shoot him if you have to.' He walked out into the passageway.

The frightened man held on to the gun, pointing it in Paulo's direction. He despised the man.

'Are you going to shoot me, Bill?' Paulo asked evenly. 'Have I not always protected you?'

'Shut up,' Bill responded. He knew he would not shoot the man however much he might want to, but he was not about to tell Paulo that.

Paulo edged forward toward him. 'Give me the gun, Willington! Let me go!'

'Get back!' the frightened man shouted, 'I don't want to

kill you, but I will if I have to!' but he knew he could not take a life. He moved around the room as Paulo moved again toward him. Suddenly, the man grabbed the gun, pointed it at Bill and fired.

'You fool! You should have shot me while you had the chance!' as he disappeared into the passageway.

Bill collapsed onto the floor.

Neko was in a cave which was normally kept permanently padlocked. Paulo and he stored all their valuables in it, including the money they used to pay their men. He knew he would not be able to carry it all away, but he would be able to bury it. He would find it again because he knew where to look. It took him only five minutes to set up the explosive in the passageway. Once the roof collapsed their fortune would be safe until they could return one day to reclaim it.

Seconds later the sound of a loud explosion reached the ears of Paulo, Mike, Piers and the Major's men. They all made their way to the source. The dust in the air made it almost impossible to see very far in front of them.

Paulo arrived first, nursing his bleeding arm. His eyes took in the collapsed roof in front of their strong room. 'What have you done?' he asked Neko.

'I have made it safe. We can come back and find it again. We have not lost it!' his brother comforted him. He looked at the blood on his arm. 'What happened?'

'There is someone in the cave. He shot me. I escaped but I had to shoot Wellington. I think he is dead.' Paulo was losing blood and feeling decidedly weak. 'I need your help, brother.

Let us leave this place.'

'I think not!' a voice from behind them spoke, 'You are going nowhere!'

Mike appeared in the doorway, aiming his gun at the men. Piers and his men also appeared. The major's men dragged Neko along one of the passageways, intending to take him out of the cave where they entered it. It was the only way out of the cave after the desert entrance had collapsed.

After Piers' arrival, Mike had grabbed Paulo, 'What do you mean, you think Bill is dead? Where is he? Take me to him!'

'He is where you left him.' Paulo snarled, knowing he was beaten.

'Is he dead?' Mike asked.

'I don't know and I don't care!' the man replied spitefully.

Mike ordered Piers and two of the three men to take Neko to the waiting helicopters, which Jameson and Schmidt had rescued from the cave before it collapsed.

The Major sent two Seahawks back to transport his men and any prisoners back to the ship. As all of Paulo's men had been buried alive, they were not required. The men had been trapped by the falling sand and rock. They had no way out from their end of the cave. It was a dead end.

With Paulo in front of him with his gun in his back and Dave, one of Winter's men holding on to him, Mike arrived in the cave where Bill sat against the wall, in pain from a wound in his chest. He had the presence of mind to grasp a cloth as he fell and had pressed it to the bleeding wound, then dragged himself to a sitting position to reduce the blood flow. Dave picked up the doctor, supporting him with his arm as they left the cave and headed for the exit ramp. Progress was pitifully slow but they eventually made their way to the cave with the lake. Paulo was in front of Mike and Bill and the soldier brought up the rear.

Paulo was struggling to walk as blood seeped down his arm. He knew he was not going to escape but he wanted to be with his brother and this fed his determination to continue walking. Eventually, the balance of life in him fell into the negative and he collapsed. Mike picked him up and, supporting him with his good arm around his shoulder, they continued to head toward the ramp.

The air was warming up as they eventually approached it. The sun poured its bright rays down into the cave and torches were no longer required. Mike could see Neko, handcuffed to one of the majors' men, standing at the top of the ramp.

Neko watched as Mike approached with Paulo. He tried to get down the ramp but the soldier refused to allow it. He could see that there was something not right with Paulo and he was concerned about him.

'My brother! I must see my brother! You must let me see my brother!' he shouted at the soldier. Piers nodded at the soldier, 'Let him go but cuff his hands.'

The soldier did as he was asked and Neko walked carefully down the ramp to his brother, whom Mike had laid on the floor of the cave. It was almost over. He had lost too much blood to survive, despite Mike's tourniquet. The main artery had been severed and it would be too late for Paulo by the time he was flown to the ship. There was nothing they could do for him.

Tears fell from Neko's eyes as he saw his brother struggling to speak. He leaned over him, 'Brother... Paulo..., stay with me! Don't leave me alone!' He was all he had.

Paulo watched his brother with gratitude. He admired him so much. His mind drifted back many years. When his father was alive, their childhood had been magical. Their father and mother were archaeologists and they often took them into the desert on their search to find long buried towns and tombs which had been eaten by the desert over centuries. The boys loved to go with them.

One day, when Paulo was eight and Neko was ten and their father was busily working on an excavation, they had wondered off much further than they should have and spent hours playing around a large sand dune, which was covered with rocks. They buried each other and threw rocks in the air at each other until none of the rocks were left, except a large rock which was too big for both of them to lift. It was lying on its side, trapped under another rock, which was even bigger. The boys decided to excavate the rock themselves and dug away underneath it until, to their surprise, the rock started to slide backwards and the sand in front of it followed.

Paulo was nearest the sliding sand and he was sucked into a huge gap which developed under the larger rock, and soon disappeared. Neko was shocked to see the large hole open up underneath the larger rock and even more shocked by his brother's disappearance. He could not leave his beloved brother to die under the sand, so he crawled underneath the rock to find him.

That was how they found the cave. It was not dark. The

sunlight reached part of the way into the cave, which was huge! The boys had never seen anything like it, even when they explored some of their parents' excavations. When Neko found Paulo, he was running around the inside of the cave, shouting with glee at his discovery.

Neko laughed at his brother as he clambered up a rock three times as tall as himself and shouted as loud as he could, 'I'm the King of the moon! I'm the King of the moon!'

It was true. Paulo had quite an imagination. The landscape in the cave was desolate, dry, dusty, and at the back of the cave, very dark. It was just like the pictures of the moon which they had seen in their school books.

The cave became their secret. Their parents never knew about it. Over many years, as they grew up they continued to visit the cave, storing anything they thought would be useful to them when they camped in it. They saw how the wind swept away the sand from the entrance to their cave until the gap became so large they could drive a truck into it.

Their childhood fantasies disappeared forever after their parents were killed in a bombing raid when they were working in Iraq. They swore they would get even with all westerners for the loss of their parents. After joining a terrorist group, they left Iraq and returned to Yemen but they found it easier to participate in the group's unholy deeds after moving into their childhood hideaway. They felt safe in the cave. Many men followed them and they built up a strong army, making their money with their mercenaries, and later with drug trafficking. They knew the desert well. Meeting up with Garcia in San Diego, where they had planted a bomb, was a stroke of luck.

The man would do anything for money. That was how they found out about genbriotic hypnotherapy.

Now it was all gone.

Paulo gasped, 'Get them back for me, brother. Make sure they pay!'

Neko sobbed as he watched his brother dying, 'I will. I will, I swear it to you!'

Murmuring, 'I'm King of the moon! I'm King of the moon,' Paulo was back in the cave, on top of the rock.

Two minutes later, the King of the moon was dead.

Epilogue

One month later

'So what happened?' JP asked.

'Neko is incarcerated. Bill is recovering, and Piers has a date with Lana. Oh, and by the way, Geordie says 'thanks' for the DS but he'll stick with his camels if you don't mind.'

'What's wrong with the DS?' his boss was miffed. The DS was the best money could buy.

Mike laughed as he drank his coffee, 'They don't make good detectives. Apparently camels are better. If it wasn't for the camels we would never have found Bill, or the soldiers.'

With raised eyebrows, JP asked, 'Camels? How can camels be detectives?'

'It's a long story, I'll tell you sometime,' Mike picked up a ginger crunch cookie and dunked it in his coffee before taking a bite. 'Kassar was right, they are nice!'

'Did you find the aircraft?' JP hoped he had. It was an expensive piece of hardware.

Mike was thoughtful, 'No... not yet but Rosa's pals at NASA are using satellite and infra-red imaging over the desert near the cave to look for it.'

JP was fascinated, 'Really?'

Laughing, Mike said, 'No, of course not! It looks like that has gone AWOL, but that's another mission, I'd say!' He took an envelope out of his briefcase and handed it to JP. 'You are summoned!'

Three months later

Sunlight streamed in through the windows of the modern, colourful church, spreading patches of coloured reflections on the walls and floor and on the people sitting on the seats watching the ceremony.

John and Caroline sat with their video cameras running. Bill sat beside JP, Craig and Maddy. Piers and Lana watched, happily holding hands.

It was a day Craig had thought would never arrive.

Mike gazed into Rosa's eyes as she replied happily, 'Yes, I mean... I do!'

The minister looked at them both. 'By the power vested in me, I now pronounce you husband and wife.'

The groom looked quizzically at the minister who laughed. 'Yes, you may kiss your bride!'

Without another word, Mike put his arms around Rosa, and tilting up her chin he kissed her passionately then said, 'Where do we go from here, Mrs Forde?'

'Anywhere you like, Commander!' she replied.